Praise for the Novels of J.J. Murray!

I'M YOUR GIRL

"Murray writes a gentle romance about cultural differences and deep commonalities in a unique tale about white/black relationships."—*Booklist*

"In this unusual book, humor and heartbreak are side by side. Murray movingly shows emotions . . . second characters are well developed and have their own surprises . . . a wonderful book."—*Romantic Times*

ORIGINAL LOVE

"Thoughtful and well done."—*Library Journal*

"Touching, soul-searching . . . not only entertaining, but enlightening as well."—*RAWSistaz*

SOMETHING REAL

"*Something Real* is about a woman finding herself and finding her voice in a community too quick to judge. *Renee and Jay* was a promising debut. *Something Real*, which is a more mature and richer work, is even better."
—*The Roanoke Times*

"Delightful! Sexy! Touching! *Something Real* is like a burst of sunshine. This release is definitely something special and something real! This is a story that readers must experience for themselves."—*Romance in Color*

"Funny and gratifying . . . Murray gives the reader plenty of characters to care about, get angry with and have a good laugh with."
—*Book-Remarks.com*

RENEE AND JAY

"A charming, funny romance and a promising debut . . . This *Romeo and Juliet* story is sweet and romantic with lively characters."—*The Roanoke Times*

"*Renee and Jay* was hilarious . . . and the author is definitely talented . . . if you are looking for a quick read that will give you some laughs, then I would highly suggest this one."—Zane, author of *Addicted* and *The Heat Seekers*

"An update of Shakespeare's *Romeo and Juliet*, with a twist."—*Essence*

Books by J.J. Murray

RENEE AND JAY

SOMETHING REAL

ORIGINAL LOVE

I'M YOUR GIRL

CAN'T GET ENOUGH OF YOUR LOVE

Published by Kensington Publishing Corporation

Can't Get Enough of Your Love

J.J. Murray

KENSINGTON BOOKS
http://www.kensingtonbooks.com

KENSINGTON BOOKS are published by

Kensington Publishing Corp.
850 Third Avenue
New York, NY 10022

ISBN-13: 978-0-7582-1399-0
ISBN-10: 0-7582-1399-9

First Kensington Trade Paperback Printing: November 2007
10 9 8 7 6 5 4 3 2 1

Printed in the United States of America

For Amy

Chapter 1

I am not a whore.

I am not a lady of the evening. I am not a floozy. I am not a harlot. I am not a hooker. I am not a pickup. I am not a skank. I am not a nymphomaniac. I am not a pavement princess.

I am an average, ordinary woman.

I just have needs, and because of these needs, I have several men in my life. That doesn't make me a player, nor does that make me nasty. I have . . . friends.

Friends with benefits.

It is a natural human need to be wanted, to be held, and to be caressed. I *need* to want a man, I need to hold a man, and I need to caress a man. I *like* to be wanted by a man, I like to be held by a man, and I *love* to be caressed by a man.

In fact, I like it so much that one man just isn't enough for me. I need a great deal of love, even if it isn't love at all. And while many people may disagree, it isn't all physical, this friends-with-benefits thing. We don't always end up in the bedroom.

Sometimes we end up in the kitchen, in the tub, in the shower, in the car, outside . . .

Let me first make one thing perfectly clear: I am *not* addicted to sex. I lived more than half my life without sex, so I can live without it. I was not molested as a child, and I was not raped as a teenager. I did not sleep around in middle school. I do not need therapy. I do not have a screw loose. I am not nor have I ever been on medication other than an occasional aspirin. I am, as far as I can tell, a normal, healthy human being who likes to have sex.

There, I've said it. I like sex. It's one of God's greatest inventions. I like the way I feel when I'm having sex, and I love living forever in the time it takes to have sex. Why is it so wrong for a woman to enjoy what got us *all* here in the first place? My men obviously like to have sex with me, I feel sexy as hell (and I'm *not* any magazine's definition of beauty), and for a little while at least, I feel immortal.

As a normal, healthy human being, I was one of those people who used to think, *Nah, that kind of thing would never happen to me. I'll be lucky to get and keep one guy.* I believed in all that one-man, one-woman monogamy hype. I believed that it was not possible for a lady to see two or more men at the same time and remain a lady.

I don't believe any of that anymore. I'm all about breaking traditions and stereotypes, and I know I'm not the only woman out there doing it.

At least I *hope* I'm not the only woman doing it.

I can't be the only woman who enjoys the chase, the anticipation, the foreplay, the pawing and gnawing, the raw emotion, the grunting, and the sweaty sighing. And if I *am* the only one, so be it.

I know that I'm *not* supposed to enjoy sex because centuries of conditioning (I paid attention in my psych class at Virginia Western) have taught women *not* to enjoy sex. Just lie back and take it, we've been told.

I do not just lie back and take it because I do not live in the past.

I do not live in a past that said women could not own land, testify in court, vote, smoke, drive, play sports, have their own orgasms, get jobs, run corporations, or campaign for president. To people who think that way I say, "Get over yourselves. The twenty-first century is the century of the woman. We still need equal rights in the boardroom and the bedroom. We still need equal rights in the workplace and the sleeping place."

I doubt that *Time, Newsweek,* and *U.S. News & World Report* will see it that way and run nice cover stories on my new sexual revolution, but . . . that's how I feel.

So who are these men in my life? I call them Earth, Wind, and Fire. Roger McDowell ("Earth"), Karl Henderson ("Wind"), and Juan Carlos Gomez ("Fire") are friends first and lovers second, and a person can never have too many friends. A friend in need is a friend indeed, right? Even the Bible says that a friend loves at all times.

I just get more, um, *friendship* than most women I know.

Men who do this kind of juggling get nothing but praise and envy from other men and even from some women. They get called "Casanova" or "Don Juan" or "Prince Charming," or, well, Hugh Hefner. They get to be called "studs" and "wolves," not "pavement princes." Not all men act this way—now, not even a majority—but I guarantee there are a *lot* of men who *wish* they could keep three women on a string, and not just for the physical excitement. They all crave the praise of their peers. They want to hear, "Look at him. Look what's he's got. That man has got it made in the shade."

I guess I crave praise, too, but not from other women. I get praise from the three men I "hang and bang with," according to my best friend, Izzie. As for other women—or other people, for that matter—let's just say they don't know what I'm doing (not even my mama!) because so far I have kept everything quietly under control. Oh, Izzie knows everything, but she keeps her big trap shut as a best friend should. Izzie seems to live all of her sexual fantasies through me, and I can't let her lose those fantasies, can I?

Anyway, if my men (did I mention I have *only* three?) want to see other women when they're not with me, that's okay. As long as they wear condoms *every* time with *every* one of their hos, I'm cool with it. They have needs, too, right?

Just think: If *all* of us had friends with benefits, what a better world we could have. For one thing, we couldn't have Republicans or Democrats anymore. They don't want *anyone* to be friends. Two, the Society of Friends would increase its membership rolls. The Shakers or Quakers or whatever they're called could finally have some fun on Sundays. And three, the TV show *Friends* would still be on the air. Wasn't that show what "friends with benefits" was all about? Hmm? Who didn't do whom on that show?

I would have done Joey, Chandler, and Ross—in that order.

I have my standards.

I have three friends who, let's say, *entertain* me, who make me feel like a natural woman for a couple hours a week. Roger is my earth brother, my soul, my Mr. Meat 'n' Potatoes, who likes good conversation before, during, and after good and often kinky sex. Karl is my wind-brother, my roots, my Mr. Hot Wings 'n' Corn Bread, who has to do it loud, proud, and rowdy. And Juan Carlos is my fire brother, my passion, my Mr. Salsa 'n' Pinto Beans, who likes to make fierce, passionate, hot love to me. Put them all together and I have a man who doesn't drink, smoke, or do drugs around me; has curly hair, dark eyes, six sets of hands; speaks two languages; loves to make love to me; *always* wears a condom; and weighs over five hundred pounds.

Just kidding. They average maybe one seventy, one eighty each.

And no, I do not entertain them all at once. That can *never* happen, nor is it even one of my fantasies. Okay, I do have the fantasy involving Roger and chocolate whipped topping (the fat-free kind) and the one with Juan Carlos involving long-stem roses. Oh, and one with Karl and some chocolate-covered strawberries, but that's neither here nor there.

When I really think about my situation, I realize that I'm doing all three of my men a favor. I don't require their love and devotion, I don't require a commitment, I don't require their money (just their time), and I don't even require their faithfulness. Why ask a man for what he cannot, does not, or is unwilling to provide? Why ask a man to do what he is not wired or programmed genetically to do?

Oh, I used to want all that commitment stuff, as if my stuff was so good that a man would want only me morning, noon, and night. Four bad relationships in a row after high school taught me otherwise. My stuff *is* good, and I know how to entertain. But the men I was committed to back then had fifteen-minute (or less) attention spans. Oh, they *said* the right things, like "You're my one and only boo, Lana," and "Lana, you're my everything," and "I only want to be with you, Lana," but their body language always said otherwise. They had one foot out of the bed, one hand grasping a pair of boxers or drawers, and one set of eyes looking for the bathroom, the kitchen, and the exit, usually in that order.

Why three? Why *not* three? Four might be a little hard to juggle. There are only seven days in a week, leaving me six days to entertain and one day to rest. Three men work out just fine. Even God rested after six days, you know.

And Sunday is when Izzie usually shows up. If the world could hear what Izzie and I talk about, we'd be the most scandalous kind of reality TV. But it's not as if my three *amigos* are that consistent and I'm getting some every night. It works out to *maybe* twice a week (just under the national average) with at least one earth-shattering, window-breaking, make-the-bullfrogs-wanna-holler-at-the-moon orgasm. I get their friendship, their warmth, their focus, and then . . .

They go.

They're gone.

Goodbye. *Adios*. See ya. *Aloha*. *Ciao*.

Not one of them stays the night, not one of them has a drawer of his very own, not one of them leaves a toothbrush in my bathroom, and not one of them has a special shelf in the refrigerator.

They're here, they're not.

I even use air freshener to cover the scent of their various colognes. I prefer to use Oust, since it completely eliminates their odors.

As a result, I'm never lonely. How can I be lonely when I have *my* space, I *allow* them to invade mine (twice if they're nice), and they're cool with the leaving part? And as far as I can tell, none of my men has grown tired of me.

Friends.

With benefits.

Don't knock it—or *me*—until you put your fantasies to good use and try it.

Chapter 2

I have always had more male friends than female friends, and for that, I can blame my parents.

Earl Davidson and Lana Cole hooked up one foggy night in Norfolk (Nah-Fuck), Virginia, when they were in their early twenties, and made me, Erlana Joy Cole. There has always been more "Earl" in me than "Lana." As for "Joy," well, I believe you have to make your own joy in this world, and "Joy" makes an appearance every now and then. I have never been girly enough for my mama or boy enough for my daddy. I'm in between, though I lean Daddy's way. And after twenty-five . . . *ish* . . . years (I can still pass for twenty-*three* on a good day), I realize that my pug nose, wide light brown eyes, and peanut head are not what Mama envisioned when she started messing with my daddy.

Yes, I have a peanut head, and I've grown to be proud of it. Mama had to have a C-section when she had me, and the doctors didn't squish my head down far enough after I was stuck for three hours inside Mama's vagina. They could have molded my head as round as Mama's or made it squarish like Daddy's, but no—they made me into a peanut. I don't look like either of my parents because of that, and the shit I took from my classmates in elementary school was brutal. They called me "Peanut Head," "Mrs. Peanut

Head," and "Nutty." One kid even called me "Mrs. Potato Head," but he was one of those kids who rode the short bus and also thought he was the black Power Ranger. Eventually, I became "Peanut," which wasn't so bad except that I wasn't as small as one. I was born big, and I still kind of am. Only Karl calls me "Peanut" now. Roger and Juan Carlos call me "Lana," though the way Juan Carlos says "*Lahhh*-na" is so much sexier.

My daddy called me "E," and he was smoof. I mean, any grown man who could watch *The Smurfs* all the way through with me had to be smoof. Daddy had a voice like Sugar Bear from the Super Sugar Crisp commercials and he could mimic Papa Smurf perfectly.

It's smoof to have a daddy who can do that when you're a kid.

After he popped Mama's coochie and popped in and out of my life until I was eight, he popped into thin air, which was hard for him to do. The man was huge and had absolutely no neck—just shoulders and a head with a rectangular jaw, piercing dark brown eyes, a curly kit—and big hands, like a boxer's hands, with big old ashy knuckles. He didn't have a pimp stroll, chains, flared plaid pants, or Adidas sneakers. My daddy wore jeans, a stained hooded gray sweatshirt, and kick-ass black steel-toed boots every day. But that was because of his job as a welder for NorShipCo. He'd come home with dirty nails, dirt streaks on his face, and the smell of the sea mixed with sweat and Hai Karate aftershave after working on Navy ships, cruise ships, and even long oil tankers. He would take me to a park near his house on West 29th Street (when *The Smurfs* weren't on), and we would play football.

Tackle football.

And my daddy hit *hard*.

I didn't actually tackle him—you know, take him completely down—until I was seven, and I didn't score a touchdown on him until I was eight. Four years of shutouts, tears, bruises, cuts, and Band-Aids. Mama didn't like it, mainly because my teachers were forever calling home to accuse her of child abuse, but *I* loved it. I *lived* football, and I know more about football than most guys do. I can tell you the results from every Super Bowl since 1982. I know the difference between an H-back and a cornerback. I know that a cover two isn't what a bra does to your girls, I can tell if it's going to be a pass play just by watching the guards pull or stay home, and I have a pass-rushing swim move that would make any defensive end in the NFL green with envy.

I even play semi-pro football for the Roanoke Revenge in the National Women's Football Association. That's right. We're women wearing pads more than once a month, but only in the springtime. We don't get a paycheck—and we actually have to buy our own equipment—but at least I get to play the sport I love.

And no, I am not a wide receiver. I am a defensive end and tight end (and it *is* true!) on a lesbian team of white women ranging in age from eighteen to fifty. I am five nine and one hundred sixty pounds of black muscle, and no one says a damn thing about my peanut head when I have my helmet on.

Oh, the Revenge are horrible this year. We're 1–5 after *two* 70–0 losses to the D.C. Divas, two butt-kickings by the Pittsburgh Passion, and a thrashing by the Baltimore Burn. But I put my hand in the dirt, I get in my licks, I break some kneecaps, and I swim move and get my sacks. And if our prima donna quarterback would pass the ball to me more than to the women she wants to sixty-nine with, we might actually score a few more touchdowns before the season (mercifully) ends against the Erie Illusion, the only team worse than we are. That probably makes Erie the worst team ever to play professional football in American history.

Playing for the Revenge is like playing one-on-one football with my daddy. We'll be down 40–0 before halftime sometimes, beaten, bloody, and gasping for oxygen, but we have heart. Though we really, *really* want to sneak away at halftime to spare the fans any more misery, we always go back out for the second half, and (thank God!) no one has scored triple-digits on us.

Yet.

I think I'm the only heterosexual on the team. I have been hit-on by almost every player, not that there's anything wrong with it. Live and let live, right? I mean, I entertain three men. So what if they entertain each other. Big deal. What I don't understand is that I'm not a "dime" (Who thought up that shit? You can't get anything with a dime now!), yet I get these looks from my teammates, even while we run through drills at practice. Imagine seeing a big white woman wearing shoulder pads, elbow pads, and knee pads, and with black grease marks under her eyes. That's scary enough. Now imagine those grease-painted eyes making eyes at *you* during a tackling drill. I take these looks as compliments, and then I take my butt *home* completely clothed and sweaty instead of hitting the showers after a practice or a game. I've seen those women-in-prison movies. I know what could happen.

Izzie wants me to hang around after practice, just to see what *might* happen.

Izzie's such a perv.

I don't think I'm that pretty. For one thing, I have big feet and long toes, and you know what they say about women who have big feet and long toes—they go through lots of socks and hose. I'm well proportioned, not ripped, with long fingers, too.

Most people who look at me see a basketball player, but I cannot stand an orange ball that bounces straight up. I need the brown ball that bounces funny. Sure, coaches in high school tried to recruit me to play basketball for them, but basketball isn't for me. I once fouled out of a pickup game in gym class in only *two* minutes. And they play basketball indoors for the most part.

I need grass, dirt, and chalk lines.

I also need a struggle. Basketball isn't much of a struggle. If you break it down, basketball is all about five people playing keep-away against five other people who are trying *not* to touch them. I can't play a sport in which I can't physically abuse the enemy, grinding, grunting, and grabbing, trash talking, cussing, scratching, gouging, poking, plucking, chasing, diving, and crunching. Football to me is a human symphony involving lots of percussion, while basketball is more like a squeaky dance with an occasional "swish." I mean, in basketball you actually get to score without any interference when you shoot a free throw.

There isn't anything free in football.

You have to earn every inch with blood, sweat, and guts. So instead of popping a J or making a breakaway layup, I grab me some dirt, and as soon as the center moves the ball, I'm going to turn the player in front of me into a human bruise, sack me a lesbian with bad hair and worse skin, and make bowlegged women limp worse.

So, after tackling other women and not catching *any* passes (football or otherwise) from other women, I go home to my little plot of paradise on a tiny little pond in Bedford County just east of Roanoke, Virginia. The pond is so tiny it doesn't even have a name.

I just call it "Mine."

Chapter 3

When Mama and I first came to Roanoke fifteen years ago so she could take a job with First Virginia (which became First Union, then Wachovia), I thought the real reason we came was so she could steal me away from my daddy, one-on-one tackle football, and easy trips to the beach. I also thought Roanoke was a boring city in the mountains.

Now, I think Roanoke is a boring, small-minded *town* masquerading as a city full of folks who occasionally notice that, indeed, there are mountains all around them. And the only beaches around here are the sons-of-beaches driving to and through the parking lots of Valley View Mall, which is a *stupid* name for a mall *surrounded* by mountains. They should have called it Mountain View Mall, but since folks around here don't see the mountains anymore . . .

We lived near Towers Mall on Colonial Avenue, an extremely busy street, in a three-bedroom ranch with a huge basement, decent backyard for Mama's flowers, and a deck out back. We weren't in the 'hood, so I went to elementary and middle school with a bunch of white kids before getting to Patrick Henry High School, where I finally was allowed to be black.

I earned an associate's degree from Virginia Western

Community College after high school so I could be a legal assistant, which I will *never* be. Paper pushing is *not* for me. So, I took a job as an instructional aide for special education students at Patrick Henry, mainly so I could have my summers off. But after living too long in the city under Mama's watchful eyes and worrisome mouth, I had to get out of Roanoke, mainly so I could save money on gas. It isn't cheap going from one friend-with-benefit's place to the next. I needed a place of my own so *they* could come to *me*.

As it should be, right?

Who am I kidding? I was paranoid and needed my own place away from Roanoke so my men would never accidentally meet. I needed to control the situation, all right? I had had too many close calls, most of them involving my cell phone. At first, I kept it on vibrate, but one night with Roger, it buzzed so often that I had to return the call "to my mama," who was really Karl wanting to get a leg up. I hated lying to Roger, especially when he heard me say: "I'll be there soon, boo." I then had to explain why I called my mama "boo," and that wasn't any fun. Now I keep my cell off when I'm with one of them and on at all other times.

When I remember, that is, and I don't always remember.

I also got tired of doing and redoing my hair, wearing certain clothing, and putting on different makeup for our various nights out on the town. For Juan Carlos, I usually wear dark eye shadow and eyeliner, spiked heels, tight jeans, and "you-can-see-my-girls" blouses, stacking and pinning up my hair . . . so he can unstack it later in the heat of passion. For Karl, I usually wear light eye shadow and eyeliner and baggier clothes, and I braid my hair as best I can . . . so he can unravel it (and me!) during our aerobic lovemaking. And for Roger, I usually wear no makeup at all, choose conservative "yes-I-have-a-decent-job" outfits, and keep my hair combed out to my shoulders . . . so he can grab it and . . .

Whoo.

I, uh, I sometimes get a little moist just while I'm doing my hair.

And keeping up with the bling has been murder. I have to remember to wear two silver hoop earrings, a silver herringbone necklace, and a silver pinkie ring for Roger, all of which he gave me for our third-week anniversary. Celebrating every little anniversary is fun, but when you have to keep track of three different timelines, you lose your damn mind. I have to wear two gold hoop earrings, a gold herringbone necklace, and a gold thumb ring for Juan Carlos, who has yet to give me any bling. I just happened to be wearing all that the day we met. As for Karl, who gives me the most bling, I have to wear as much gold bling as my ears, neck, fingers, and wrists can hold. Karl likes me to bling. He's even trying to convince me to get my eyebrows, nose, belly button, girls, and stuff pierced, but if I did that, I'd be a metal detector's dream. I'd also have a lot of explaining to do to Juan Carlos and Roger because all those holes aren't easy to hide. Karl also wants me to tattoo his name on the inside of my thigh. Not only would that hurt (I'm scared of needles), but that would also lead to discussions with Juan Carlos and Roger that I do not want to have when a man is down there talking to my stuff. I want him concentrating, not reading.

Because of all this stress, last month during spring break I went searching for a new place. I needed to live as far away from Roanoke (and my mama) as I could get and still have an easy commute to work. I also needed to save myself the trouble of becoming someone else every other day.

I was feeling "tri-polar" or something.

But at first, I couldn't find anywhere to live that wasn't too expensive, too small (I need my space), or too close to Mama. I needed to find a cheap place in a remote area, and that meant looking to the hills.

One late March day I called a man advertising "a cottage on a pond" (what could be more isolated and romantic?) and drove to Bedford County.

Yeah, this city girl went to the country so she could get herself done on a regular basis.

Chapter 4

I met Mr. Wilson in front of his farmhouse about twenty miles north and east of Roanoke. Tall, lean, and rugged, Mr. Wilson could have been an ancient black cowboy, a Buffalo soldier, looking all country in his stiff blue jeans, matching jean jacket, black cowboy boots, and black leather cowboy hat.

"We'll take your car," he said, and away we went down a dirt lane that shot off from his farm off Route 460.

We passed through mini-forests and drove through fields of green sprouts until he said, "Turn . . . left, I think, at the first oak tree."

I slowed at the first tree I came to.

"That's a beech tree."

How was I to know? I was a city girl! A maple, two sycamores, and another beech later, I saw the oak tree. Gravel roads led right and left around it. I stopped in the shade of the tree, and like something out of *The Wizard of Oz*, the tree spread out against the sky, a swarm of daffodils surrounding it.

"My granddaddy planted that one," Mr. Wilson said. "And we planted Granddaddy right under it."

What do you say to that? I didn't say anything. I was thinking, *No shit.* Or was it, *Oh, shit!*? Hmm.

At least I knew I would have quiet neighbors.

Mr. Wilson slumped down in his seat and closed his eyes, pulling down his hat. "Wake me when we get there."

"Is it far?"

"No. I'm just old and need my naps."

I took the left gravel path, which narrowed to a car width, and brush scraped the sides of my VW Rabbit. I crept along for half a mile, the speedometer below ten, until the path widened around some boulder-infested curves. I was worried that the muffler would fall off, drag, and muffle no more.

A few S-turns later, I saw a pond lapping on the shore mere feet from us. I stood on the brake. "Mr. Wilson?"

"Hmm?"

"I think we're here."

He didn't look up or open his eyes. "You see the cottage?"

I saw only some cold, greenish water. "No."

"Then we're in the wrong place. Turn around, go back to the oak, and turn right this time."

I was almost out of gas, paint and primer from my car had decorated every piece of scrub brush in the county, and Mr. Wilson was snoring. I felt like screaming.

The right gravel path was smoother, though little saplings grew at intervals in the road. I felt like some Olympic skier going around (or through?) all those little gates. Not that I watch the Winter Olympics. There are so few black people in those events. I mean, where is a black person going to practice cross-country skiing and shooting at little targets without getting arrested in this country?

After a gradual descent, I saw the top of a cottage peeking out from a stand of pine trees.

"Mr. Wilson?"

"Hmm?"

"I see the cottage."

"What color?"

I squinted. "Looks like red brick with a black roof." And it wasn't a cottage. It was a two-story *house*.

"That's the one." He sat up. "The old girl's still standing. I haven't been out this way in years. I thought a storm might have done her in. Just park as close as you can."

That wasn't easy. The gravel path ended, and a swampy area of high grass began. The Rabbit struggled over thick stalks and heavy grasses until it bottomed out and stopped on its own.

"Close enough," Mr. Wilson said, and he got out. "Show yourself around. I'll be in the barn." He pointed at a squat, dark brown building behind the house. "Have to see if she's still there. The doors should be open."

As he walked away, I hoped to God that "she" wasn't his grandma. Then I thought up a little song: "Paw-Paw's under the old oak tree, Mee-Maw's in the barn . . ."

Acres and acres of thick grass surrounded me, a scene right out of every werewolf movie I'd ever seen. I expected to see wild dogs lurking here nightly. Even stray cats would be happy here, gorging themselves on field mice. If I harvested it all, there might actually be a lawn underneath. I looked down and saw a couple red tulips peeking up at me, and the more I looked, the more flowers I saw struggling to come up through the grass to the sun. Daffodils, irises, and more tulips than I could count surrounded the house and a nearby pond. It seemed that the whole property was some-one's garden.

The wooden dock jutting out into the pond needed work. Buckled planks drooped into the water, and the four support posts in the water tilted in all directions. It would be easier to tear it down and start from scratch. And why would anyone have a dock on such a small pond? If you dive off, you're almost to the other side!

I knew I'd have to create a driveway or carve out a sidewalk somehow. And the roadside scrub brush would have to be cut back, the cart path leveled, and the saplings removed. My back ached at these thoughts. Or, actually, my hands ached, because I knew I'd have three strong men's backs to rub down after *they* did all this work for me.

Friends with benefits have other uses, too.

The soil had to be rich. I could plant more crocus, tulip, and daffodil bulbs in the fall, and I could even dig out an area for annuals under the picture window near the front door. I looked up and saw empty white flower boxes under five windows. They could be filled up with petunias or something. Not that I had ever actually planted all that shit. That was Mama's domain. There wasn't a *gladiolus humongous* she couldn't plant, tend, and talk to more than her own and only daughter.

Mr. Wilson stepped out of the barn. "Been inside yet?"

"Not yet."

"Take your time. I'm trying to get Sheila going."

"Who's Sheila?" *And*, I had thought, *Sheila had better not be the sister you chained up in the barn.*

"You'll see." He vanished into the barn.

Black shutters, dark red brick, all of the windows uncracked—so far so good. A rusty oil tank hugged the back of the house, but it wasn't leaking as far as I could tell. I used a stick to see if it had any fuel, but it came up dry.

What amazed me most were the doors. There were only two, one in front on the right side and one around the left corner, and neither had deadbolts or keyed knobs. Though the house was far from civilization, I knew I'd have to do something about that. Who puts in outside doors without locks on the knobs? Country people sure were trusting.

It was then I noticed there were no power lines. A thick black rope of a line connected the barn to the house, but there weren't any other lines. I had visions of hurricane lamps and candles inside, with a working butter churn in the corner by the wood cookstove.

The rumbling of an engine abruptly interrupted my visions. Mr. Wilson had gotten Sheila to turn over. I walked toward the roar and entered the barn through a heavy side door. Piles of firewood four feet high lined the wall to my immediate right. Mr. Wilson stood in the middle of an amazing machine, hands and jeans greasy, a broad smile on his lips. The machine made a U around him and filled half the barn.

He noticed me and shouted, "This is Sheila! Ain't she a beaut?"

Sheila would have been a "beaut" if I knew exactly what she was. Sheila was a mass of hoses, wires, and gears. Sheila looked like an aircraft engine on crack.

He crossed two fingers on his right hand and held the hand high above his head. With his left hand, he reached into a mass of hoses and wires, and flipped a switch. A light hanging from a beam flashed on and off, flickered orange, and then stayed a steady, bright yellow. Sheila was a generator, and probably the world's largest.

He motioned me outside the barn, leaving the door open. "Always leave this door open when Sheila's percolating," he said, wiping more grease on his pants. "The fumes can get bad. I rigged Sheila to work up to twelve hours a day on a single gallon of gas."

"Wow," I said, though at the time I didn't know why. Now, I know. Mr. Wilson's invention, while huge, is incredibly efficient. He should work for NASA.

We walked toward the house. "Sheila runs your lights, stove, fridge, and water pump."

"Is there a washer and dryer?"

"Not yet. My wife, Jenny, God rest her soul, she liked to use the Laundromat over on four sixty, or she'd scrub 'em up in the pond."

That wasn't going to happen. The pond had greenish water, and I don't look good in green. "No problem." And it hasn't been a problem. Mama has a nice washer and dryer.

"Let me show you Jenny's dollhouse." We paused at the door. "You married?"

"No, sir."

"You got a boyfriend?"

"No," I said, and I didn't lie. I didn't have *a* boyfriend. Besides, country folks might not understand a concept like friends with benefits.

"A cute gal like you doesn't have a boyfriend?"

I had to tell him something. "I have a few friends."

"Hmm. Not ready to settle down yet, huh?"

"No."

"City girls are like that."

"Yes, sir."

"Jenny was a country girl." He smiled. "Hmm." He wiggled the doorknob. "I'll get you some locks, city girl." He pushed the door, and it swung easily on its hinges. "Come on in."

I expected must, mildew, and decay. I expected bats to swoop down, critters to scurry, and cobwebs to block my path. I expected a nest of mice to look up, smile at me, and say, "How ya doin'?" But Jenny's dollhouse was immaculate and smelled like pine, as if someone had sealed it with Saran Wrap.

Directly in front of me were shiny wooden stairs rising to a landing before continuing to rise to the left. I stood on a sparkling red-and-brown print linoleum floor. To the left of the stairs, four high-backed chairs surrounded a rough-hewn oak table shellacked to a glassy shine. The rest of the ground floor, it seemed, was the kitchen.

"Big, ain't it? Jenny loved to cook." He rubbed his stomach for effect. "I used to be a bit larger. Jenny could cook all day, and I could eat her cooking all night. Storage room's behind that door there. Bedrooms, bath, and sitting room are upstairs. Do you like to cook?"

"Yes." And I do more cooking in the kitchen than in the bedroom. And trust me, that oak table is sturdy enough for two people to, um, entertain each other on.

He showed me the little four-burner electric stove, the oak cabinets that needed refinishing, the skinny but adequate "icebox," and the shiny sink and the plumbing underneath. Every cabinet contained pots, pans, and glasses, and each drawer bulged with silverware and other cooking utensils. The ad didn't say it was a completely furnished cottage. I have saved so much money because of that.

"I did everything myself," he said. "And I passed all the inspections the first time. You got a microwave?"

"No, sir."

"Just as well. It ain't cooking at all, you ask me, and the electric couldn't handle it, anyway." He opened the storage room door and reached into the darkness, grabbing and pulling a string.

"Let there be light," I said.

He turned to me sharply. "Are you a religious gal?"

"I pray a lot." And I do. Hell, it can't hurt, right? Izzie says I call on Jesus only when I'm getting my swerve on. I call on Him other times, too, like when the Rabbit won't start on the first try on a cold day, or when I'm late for something and the jerk in front of me is creeping along at the damn speed limit.

"Hmm. Jenny would have liked you." He winked at me. "I haven't yet reformed."

I followed him into the room, extremely large for a storage room. "This is your oil heater, though you won't need it because of the woodstove. There's your water tank and pump, and this is your woodstove. Puts out a nice, even heat throughout the house once you cut off the generator."

That explained all the wood in the barn.

"The fuse box over there needs to be updated, but I'll take care of that. I've left that space over there so you could have a washer and dryer one day. I'll have someone inspect the well and the septic. They ought to pass." He tapped the top of the woodstove. "This is my greatest invention."

The woodstove didn't look that different from any other. Squat, cast iron, a grate, a large pipe up, and . . . a dozen little silver pipes snaking in and out.

"You've noticed the pipes, haven't you?" He blew some dust off some pipes going into and out of the back of the stove. "As you've probably figured out, if you shut off the generator, you shut off your ability to have hot water."

I hadn't noticed, but I nodded as if I had.

"Jenny hated taking cold baths in the morning, especially in the winter, so what I did was run these pipes from the water tank to the woodstove and back. Now, all the water in this house has to pass through this stove."

"Does that mean I have to keep the stove going all summer?"

He smiled. "No. Once you turn on the generator, the water heats up to a hundred forty in about half an hour. If you're like Jenny, though, you'll want your bath as soon as you wake up, so you'll have to go out to the barn at least thirty minutes before your bath. You got anywhere you got to be?"

"No. I'm on spring break."

"Are you a student?"

I couldn't tell him "teacher's aide" and expect him to rent the cottage to me. "No, I'm a teacher at Patrick Henry." And I sort of am.

"A young thing like you?"

I blushed. I like getting hit on, even if the man has wrinkles older than I am. "Yes."

He smiled. "Any questions so far?"

I had yet to see a phone or a phone jack. "How would I make a phone call?"

He furrowed his gray eyebrows. "Well, you dial the number on a telephone."

"No. I mean, is there a phone here?"

."Oh. No. We never had one here." Mr. Wilson raised his eyebrows. "You'd have to call from Gordon's Store out on four sixty."

I pulled out my cell phone. "I have a cell phone."

And the charges are a killer! I'm twenty miles from Roanoke, a decent-sized Virginia city, but all my calls are out of the network until I hit the Roanoke County line.

"Let's see the rest of the house," he said.

Upstairs, first door on the right, was the sitting room. "Just for sitting, reading," he said.

And entertaining in a small space when we're too, um, caught up to make it to the bedroom.

A beige two-seater sofa centered the left wall, identical brass lamp stand/magazine racks on either side, a matching easy chair hugging the far right corner near a bookcase. Framed needlepoint pastoral scenes were spaced around the room.

"Jenny and her needlepoint, and she never used a pattern," he said, rocking in the easy chair.

I want to remove those scenes of cows, horses, and sheep, I really do, but I'm afraid Jenny will return from the grave (or from under a beech tree somewhere) to visit me. I don't say "Jenny" three times in a mirror, either.

I squatted at the bookcase and found it filled with *Reader's Digests* starting in 1957 and ending in 1972.

"We stopped subscribing for some reason or other. It might have been Watergate. Either that or we simply couldn't get any more of 'em packed in there." Beige drapes shrouded the windows, one of which faced the road, the other the barn. "We usually kept these drapes closed. Not much of a view. Except for each other, that is."

I've replaced all those dusty *Reader's Digests* with *Essence, Honey,* and *O* magazine. Oprah is one of my role models, and I plan to stay unmarried like her until I'm fifty. The other magazines are to help me know what I should look like, as if that will ever happen. I flip through those glossy pages and shake my head mostly. Where do they find these flawlessly skinned, buxom black women with perfect teeth, nails, and hair? *I've* never met any of them. They must live outside Virginia or something. Roger wrote me a poem about my "issues" with these women called "She Is Beautiful."

When she wakes,
she is beautiful,
flashing a little leg
and yawning shyly,
her mouth a delicate O.

When she does her hair,
she is beautiful,
Golden Hotting with practiced hands
around tender ears,
steam rising into the air.

When she sings,
she is beautiful,
flashing teeth and singing strong,
her neck arched as her lips
whisper sweetness into the air.

When she bites her lower lip,
she is beautiful,
softening bad news
with wide eyes and a pout.

When she plays football,
she is beautiful,
flashing hands, arms, and legs
as the dust and turf fly
behind her.

When she swats the remote control from
my hand to hold my hand,
she is beautiful,
sighing to tell me she wants to hold
more than my attention later tonight.

And when she walks,
Lord God!
she is beautiful,
swaying with hips and legs and back
in time to a rhythm she wants
only me to hear.

I don't need a magazine
to tell me
she is beautiful
because
her body, soul, and mind
fill all the glossy pages
of my heart.

I have the poem, um, hidden between the mattress and box spring of my bed. I doubt Juan Carlos or Karl would appreciate it as much as I do. I sometimes take it out to feel special when I'm alone.

Opposite the sitting room was a bedroom in navy blue. Two
bookcases housed quite a collection of African-American books by
Zora Neale Hurston, James Baldwin, Langston Hughes, and Richard
Wright, among others. A simple gray-and-blue quilt lay neatly folded
at the foot of a single bed.

. "Believe it or not," Mr. Wilson called out as he rocked, "we
stacked all three of our boys in there using a bunk bed and that little bed. They were hardly in here except to sleep, of course. As
soon as they were grown and gone, I turned it into my reading
room. It was also where I slept when I came in too late."

Everything in the room matched. The dresser, mirror, nightstand, and headboard were whitewashed pine, matching the color
of the drapes. The window provided a nice view of the pond.

"Hope you don't mind if I rest a bit," Mr. Wilson said. "You won't
get lost."

I have touched all the books in that reading room, finishing
every single one, and when I have my four children (and I will—
and they *all* will play football), I will name them James, Langston,
Richard, and Zora. Hell, I might name them all Zora, even if they're
all boys. I'll have Zora James, Zora Langston, Zora Richard, and Zora
Zora. They'll be called "The Four Z's," and I'll have the TV cameras
on me whenever they win the national championship or the Super
Bowl. I won't wear embarrassing clothing that proclaims they're
mine, though, nor will I overdo the bling like some of these women
do. I saw the mama of one basketball player looking like a hood rat,
her hair a mass of extensions, wearing his jersey. Scary.

I continued down the hall, opening the first door I came to on
the right. I entered a huge closet filled with old women's clothes,
shoes, and hats, all encased in plastic. At the time, I thought,
Grandma Lula lived here? At the far end of the closet was a window with a nice view of the woods. If I removed all the clothes, this
closet with a window could be my office or my studio. Not that I
needed either. I just thought it would be cool to say that I had one.
Now, however, it's still a closet, filled mostly with shoe boxes.

"I'll get all Jenny's clothes out of there," Mr. Wilson called out.

I left the closet and crossed the hall to a larger bedroom to see a queen-size bed. But everything was too yellow. The bedspread, the drapes on two windows, the quilt, and even the wastebasket were shades of yellow.

"Bright in here, isn't it?"

I jumped. Mr. Wilson was in the doorway behind me. Country folks can be sneaky like that. "Yes, sir."

"Jenny's favorite color. She loved lemons, daffodils, and ba-nanas, too." He stepped to a window. "The best views of the pond are from this room. We used to watch sunsets in here."

I was in a shrine to Jenny Wilson. Her combs and brushes were still lined up in front of the mirror on the dresser.

He crossed the room to a small closet door and opened it. "Well, looky here. All my old suits." He pulled out a black suit on a hanger and held it in front of him. There was no way it would fit him now. "Jenny liked me plump." He returned the suit to the closet. "I'll get these out of here, too. Check out the bathroom."

The bathroom was a simple white. A beige room, then a blue room, then a yellow room, then a white room—Jenny's dollhouse had simple colors for a simple home. I opened the only closet in the bathroom and saw stacks of towels and sheets. I pulled back the shower curtain and laughed when I saw a window.

"You laughing at my window? There didn't used to be a window there. I mean, who puts a window in a shower?"

"Exhibitionists?" I had wanted to say.

"I put that there for a reason." He leaned on the edge of a simple pedestal sink, a mirrored medicine cabinet above. "Jenny's greatest fear was that one of our children would fall off that dock out there and drown, even though all of them could swim just fine and that pond isn't but seven or eight feet deep at its deepest. My oldest, Thaddeus, he used to get up before sunrise every morning and fish off that dock for his breakfast. He usually caught something worth eating, sunfish mostly. Anyway, this was the only room in the house without a window, so I cut windows for her over the tub and over there beside the toilet."

I have a heavy curtain on the window next to the toilet, but no-thing covers the window in the shower. It's not as if anyone's out here looking at me, and, well, it gives me a cheap thrill every morning to know that someone *could* see my girls in all their soapy glory.

"What kind of rent are you paying back there in the city?"

I groaned inside. "Three hundred a month." That I had to pay to my mama for half a house note and half of the utilities and groceries.

"That much? Times sure have changed. I won't charge you that much for this old barn, though. It wouldn't be right."

I tried to keep my eyes from popping out of their sockets. A furnished two-bedroom cottage on a pond with acres and acres of privacy and solitude for *less* than three hundred dollars a month?

"What do you think is fair?" he asked.

I shook my head. "Mr. Wilson, a place like this would go for up to a thousand dollars a month or more down at Smith Mountain Lake."

"You don't say. Hmm."

I regretted telling him that the second I said it, but then . . .

"Tell you what. You pay me what you think is fair minus whatever work you do on the place. With the amount of work that needs to be done around here, I may as well rent it to you for nothing. Have you seen anything that needs fixing?"

My eyes did pop then. For nothing? Was he kidding? "Um, not much inside needs fixing, though those cabinets could use some refinishing." And Karl would be the man to do it. He likes working with his hands. He's good with his wood, too.

Mr. Wilson nodded. "How about outside?"

I told him my plans for the grass, the sidewalk, the dock, and the brush along the road. He listened, nodding often. It was strange, but in a way, Mr. Wilson had been interviewing me all along to be the caretaker of Jenny's dollhouse.

"You could get up a garden somewhere, too," he said. "The richest soil in the world is around here. You'll also want to chop some more wood, keep a fresh cord drying out." The light in the bathroom flickered and died. "Surprised Sheila lasted as long as she did. Not bad for ten-year-old gas, huh?"

We walked down the stairs and out the front door. "When can I move in?"

"How about now?"

"Great. Do you have a lease I can sign?"

"I trust you. Just stick the money in my mailbox, say, the first of every month?"

"Okay." This was too easy. "Um, don't I need to pay a damage deposit or something?"

"What for?"

"In case I damage something."

He shook his head. "This cottage has been standing since just after the Civil War. It can survive anything."

We waded through the grass to the Rabbit, the horizon teeming with bulbous black clouds. "It is going to rain something fierce," he said. "Maybe you ought to wait till tomorrow to move in."

"I don't have much to move." That belonged only to me. One trip with the Rabbit, mainly with clothes and shoe boxes, was all it took.

"Suit yourself. I'll reveal all of Sheila's secrets to you when you move in, and since the house is open, you can move in any time it's convenient for you."

"Thank you."

"Don't mention it."

We got in the car. "No, really, Mr. Wilson. Thank you. This is a miracle."

"Just take care of the dollhouse and Jenny will take care of you," he said. He pulled his hat down and took a snooze until we reached the farmhouse, and I didn't take a single wrong turn on the way back to his farm.

I shook him gently after I parked. A few raindrops plopped down.

"It's fixing to be a real bad storm," he said as he got out of the car. "A bad storm with heavy rain, maybe with hail. You better be getting back to Roanoke. Best you not move in until all this passes, Ms. Cole. I'll have the place ready for you. The day you're ready to move in, you just go on and move in."

"Shouldn't I call you first?"

He shook his head. "Jenny will tell me."

And with that, I roared away as the rain thickened, the wind picked up, and hail filled the air.

Chapter 5

Imoved in *two* days later after first surviving a hail of words from Mama.

I would have moved in the very next day, but I just had to have an argument with Mama. I'm sure it's in some "how to raise your mama" book. First, you have to shock your mama with "Mama, I'm moving out after twenty-five years of sponging off you." Second, you have to watch her mouth drop to the floor. You will be amazed how far a mama's mouth can drop, and when it comes back up, it has dust bunnies all up in it. Third, you have to begin packing as the lecture rages all around you and *keep* packing no matter how much sense she makes.

It was actually one of the better moments in my life.

"After twenty-five years," Mama raged, "*twenty-five years*! You suddenly get it into your head, just *suddenly get it into your head*, to go off on your own, just *go off on your own.* . . ."

Mama has this need to repeat everything twice, the second time louder. She has conversations with herself like this all the time, even when she's asleep and even when she prays. I wonder if God hears her original prayers, or does He hear the echoes? I'll bet He hears the echoes. They're always louder.

"You think you can take care of an entire house when you can't even take care of half of this one?"

She had a point, but I didn't say anything. I waited for the repeat, but she didn't give me one that day.

"I asked you a question, Erlana!"

Again, I waited for the repeat. None came. "Mama, there's not much to take care of at that house." And besides, I had three strong men who would do all that for me.

"You know, Karl, if you refinish those cabinets, I might be up for that special thing you want to try. . . . Roger, boy, you need some sun! You know how I love your freckles. Go make me some new ones to count with my tongue. See all that grass out there? . . . Juan Carlos, want to go skinny-dipping? You do? Well, before I join you, why don't you do something about that dock over there. . . ."

Yeah. I can take care of that house all by *myself.*

"Erlana, you know you can't multitask."

She made another point. I can barely pee and brush my teeth at the same time. I've lost a few toothbrushes that way.

"Taking care of a house is multitasking all the time."

"I'll manage." After all, it takes skill to multitask three men. I smiled. "I'll be fine, Mama."

"And you think you can afford to stay at that house making only seven fifty an hour and not working in the summer? *Not even working in the summer!*"

That calmed me down. The repeat had returned. All was right and well with the world again. "I'll manage. Any work I do on the place gets deducted from the rent."

"You are actually going to do some work around that house?"

It did sound kind of funny when I said it. "Yes."

"I'll believe that when I see it. But it still takes money to fix up a house, Erlana."

"I have a couple thousand saved up in the bank." I had been saving for a new car, but the Rabbit will just have to do for a little while longer. "I'll be paying around sixty a month in utilities, sixty for my phone, the Rabbit is paid for, I have low car insurance"—since I have a five hundred dollar deductible—"I have no furniture to buy, no drapes or . . . okay, maybe all that yellow can go—"

"And what is it, thirty miles from your job?" Mama interrupted. *"Thirty miles!"*

"Twenty," I said as I began to empty my drawers into two big old duffel bags, the only luggage I have ever owned.

"Twenty! That's forty miles a day, two hundred miles a week, over seven *thousand* miles a school year! Seven *thousand* miles, Erlana!"

Mama's really good at math.

"That car of yours can't handle that!"

But Juan Carlos can. He's a mechanic. He's *really* good with his hands. I want to tell Mama about Juan Carlos, Roger, and Karl, but that would cause trouble. . . .

Though introducing them to her might be fun. Hmm . . .

"Mama, this here's Juan Carlos. You like the little mole on his cheek, his thin moustache, and his soft skin?"

Mama grabs her chest. "He's a . . . C-c-catholic who barely speaks English!"

"I understand him just fine, Mama. And this is Karl. You like his little shaving bumps and the dimple in his chin?"

Mama slumps onto the couch, still clutching her chest. "Where'd he get all those tattoos? In prison?"

"Karl graduated Hampton U, Mama. He's no felon. And this is Roger. You like his big pores, freckles, and goatee?"

Mama goes into convulsions mumbling, "He's white? He's white?"

"Yes, Mama, and guess what? I'm dating all three of them . . . at once!"

Once the introductions were over, we'd have to pay a couple hundred for the ambulance, so . . . Hmm. Which of the three would give her the *worst* heart attack? Probably Karl. He's black with the most beautiful Afro, which I love braiding—or only half-braiding, depending on how horny I am. He also has more tattoos per square inch than the average tattoo artist.

And I've checked out each and every one of those tattoos, mainly looking for other women's names. I haven't found any yet, but if I do, I got me some strong teeth and sharp nails.

"The Rabbit will be fine, Mama."

"And how are you going to feed yourself?"

I had shrugged. I mean, it didn't matter because I was going to get fed in bed. Wait—Roger usually likes to eat at the table. "I'll manage, Mama."

"Child, you can't cook."

True. "I will manage, Mama, okay?"

"Well, what about—"

"Why should I stay here, Mama?" I interrupted.

More jaw dropping. I rarely interrupt her. She picked up her jaw and blinked at me. "You should stay here because it's the . . . because it's the *sensible* thing to do."

"It's sensible to pay rent to your own mama for seven years?" I asked.

She had sighed. "Is that what this is about? Is *that* what this is about? If this is about money, Erlana, I can—"

"It's not about money, Mama."

"It isn't?"

"No." Simple answers are the best for jaw-dropping, repetitive mamas.

"Then why do you have to leave?"

She had finally asked the right question. "I am twenty-five years old. All these years you've been saying that I need to grow up"—definitely repeated to me more than twice *a day*—"and when I finally do something grown-up, you tell me it's not sensible. Now Mama, I know you're not bipolar"—though she eerily fits most of the clinical descriptions. "And I know you don't like to contradict yourself"—although she does contradict herself as often as the sun rises. "So what did you really mean all these years when you said that I needed to grow up?"

Lots of blinking, ending with her eyes sealed shut, her lips twitching. Her eyes opened with a little roll, a few nasally exhaled breaths escaping. "I meant . . ." Arms folded, head shaking, eyes closed again. "I meant that you should settle down."

With a man, a house, and a baby. It was time to drop the hammer. "Like you did, Mama?"

Eyes open. More whites than browns. Eyebrows stitched together. "Erlana Joy Cole, you will not *sass* me in this house, I will not have sassing in *this* house, you will *not* sass me in *my* house!"

And she said it *three* times *three* different ways! I had looked away and started on the next drawer. "It isn't sassing if it's the truth," I whispered.

"What did you say?"

My mama can hear the click of a car door gently closing five blocks away and know that it's me coming home really late from a date with a boy. My mama can hear me whispering on the phone under my covers while she's working in her garden outside on a windy day. My mama can hear ants fart and fleas sneeze. She can hear snow falling in Maryland. She had heard me, so I didn't repeat it.

Her hands dropped to her sides. "I don't want you to go."

My heart hurt a little when she said that, but I haven't watched half a lifetime of *Oprah* and *Montel* for nothing. "I'm only twenty miles away."

"Twenty miles . . . I want you to stay."

"I'm not a dog, Mama." I couldn't help myself.

"I didn't say you were!"

I turned to her. "I am leaving this house, Mama. I am moving into another house. I have been here long enough. I—"

"Your daddy put you up to this, didn't he?"

No matter how often I tell her, she still won't believe me. "Mama, I haven't spoken to Daddy in almost seven years. You know that." He called and talked to me for all of two minutes the day I graduated from high school. "I am putting *me* up to this."

I had finished packing my dresser and opened the closet door. I didn't have much in there, so with one swoop of an arm, I had emptied my closet of "dress" clothing. Man, do I hate wearing church dresses. As for the shoe boxes stacked floor to ceiling, though, that would be tricky. My feet stopped growing ten years ago, and I religiously take care of my shoes, saving all the boxes.

"What am I going to do without you, Erlana Joy?"

Another shot at my heart. I had to be strong. "You have your flowers, Mama. They're starting to come up now, right? And like you've always said I'm not worth lint around here." I also wasn't worth a pickle, a penny, and later (after inflation) a nickel.

"I didn't mean . . . You know I didn't mean any of that *literally*, Erlana. I was just trying to . . . to motivate you."

I removed an old framed snapshot of my daddy from my nightstand. "You *have* motivated me, Mama, and this is the result. You have motivated me to grow up and move out."

"You hate me," she said.

That one bounced right off my heart. Is this a line all mamas use as a last resort? "I don't hate you, Mama. I'll never hate you."

"Then why are you running away?"

Oh, I suppose I could have said something lame and melodramatic like "I am going out into the world to find out who I truly am, Mama," or "I am going out into the great beyond to find *me*, Mama," or "I want to see what I can possibly be in this wild and wonderful world." None of that would be true, and I try never to say anything too melodramatic like that.

I just wanted a place where I could be loved, without restrictions, without strings, and without daily lectures, where I could be worth more than lint, a pickle, and some change.

I simply said, "I am not running away, Mama. I am growing up. There's a difference."

"You're running away from me."

"Mama, if I had wanted to run away from you, I would have left long ago." When I was eight years old. "I have overstayed my welcome at your house, that's all, and it is time I was moving on."

"Oh, you're exactly like your daddy, despite all I've tried to do for you. Just exactly like your daddy."

I took that as a compliment. "Thank you, Mama."

And that's how I left her. I didn't feel bad about it. I mean, twenty-five years is probably seven years too long to stay at home. After high school, I could have gone to Radford University—they accepted me and my measly 2.8 GPA—but I stuck around Roanoke because I really didn't have an escape plan for *after* Radford. I would have probably gotten a business degree and worked customer service at the bank for the rest of my life, maybe with Mama as my boss!

It's still one of my recurring nightmares. Not very pretty.

Now, I had an escape plan, and the day I moved, I introduced Jenny's dollhouse to Juan Carlos.

And the housewarming gift he gave me—repeatedly—didn't warm up just the house.

Chapter 6

After dumping what little I had and setting up my entertainment system (a twenty-inch TV/DVD player and a boom box) at my new house, I drove back to Roanoke to pick up Juan Carlos at Berglund Auto World. Yes, he is a mechanic without his own ride. Karl at least has an old Chevy Blazer, and Roger has a Nissan pickup. Almost every day, Juan Carlos's mama drops him off at work in her old Pontiac Bonneville or he takes the city bus to work. His mama also gets most of his money. At first, I thought it was sweet, but now . . . He is definitely too attached to his mama, and though I have never met her, I want to smack her for not severing the umbilical cord. A man pushing thirty should not be living at home with his mama.

"Where are we going?"

"For a drive."

He licked his lips. "You have something . . . planned?"

"Maybe."

"Well, okay."

Juan Carlos isn't exactly a conversationalist, but he's very good with his tongue.

I watched Juan Carlos's eyes for any signs of life when we got to the cottage, but there were none. When the road finally ended at the beginning of the tall grass, he turned and stared at me. "What is this all about?"

I raised my eyebrows and got out.

"Who lives here?" he asked as he got out.

I turned and stepped into his arms, resting my forehead on his chest. "I do." He started to speak but stopped. "Come on," I said.

"Wait," he said. "Is this your house?"

I kissed his nose. "Yes. And it's a cottage, not a house." Okay, it's a love shack, but I doubt Juan Carlos would understand. "And I'm staying here nearly rent-free as long as I do a few things around the house."

"Like cutting all this grass."

I kissed his lips. "That will be the first thing *you'll* do." Though Roger really needs the sun worse. Juan Carlos's skin is like hot coffee laced with jalapeño peppers. He doesn't need any more sun. "Do you like it?"

"I have not seen it yet."

"Well, do you like what you've seen so far?"

He looked around. "Where are your neighbors?"

"There aren't any. Maybe a deer or two will come sniffing around."

"And it is nearly rent-free?"

I nodded.

"Well, show me this place."

Since it was only five o' clock, we had plenty of light to see inside the house without having to crank up Sheila. Juan Carlos didn't say much as we moved from room to room. Mr. Wilson had cleaned out all the closets, so I had a better idea of what my office/studio/future glorified shoe rack would look like.

"Well?" I asked as he sat on the bed in the master bedroom.

"This place is like a museum," he said.

"I like it just fine."

He raised and lowered his eyes. "It is so far from Roanoke."

I straddled him, wrapping my legs around his back. "It's only twenty miles."

"Yes, but . . ."

"If you'd only get yourself a car. Doesn't Berglund give employee discounts?"

"Yes, but . . ."

But Mama needs the money. I didn't want to go down that road.
"Aren't there loaner cars you can borrow?"

"Yes, but they do not like employees to do that."

"Well, you know I don't mind picking you up." It was kind of how we met in the first place, only the other way around. Sort of. More on that later.

"I do not like you picking me up."

"Because it's not macho," he was about to add, and I didn't want to have *that* conversation again. Juan Carlos has a *long* list of what a woman should and shouldn't do.

"I don't mind picking you up, you know that." I kissed him on the neck. "As long as I can have you here all to myself more often, I don't mind at all."

"But I must work," he said.

I unbuttoned his shirt and unbuckled his belt. "Let me do all the work, baby. . . ."

Forgive us, Jenny, I prayed while we made love in a yellow room as the orange sun set over the green pond, rocking Jenny's bed as the waves gently kissed the shore. And afterwards, while we cuddled without speaking, I realized something monumental.

I like this, but I don't really like Juan Carlos.

I couldn't put my finger on it at the time, and I still can't. There's something . . . wrong with him. The loving is better than good, but the conversation is butt, and it's not because he doesn't speak English that well. He's just too . . . something.

I spent the rest of that spring break breaking my own back, since Roger was busy with his job (more on that and him later), Juan Carlos was working double shifts because of another damn GM recall (which makes me glad I own a VW), and Karl, well, I couldn't find Karl. I paged him to death, but he never answered my page, which most likely meant he was on the road somewhere.

Mr. Wilson came to my rescue. He just . . . showed up, real

sneaky and freaky like, saying, "Jenny said you might need some help."

I was beginning to like Jenny, though it's beyond freaky at night to know a ghost might be walking around *her* kitchen downstairs.

Mr. Wilson and I reduced the dock to a stack of wood on the left side of the barn, talking mostly about the wildlife around the pond. He told me about anemones, arbutus, Indian pipes, and blazing stars, and all their medicinal properties. He recounted stories of white-tailed deer, red foxes, mink, muskrat, ground squirrels, and even a few wild turkeys that visited the dollhouse. I know I have a ground squirrel living in the attic, which really makes no sense. He should be living on the ground, right? I hear him rooting around up there every night, but he (or she?) is usually quiet after eleven. Maybe Jenny quiets him down, too.

I then asked Mr. Wilson about snakes.

I wish I hadn't.

"There are some gopher snakes around here, but they're harmless," he said. "They'll keep the field mice down, though. I remember when we had to use an outhouse behind the barn before we had the septic put in. One day, I was sitting there taking care of my business when I felt something poking me from below. I stood up, and sure enough, a gopher snake six feet long came up out of the cesspit. I don't rightly know why it was down there. . . ."

I *always* check the toilet bowl now, even though the bathroom is on the second floor. Shit, I even check it at work. Roanoke isn't that far from the country.

"That pond out there," he said as we took an iced tea break a little later in the day, "is full of largemouth bass, but if anyone asks you, you tell 'em that there's nothing but bluegill and sunfish in it. We don't want our secret getting out."

He pointed to a long aluminum canoe balanced between two rafters in the barn. "That there's the best way to fish the pond, if you ask me. Shove off, drift a bit, and move with the water like the fish do. Some of the best spots to cast are within twenty feet of this dock."

I've never done it in a canoe. That might be interesting. Roger would try it. He's the most adventurous. We'd probably tip over that canoe fifty times . . . and we'd have a million mosquito bites for our troubles. Hmm. Maybe there *are* some places where a lady cannot entertain her man properly.

Mr. Wilson then took me around the front of the house. "There's a sidewalk under all this grass. It's just a bunch of concrete squares that run from the house to the driveway." He took a few steps from the door, kneeling and pulling up a clump of sod. "Here's one. There are even a bunch leading down to the dock, spaced about a foot apart."

Jenny's dollhouse is like a good mystery novel. The more I dig through the layers and the dirt, the more mysteries I solve. I feel more like a detective than a tenant, gradually revealing the secrets of the house.

I spent the better part of spring break hacking, carving, and digging until a parking area appeared. Then I trimmed and cleared bushes, saplings, and tree branches from the worst section of the long driveway. I was sweaty and sticky, bugs dive-bombing me as the sun started to set, but I felt wonderful.

But Juan Carlos wasn't havin' it.

"Why did you not wait for me to help you?"

"I had nothing better to do," I said as we ate some grilled cheese sandwiches, our first meal together in my new house. Besides, I had thought, if I waited on his ass (or Roger's or Karl's), nothing would get done.

He didn't ask to move in with me, but I didn't think he would. What would his mama say about that? However, I have to entertain the possibility that Karl or Roger may ask me that very question. I already know my answer: *No.*

How would they react? Hmm. Karl would probably shrug it off. Yeah, Karl's a roughneck. He wouldn't care. He would just ask to ask, you know? To be polite. Roger . . . Hmm. Roger is more of an enigma. He would probably go away hurt, hardly saying a word, and that would hurt me the most, since we have the best conversations. But then . . . then he'd be back as if nothing had happened.

At least I hope he'd come back.

I was so happy and unparanoid that first day—I finally had one of my men visit me at *my* new house, far from Roanoke—that I did something stupid. I promised Juan Carlos that I'd cook for him whenever he visited, and I regretted it once school began again. I was too tired to cook anything special, since I was also going to football practice for the Revenge after school. I made hot ham-and-cheese sandwiches and home fries one night and baked spaghetti another night. But no matter what I cooked, Juan Carlos rarely said anything positive about the meal.

"Is there something burning?" he'd say as he walked into the kitchen.

"No."

I found myself talking to the pots and pans on the stove. I hoped they wouldn't take it personally.

He did the same thing each day he visited. First, he commented on what he wanted for dinner, always something he knew I didn't have, like steak or rice. Then his nose detected some stench that only he could smell. After that, he'd lounge in front of the TV, flipping back and forth between the only two channels that came in clearly because I didn't have an antenna. After watching or finding nothing on the "stupid TV," he'd share that information with me and bellow, "I am hungry!" from the top of the stairs.

Meanwhile in the kitchen, I slammed cabinet doors and cursed the walls. We didn't eat like a proper couple—in the kitchen—but instead used TV trays upstairs. After the meal, finished without my receiving so much as a "thank you," I descended to the kitchen, washed and dried the dishes, straightened up, and tried to read some of Hurston's *Their Eyes Were Watching God* while he cursed the TV in Spanish.

I had become Juan Carlos's *other* mother in a matter of days. My "love shack" was fast becoming Juan Carlos's "snack shack."

If I wasn't interested in the "nothing" he found on TV, I'd sit in the easy chair reading about Janie Crawford, Hurston's magnificent heroine, and the three men in *her* life. Juan Carlos was beginning to sound and act more and more like Jody Starks, Janie's second husband, who treated her just a tiny bit better than a slave. *I feel you, Janie Crawford,* I thought as I read. *I know what you're going through because I have a man over here commanding my sofa, waiting, on purpose, until I'm in the middle of an interesting passage to announce things.*

"I will be working double shifts until June starting next Thursday."

I ignored him.

"Lana?" He hit the mute.

"Huh?"

"I said that I will be working double shifts until June starting next Thursday."

"Oh."

"It will be difficult for me to see you."

I shrugged. "We'll find a way." I put down my book. "Why don't we do something special while we have the time?"

"Like what?"

"Like . . . let's go to the movies and then come back here to mess around."

"We do that all the time. It is not special." He nodded. "We will go dancing Friday night. I know a good place to go."

"Where?"

"In Roanoke. It is a small club run by my friend."

That wasn't going to happen. That *couldn't* happen. I mean, just going to a movie, where I insist that we sit in the last row, is hard enough. I have to first find out where the other two are so we can see a movie where they aren't. Even so, half the time I spend more time watching the folks around us than the movie.

"Yes," he said with a smile, "we are going dancing."

I like a decisive man, but I had to think quickly. I hadn't been dancing in so long. I really like dancing, and with tall, sexy Juan Carlos as my partner, I envisioned having his long, strong hands around me, grabbing my ass . . . looking up into his sexy unshaven face, his dark eyes . . . grinding on him all night long.

But not in Roanoke. Roanoke likes to talk. Roanoke has no life, so it sucks the life out of others' lives by running its mouth.

Roanoke is a gossip, a perpetual Nosy Parker at the beauty salon of southwest Virginia.

"Why don't we go down to Greensboro? They have better clubs than Roanoke." For black folks, that is, and Juan Carlos is just dark enough to pass for black. "And the Revenge doesn't play this weekend, so . . ."

"I do not understand why you must play football," he said. "It is not for a lady to do."

It is for *this* lady. Only Roger has ever seen me play football, and the massages he gives me after my games are heavenly. In fact, only Roger and I have ever sat down and watched football together, making all sorts of silly, um, sexual bets. If my team makes a first down, he has to go down on me. If my team scores, I score. I always pick the team with the best offense, and he always seems to choose the team with the worst defense for some reason.

I, um, I really like it when my team scores lots of points, and Roger doesn't seem to mind if his team gets shut out.

I guess if I really think about it, I play a little football in bed, too. For me, either a man is going to pop me with a kiss or he's gone. Either we're going to be tackling each other or he's going to be stepping. If I don't sweat or end up dirty, bruised, or cut, we aren't trying hard enough. If afterwards I don't ache, the love didn't take and I might not be awake. If a man gets with me, he had better like to shake and bake all the way into my end zone.

Juan Carlos used to think he might break me in two during sex. "That's not going to happen, Juan Carlos," I told him. "You can shake and bake me, but you're not going to break me."

I can't say the same thing to Karl. He really knows how to party in my end zone.

Juan Carlos and I often argued about my "hobby," as he called it, and that night was no different.

"You know I want to stay in shape for you, Juan Carlos," I had said. "You like me to be athletic in bed, right?"

"In bed, yes." He smiled.

"So I'm just trying to stay in shape for you." And Karl. And Roger.

"But you will grow out of this."

"I am not a child, Juan Carlos."

"You will grow out of this," he repeated.

Nope. "Look, I want to go dancing with you, but only in Greensboro, okay?"

"But why do we have to drive all the way to North Carolina to go dancing?"

It took a lot of convincing—and several condoms—but Juan Carlos gave in after lots of horizontal dancing.

On Friday, I prepared for our night of dancing. I picked out an electric blue, backless, one-piece short set. The neckline plunged, revealing the top of what cleavage I had, and my long sexy legs smoldered out of my shorts. I modeled in front of the mirror and said, "Girl, I see a whole lot of you leaking out all over."

Juan Carlos didn't like what he saw at all. "You are wearing that?"

"What's wrong with it?"

"It is too revealing. I want you to change."

I rolled my eyes and neck. "No."

"No?"

"No." I can be decisive, too.

He said nothing for two straight hours, until we got to a club in Greensboro, where I discovered that Juan Carlos could not dance a lick. Not a lick. He was too stiff, he didn't know what to do with his hands, and he couldn't keep up with the hip-hop beat. Meanwhile, I jiggled, undulating smoothly in rhythm to the music. A couple of black guys with a whole lot more rhythm than Juan Carlos bounced and shook their way between us, and for a moment, Juan Carlos disappeared.

And I didn't give a shit.

Four songs later, I looked around, located Juan Carlos at a table, and walked over. "Did I wear you out already?"

"No. I disappeared, and you did not notice."

I sat across from him. "This place is jamming! Do you mind if I dance some more?"

"Yes, I mind if my girlfriend dances with other men."

He was one-third right, anyway. Each one of my men thinks he's my boyfriend, which means, I guess, that I'm not duplicitous, but "tri-plicitous," and it definitely makes me trip sometimes.

I took his hand. "Come out and dance, then, Juan Carlos. You asked me out to go dancing, so do some dancing with me."

He tried to pull his hand away from mine. "I cannot compete."

He had that right. I dropped his hand. "Well, if you hear a slow song, come on out."

That club didn't play a single slow song that night, most likely to keep people sweaty and drinking their overpriced drinks. Juan Carlos had bought us Cokes, and the ice cubes in my glass had all melted by the time I came over for a rest.

"You're not having fun, are you?" I asked.

"I am having the time of my life sipping a flat Coke in a smoky room while black men make moves on my girlfriend."

Two of my dance partners came over to our table. Both of them were tall, black, and sharply dressed. "Yo, girl, you comin' back out?" the one with the gold earring asked.

I looked at Juan Carlos and raised my eyebrows. "Can I?"

"No. It is not all right."

"What you askin' him for?" Golden Earring asked, putting his butt in Juan Carlos's face.

I looked at Golden Earring with eyes that said "I'd remove that booty from his face if I were you."

I focused on my hands. I started to speak and stopped. I looked at Juan Carlos quickly, then back down at my hands. "I'm tired, fellas."

"What's your number?" the other one asked. "We'll hook up sometime."

Juan Carlos stood. "My girlfriend is tired."

Golden Earring turned and frowned at Juan Carlos. "Yeah, right." He leaned in toward me. "So how about that number?"

Juan Carlos grabbed me by the wrist. "Come on, Lana. It is time to go."

I looked at them and stood. "I have to go," I said, and I squeezed by them, my eyes on the floor all the way to the exit.

Juan Carlos didn't speak to me all the way back to Jenny's dollhouse, another silent two-hour ride, and when I asked if he wanted
to fool around when we got there, he said, "You must be too tired
from all that dancing."

"I'm not tired, Juan Carlos."

"Well, I am. What was that about back there, Lana?"

"What was what about?"

"Those two guys. You did not say I was your boyfriend."

I shook my head. "We shouldn't have gone."

"Because you think I cannot dance?"

I stared holes in his head. "We just shouldn't have gone. And
anyway, why'd you take me dancing if you can't dance?"

"I can dance. Just not like them."

Not like anyone I've ever seen, actually. "So they were good
dancers, Juan Carlos. You know I'd never hook up with them."
Unless they moved to Roanoke, but Roanoke has no good dance
clubs. Hmm. Maybe I should start one. I'll call it "The Spot," and
then people will say, "See you at The Spot." Golden Earring can
come, and then maybe he can hit my G-spot at The Spot—

"Maybe you moved far away to get far away from me."

I hated having a fantasy interrupted. So, though he was right—
sort of—I stood silently in front of him for a few moments. It was almost as if we were on a blind date, and though he was one of my
friends with benefits, I didn't recognize him at all.

"Look, I moved out here to get away from Roanoke, to get a little solitude." To have my men come to me, to keep y'all separated,
to keep this good thing going good. I touched his hand. "I didn't
move here to get away from you. I moved here so that we could
have more time together alone."

He pulled his hand away from my hand. "Then why did you flirt
with the black boys?"

Because they were *fo-ine!* "I wasn't flirting. I was dancing.
There's a difference." Though from the way I dance, I'm more than
just flirting. Teacher's aides who play professional women's football
don't get out much, you know.

"We are not going dancing ever again," he said.

"Okay, we won't go dancing ever again."

"That is right."

He started to undress, and at that moment, I didn't want to do *anything* with him. "Juan Carlos?"

"What?"

"Put your clothes back on."

"What?"

"I want you to leave now."

"What?"

"I do not want to be with you tonight."

"What?"

I grabbed his shirt and threw it at him. "I don't stutter, Juan Carlos. Go home."

"Why?"

And then it all poured out. "Because you never say 'Thank you, Lana,' when I cook for you. You never say 'I'm sorry, Lana,' like tonight, when you made me feel bad for wearing what I wore, giving me the silent treatment for a total of four hours, and then making a scene at the club."

"I did not—"

"And you never say 'I was wrong, Lana,'" I interrupted, "especially when you know you are, like tonight. You are the most ungrateful, most demanding, and most controlling person I have ever known."

Next to my mama, of course, but that's her job.

"I say 'thank you' and 'I am sorry,'" he said.

"Not out loud to me, you don't. Sex is your 'thank you.' Saying nothing is your 'I'm sorry.' I'm tired of it. You weren't put on this earth to criticize me." Only Mama was. "And I won't have anyone in my life hammering away at me."

"I do not hammer away at you."

"You do."

"You are making no sense."

"Okay, I'll spell it out for you. *I ain't havin' it no more.* Not in this house. Not in *my* house."

"You are only renting it, and it is only a cottage."

I counted to three. "I'm not having any of your attitude anymore, man."

"Not having what anymore?"

"Your attitude."

"What attitude?"

I sighed. "You act as if you own me, and you don't. No one owns me."

He blinked. "Are you breaking up with me?"

I wasn't breaking up with him. I just wanted him gone so I could get some me-time. "Just go home, Juan Carlos."

"I am not going home. This is just an argument, and tomorrow you will think differently." He slipped out of his pants and pulled back the covers on the bed.

This was not going well. I decided to resort to "The List," a list of things a man is not supposed to say to a woman . . . only I have to flip it around some. "Juan Carlos, if you were a woman, you would always be on your period."

He gasped.

"If you were a woman, Juan Carlos, you would have a terminal case of PMS."

He jumped out of the bed.

"If you were a woman, you would be a bitch, Juan Carlos. The dictionary must have your picture next to the word 'bitch.'"

His jaw dropped.

"No one tells me what to do in my own house, Juan Carlos. You're . . . not . . . my . . . daddy!"

I have never seen Juan Carlos move so fast. He dressed, said "You . . . you" a couple times, eventually called *me* a "bitch" and a "bunta," and tore out of the house. I watched dirt flying up from behind his mama's rusty old Bonneville and sighed when the taillights finally disappeared.

Later, alone again with a glass of iced tea, standing at the edge of the pond, I hummed some old Bessie Smith blues as the tiny waves of the pond lapped at my feet.

The next day, Juan Carlos returned with a dozen long-stem roses

and some outstanding takeout from El Rodeo. He also apologized
to me all night long for his bad attitude.

I likes me some drama.

Juan Carlos is good for that.

And he dances horizontally just fo-ine.

Chapter 7

I have never almost "lost" Karl like that, mainly because Karl is so hard to find sometimes. But when I do find him, I usually have to take a day off from work and life in general afterward.

We, um, we tear it up.

I've been with Karl the longest, about eight months. I was between men when I first met him while jogging through Washington Park on a hot August day. Our first few conversations intrigued me mainly for what he *could* have said but *didn't* say, and for what I *could* have said but *didn't* say.

To stay in shape for the upcoming tryouts for the Roanoke Revenge, I used to park over at the Addison Middle School track and run a loop from there through a neighborhood down to a creek and up the hill to the Washington Park pool and the field beyond, where I did some wind sprints. Thus, Karl saw me for the first time at my absolute worst that hot, humid August day. I was sweaty. I was stank. I was shiny. I was funky.

He was sitting on the hood of his Blazer wearing a white wife beater, long black baggy jean shorts, and tan Timberland boots. He had a little bling going on, but mostly he was tattooed and muscled from the neck down and he was fo-ine.

And I looked like shit—except for my running shoes—in some

old green mesh shorts, an oversized gray long-sleeved shirt, and a black Nike visor, but that's how I usually work out. Why do so many women try to look cute when they can't possibly look cute, all sweaty and stank, when they work out? Why ruin a "she-she" hundred-dollar jogging outfit with sweat when any old pair of sweats will do?

Okay, okay. I didn't match that day. My "she-she" running shorts and top were already dirty, and my "outfit" (such as it was) was the best I could find. Besides, I didn't expect to meet anyone, right?

As I neared him that day, he called out, "What you running for, girl?"

I played the shy girl, pointing at myself.

He smiled. "Yeah, I'm talking to you."

I could barely catch my breath. That hill was a killer, and so was his smile. "Hey," I said. I *didn't* say, "Is this your ride?" or "Do I know you?" or "What's your name?" I just said, "Hey."

"Why are you running on such a hot day?"

"To keep in shape."

He *didn't* say, "Girl, you got a nice one." He simply asked, "What for?"

Which was a compliment, right? He was saying without saying that I already looked to be in good shape. "I'm getting in shape for football." I *didn't* say, "I'm getting in shape for you and me getting it on later."

His face didn't change, and he didn't hesitate. "You play?"

"I'm going to. For the Roanoke Revenge."

He nodded. "I heard about them. You any good?"

I *could* have said, "I'm best when I'm being bad" or "Wanna find out?" All I said was, "Yeah."

He had such a young face for someone my age, but it turns out he was twenty-two and fresh out of college at Hampton. "Maybe I'll have to come and see you play."

I *could* have said, "We can play all night long, player," or I *could* have asked him to play with me back at his place, but I could only say, "All right."

I kept on to that field beyond the pool and ran ten wind sprints. Then I half-jogged past the pool and passed him again.

He slid down from the hood. "You thirsty?"

I nodded.

He pulled some bottled water from a cooler inside his Blazer and threw it to me. I took a sip and poured some on my head.

"Thanks," I said.

"I'm Karl," he said.

"Lana," I said. "But some folks call me 'Peanut.'"

He smiled. He just . . . smiled. He *didn't* ask if I had a boyfriend, and he *didn't* rape me with his eyes, instead focusing on my eyes and not my thighs. "You run here all the time?"

"When I can," I said, "about every other day."

"I'll look out for you."

I thanked him again for the drink and jogged away real slow.

I came back two days later, this time in my "she-she" jogging outfit.

"There she is," he said from his perch on the Blazer.

"Hey."

"Catch you when you come back by?"

"Sure."

I did only eight wind sprints that day, but not because it was hot or I was tired. Karl had intrigued me by *not* using any lines or really hitting on me. I kind of wondered why any man would be sitting on the hood of his Blazer on a hot August day for maybe three days in a row, but maybe he was there only to see me again. He had a bottle of Gatorade for me when I jogged back, and I took that as a sign of something big.

"You do any weight training?" he asked.

"Some." Which was a lie and a half. I've just always been naturally muscular.

"Maybe we can work out together sometime."

I *could* have asked, "Are you asking me out on a date?" but I didn't. Who goes weightlifting on a date? I also *could* have said, "We could work out at your place right now." I'm pretty forward, but I'm not that forward. "Sure," I said. "We can do that."

"Breckinridge has a weight room," he said. "I can meet you there tomorrow around seven."

"Okay. Seven."

The next day, precisely at seven, he showed up at the Breckinridge Middle School weight room, and we worked out. He was helpful and charming, and though I made it obvious that I had never lifted any weights before, he helped me with my technique, let me borrow his weight belt, and spotted me. We were just two athletes improving our bodies, and I spent most of my time wondering what our two athletic bodies could do to each other in bed.

I was sitting on a weight bench toweling off when he asked, "You doing anything this evening?"

I was sweaty, stank, and sore, and yet he wanted to see more of me. "No."

"Want to hang out?"

"Sure. I'd like to go home and take a shower first."

He *didn't* say, "Can I join you?" though I probably would have let him if Mama wasn't at home. "Me, too. I'll meet you downtown at Corned Beef, say around ten?"

At Corned Beef and Company, which is a little restaurant and bar in Center in the Square, we drank sodas after I told him that I didn't drink. He didn't question it, didn't wonder about it, and didn't make me feel like a child because of it.

"How old are you?" I asked.

"Twenty-two."

I stared into my Coke. "I'm twenty-four."

He *didn't* ask, "You got a problem with it?" or say "Age ain't nothing but a number." Instead, he asked, "Want to go for a walk?"

"Sure."

We walked through Elmwood Park, and once we were in the relative darkness under the bridge connecting one part of the main library to the other, he kissed my cheek. He *didn't* say anything, and I *didn't* say anything. We just kept . . . walking together, not holding hands, smiling mostly.

It was cute.

We walked up to where my car and his Blazer were parked, and without him even asking, I got into his Blazer, we went back to his place, and . . .

It was very nice.

Okay, it was more than nice. I am, well, active when it comes to lovemaking, often wearing a man out. With Karl, though, I had met my match. It was as if we were in competition to see who could put a worse sexual hurting on the other. It was exhausting, it was erotic, it required several water breaks—even a little ice that didn't stay ice for long on my back.

I miss those first few meetings because they contained the *longest* conversations we ever had. He wasn't into being an entrepreneur yet. That came later. He had a marketing degree, and he was trying to figure out how to put it to use on his own terms. He despised corporate America, doubting it'd ever hire him because of his skin color and all those tattoos. He had dreams of having his own store and being his own man, and I had dreams of *us* owning *our* own store and being financially independent.

Then he started taking trips to New York to "do his thing," buying fake Coach bags and bootleg DVDs to sell down here. This led to several broken dates and many nights of me sitting by the phone. It was the same old pattern I had just been through with four other men. I received fewer phone calls *from* him and made more pages *to* him. It was so aggravating not to be able to contact him directly. I offered to buy him a cell phone, but he only told me, "I'm old school, Peanut."

That was his only explanation.

Then he started paying more attention to his body than mine. Less talk, more action, little conversation before, during, or after lovemaking. It was all "hit it and quit it." I mean, we used to do foreplay all the time, you know, flirting on the phone whenever he'd call me back, grabbing and touching in his Blazer, so that by the time we got back to his place, I was swimming in my own juices. Gradually, we flirted less, with fewer touches and grabs, did just enough foreplay to get him started . . .

It got old.

And I wasn't going to do "old" anymore.

Chapter 8

If the old Karl could have come around more often, I wouldn't have had to add Juan Carlos, who has always been more interested in my pleasure than his pleasure.

And as with Karl, Juan Carlos and I met by accident. Actually, it was the Rabbit's fault. My car broke down on Williamson Road a block from Berglund Auto World last fall. It just quit in the left lane. I put my flashers on and waited for help while cars whizzed by me on both sides. No one stopped to help me. No one.

Enter Juan Carlos.

He came out of nowhere and said, "I will help you."

"Thank you," I said, looking at his nice ass and little thin moustache.

"If you steer, I will push," he said.

You know I was thinking nasty thoughts when he said that. I hadn't had any good loving for weeks, since Karl was off doing "his thing."

Juan Carlos first stopped traffic in both lanes simply by holding out his hands, and then he pushed the Rabbit smoothly into the lot at Berglund.

"You're only doing this so y'all can fix it and charge me an arm and a leg," I said when I got out.

"I will fix it for you," he said. "Pop the hood."

And then . . . I watched him work on my car, pulling this, adjusting that, getting all greasy. I also watched his ass and fantasized. He ended up adding two quarts of oil, some coolant, and some water to my radiator. He added something to my oil, closed the hood, and told me to start it up.

It didn't start. It only clicked a bit, then nothing.

"You need a battery, too," he said.

No, I thought, *I need my hands on that ass of yours.* I had so many hoochie thoughts that day.

"Do you have my size?" I asked, staring directly at his package. I was sure he had my size. "I mean, do you have batteries for VWs?"

"I am sure we do. Wait inside where it is cooler, and I will get you a battery."

"I'll wait right here," I said. I enjoyed watching him work.

He put in a new battery, and the Rabbit came back to life. He came over to my window. "No charge."

I didn't have any money on me, anyway, but I protested. "I have to pay you somehow."

"It is okay. You needed help. I helped."

I liked his attitude *then.* "Well, don't you want to . . . test it out? You know, make sure everything else is working." I licked my lips. "I'll even let you drive."

He shrugged. "Okay."

So . . . we took a drive, and he drove the hell out my Rabbit, zipping us up Williamson Road. I watched him shift gears with those big hands of his . . . imagining those big hands squeezing my girls.

Yeah, I was horny.

I had him pull into an empty lot on Plantation Road so I could drive. He parked, got out, came over to my side, opened my door . . . and I pulled him in.

There wasn't much room on the passenger side, even when I pushed the seat all the way back, but somehow I managed to get his pants off, my pants off, his stuff where it belonged . . .

I, um, I attacked his ass.

Twice.

When he was through—I could have gone another round—I drove him back to Berglund.

"I want to see you again," I said.

"I would like that," he said.

I didn't tell him that I had a boyfriend, and I didn't feel guilty about it. That surprised me at first, but then I reasoned, "I don't have a ring on this finger."

Later, I didn't have to pay full price for a new radiator, new struts, or new brakes thanks to Juan Carlos's employee discount. I'm lucky that way, I guess. My Rabbit has had more oil changes and, in general, I have had better maintenance on my car *and* my body with Juan Carlos, but I get to pick and choose when I get "serviced." I didn't have to sit by the phone anymore after that. If Karl was AWOL, Juan Carlos was on.

And if Juan Carlos didn't have such a bad attitude, I wouldn't have had to add Roger.

See, it's all Karl's fault.

Okay, I know I'm rationalizing. I probably would have added the other two even if Karl had been faithful (I doubt he has been), had been around more than once a month, and had been a better conversationalist.

When it comes to body and sex, Karl is the clear winner. He treats his body like a temple, I am his worshipper, and when we get busy, it's a religious experience, just me and my African god. He's so good, um, pelvically (if that's even a word) that he has to be practicing elsewhere to keep his "thrusters" in tune.

When it comes to sheer passion, Juan Carlos has the others beat. He knows how to romance me with the occasional flower, to sing to me in a language I don't understand as much as I *feel,* to warm me from head to toe with his hands.

And when it comes to my mind and soul, Roger fills me to bursting, listening to my rants and criticisms, writing me poetry, giving advice only when I ask for it, and massaging my cares away with his hands and his words.

I've made them sound perfect, huh?

Well, they aren't perfect.

Karl chews his nails, Juan Carlos's nails are sometimes caked with grease, and Roger's nails are usually too long. Karl bathes in cologne, Juan Carlos sometimes smells like exhaust fumes and gasoline, and Roger nearly always smells like the great outdoors. All three make some seriously strange faces when they're angry—and sometimes during sex—that are not attractive at all. Juan Carlos's nostrils flare, Roger's ears wiggle, and Karl's upper lip curls until it touches his nose. None of them dresses all that well (not that I care, since I'm more interested in what's under their clothes), every last one of them wearing jeans and boots. And none of them is particularly smooth when it comes to the "right" thing to say to me to turn me on. In fact, most of the time I spend with Karl and Juan Carlos involves no dialogue whatsoever.

We just . . . get it on.

Now as for Roger . . . Damn, he makes me sigh, and though I know it's wrong to think this, I wish to God he was black. If he were black, we'd be married with 2.1 kids, a dog, and a picket fence already. Thinking that doesn't make me a racist, does it? I mean, Roger has soul, he has heart, he has this soft way of talking, those hazel eyes, that flaming curly red hair and matching goatee, which I've secretly nicknamed a "man-gina"—

Boy looks like his head is on fire even at night.

Of the three, he speaks to me, and I don't mean talking. He's not as—and *don't* be thinking I'm about to say "as big" or "as endowed" as the others . . . because he *is*—he's just not as fiery. He takes his time. He worships my body slowly, and after Juan Carlos and Karl, it's nice to be devoured slowly, as if I'm a seven-course meal he has to savor carefully, tenderly.

Though his hair could signal the space shuttle, Visine could use his entire head in an eye drops commercial, circus clowns are envious, and Ronald McDonald wants to sue him for hair-rights infringement.

Enough of the hair jokes.

Roger's passion just burns slowly, like that candle you keep in your bathroom for show that you decide to light one day and, for whatever reason, just won't burn itself out for months and months.

Roger's like that.

I just wish he didn't sell death.

Chapter 9

He doesn't "sell" death exactly, but he makes such a creepy living.

His family runs Fairview Cemetery, which isn't that creepy. I mean, someone has to do it, right? And it must be a good business. It's just creepy that folks have to die to give him and his family a living.

I first met Roger at the front door of my mama's house one cool Saturday in late February while Mama was working overtime at the banking center. I had just gotten out of the shower, so I was barely wearing anything—no bra, no drawers, just some shorts and a T-shirt. And as soon as that cool air hit my girls, my nipples jumped to life.

"Good afternoon," he said.

"Is it?" I asked.

"What?" he said.

"Afternoon."

He looked at my toes, and they are some ragged-looking things. "Yes, ma'am. It's after three."

"Oh." I had had a wild night of passion at Karl's apartment the night before, so I had just gotten up.

He was still staring at my toes so much that I crossed one foot over the other, giving him a glimpse of only the five less crusty ones.

"Do you have a reason for ringing my doorbell?" I asked.

"Oh, yeah," he said, looking all good in a dark suit and tie and shiny black church shoes.

I thought he was a religious boy selling God, maybe half of a pair of Jehovah's Witnesses. I like messing with them, flirting with them mostly, and that day, my "outfit" left nothing to his imagination.

There's not much else to do in Roanoke in February, you know.

"Well, I'll get right to the points, I mean, point, Miss, um"—he looked at a card—"Cole."

He had noticed my points. I checked my girls, and my points were still right pointy. Karl says they're "half dollars." Juan says they're *pesos* or something. Roger would later call them "pepperoni."

"You have a name?"

"Oh. Yeah. I'm Roger McDowell. Um, Miss Cole—"

"Lana."

"Um, Lana, have you ever thought about where you might go when you die?"

"Heaven, I hope," I said.

His face got all red. "No, um, I meant, have you ever thought about where your body would go?"

"Huh?"

He smiled, and he had a decent smile, a little toothy but not bucktoothed. "I get that a lot."

"Get what a lot?"

"That 'huh.'" He handed me his card. "I represent Fairview Cemetery, and believe it or not, we're having a sale."

That's when I started cracking up.

"That's right, Lana, for a limited time, you can get two plots at Fairview Cemetery for the pre-need discounted price of seventeen hundred dollars, and if you act quickly—"

"Before I die, right?"

"That's right. If you act quickly before you die, not only will you pay as low as twenty-five dollars a month, perpetual care included, but you may also qualify for thirty-six months of interest-free payments and"—he raised his eyebrows—"you can pick out a pair of nice plots in the front row."

I liked him and his sense of humor immediately—I'm impulsive like that—so I invited him inside and had him sit on Mama's favorite couch. The couch is black-and-white checked, and Roger was red, white, and embarrassed all over it.

"I knew you weren't interested," he said, "so I went off the script."

"There's a script?"

"Yeah."

"That's creepy."

"I know."

"Does it work?"

He nodded. "But it only seems to work if the person I'm talking to is sixty or older. It's usually the discounted headstone that seals the deal."

"No way."

"You'd be surprised how often people actually come out to browse the cemetery, looking for a prime piece of real estate."

"They actually come out to pick their planting places?" I know spit was flying when I said that.

He shrugged. "Some want a nice view of the valley or the mountains, and others just want some shade."

I have never laughed so much about death in my life. He told me about people who asked the strangest questions: "Where's the nearest sewage line?" "Does this cemetery have a drainage system?" "What if there's a flood?" "Do you really put the caskets six feet deep?" "Why six feet and not seven feet or even eight?" I watched Roger light up as he talked, focusing on his little dimples, his curly red hair, the red hair on his legs sprouting just above his black dress socks, the overall smoothness of his skin, his man-gina and what that might feel like on my stuff.

"I have an easier time with women," he told me, "because most of the time, their husbands precede them into the great beyond—or they're *about* to."

"It costs seventeen hundred dollars?"

He nodded.

"And that's a discount?"

"You wouldn't believe how much it costs if you wait until some-one dies, and we only take cash then."

I blinked. "How much?"

"A couple thousand."

D-damn.

"As the script says"—he cleared his throat—"your cost is always much, much less if you plan ahead."

"To be dead," I added.

He smiled. "Yeah."

"Um, isn't it kind of, well, creepy to bring death into people's houses?"

He nodded. "I get a lot of doors slammed in my face."

What a crummy job, I thought, *but he has to be paid pretty well.* "How does a person get your job, Roger?" I asked.

"I was born into it." He sighed. "It's a family business."

"Oh." In a way, I was glad. I mean, if Roger had actually gone to some school to learn how to plant people, I would have been even more freaked out. "Um, what happens if your cemetery, um, runs out of space?"

He squared his shoulders and changed his voice to someone older. "At the present rate of interment, Fairview should have burial space well into the twenty-second century."

Creepier.

"That's what my father tells people."

"And you just . . . go door-to-door like this?"

"When the weather's nice. And if I'm not doing this, I'm putting flowers out on graves—you know, the graves of those whose fami-lies have forgotten them."

"That's sweet."

"A lot of people forget. But mostly, I am the perpetual-care man, cutting the grass and trimming around the graves. I also assist my father at interments. Pretty soon I'll be supervising interments on my own."

That has to be the hardest job of all! All that pain and sorrow, maybe daily, and, what, there may be three or four funerals some days? It made me appreciate dealing with developmentally handicapped kids a lot more. All I have to do is push a wheelchair, help a kid feed himself or herself, or make sure they get in and out of the bathroom okay. Roger has to watch people at their lowest, their most grief-stricken.

"I've taken up too much of your time," he said, and he stood, all six feet of him.

I like a man who's taller than I am, and I especially like a man who has a sense of humor. He was someone I could talk to, unlike Karl or Juan Carlos, so I had to get him to come back. "My mama might be interested." I knew she wouldn't be interested at all, but at least I'd get to see him again.

He took out a little notepad. "How old is your mother?"

I blinked.

"Sorry. I shouldn't have asked."

"No, it's all right. I suppose you have to ask. Mama is pushing fifty, but she looks much older."

He wrote it down. "I'll have to come back before it's too late, then."

I nodded, biting my lip to keep myself from smiling.

"Is there, um, a Mr. Cole?"

"No. He doesn't live with us. Um, can you come back later tonight?" I didn't want to be with Karl two nights in a row, and Juan Carlos was working too late again, so I thought . . . why not?

"Sure."

"Around seven."

He smiled. "Seven. See you later, Lana."

I tripped all through dinner with Mama, asking her all sorts of questions.

"How are you feeling, Mama?"

"Fine, just fine."

"How's your blood pressure?"

She looked up from her greens at me. "Normal."

"They check you for diabetes every time you go, right?"

"Yes."

"You haven't, um, gone through the change yet, have you?"

"No. What's this about?"

"Nothing."

When the doorbell rang at seven—Roger is a punctual man, too—I burst out of the kitchen to the front door. I returned to the kitchen with my hand firmly grasping Roger's arm.

"Mama?"

Lots of delicious blinking.

"This is my friend, Roger."

"Uh-huh," Mama said.

"Roger has something to tell you, Mama."

"He . . . does?" Her eyes were like soup bowls, I swear!

"Yes, ma'am," Roger said. "May I sit?"

Mama nodded, never taking her eyes off his red hair.

"Mrs. Cole, have you ever thought about where your final resting place will be?"

I knew Mama was shook up because she always corrected people when they called her "Mrs." By the time he finished his question, however, she turned back into Mama.

"My final what?" she asked.

"Your final resting place. Have you ever thought about where you will be buried in the event of your demise?"

Mama straightened up and looked hard at me. "You're from some cemetery, right?"

"Yes, ma'am. Fairview Cemetery."

She shot a look at me. "Uh-huh." She turned to Roger. "I am *not* interested."

Roger looked at me, and I half expected him to say, "But you *said* she'd be interested." He only looked down at the table, smiled, and looked back at me . . . differently, as if he knew why he had made a second trip. "I understand," he said to Mama. He stood. "I understand," he said *to me!* "It was nice to meet you, Mrs. Cole."

"It's Miss," Mama spat.

Roger nodded to Mama, nodded to me, and then headed for the door, me trailing behind. At the door he turned, his face getting all pink. "Um, Miss Cole—"

"Lana, remember?"

"Lana. Um, normally two people go out a few times before, you know, meeting the parents, so, uh . . ."

Damn, he was quick!

"So, are you doing anything, say . . . tonight?"

I stepped closer to him and whispered, "No."

"Would you, um, like to do something tonight?"

I nodded. "And since you've already met my mama," I whispered, "maybe we can take our relationship to a whole new level. Where do you live?"

"I'm practically your neighbor." He pointed behind Mama's house to some apartments. "I live about a block away."

Perfect, I thought.

I had messed with some white guys in high school, but I had never been with any of them in the biblical sense, so that night was illuminating in so many ways.

I drove (so Mama wouldn't be suspicious) to his place, a one-bedroom A-frame apartment within shouting distance of Mama's back deck. It was a clean, neat, and sparse apartment, hardly a bachelor pad. Actually, it was practically empty. A counter with stools sectioned off the kitchenette from the rest of the apartment, which was devoid of any furniture—even a couch—save a thirty-six-inch TV on a stand containing stereo equipment, thin gauze covering the only large window, which looked out onto the second-floor walkway.

"Um, Roger," I said, but I didn't finish asking where his bed was because he took me by the hand to the back corner of the apartment to a twelve-by-twelve section of linoleum. He kissed my neck.

"Where's your bed?"

He kept on kissing. "You're standing on it."

"You sleep on the floor?"

"No." He tapped the back wall. "That's a wall bed."

"Oh."

He worked his way to my girls, introducing himself slowly with his tongue with a lot more tenderness than Juan Carlos or Karl.

"Roger, are you going to—"

I froze. Through the gauze, I saw the outline of someone walking by.

He had my shirt off.

I covered up my girls. "Roger, can they see us?"

He was working on my pants using his teeth on my zipper. "What if they can?"

I didn't stop him because the danger thrilled me right down to my stuff. I let him strip me naked, I stripped him naked, and then he devoured me, right there on that cool linoleum floor as shadows walked by and his skin illuminated the apartment. He didn't glow or anything like that, although he sweated pretty freely . . . or maybe it was my sweat that caused . . . Okay, we were both sweating like Michael Jackson at a middle school dance at an all-boys school, sliding all over each other. The sex was better than good, despite how sore my stuff was, his lips and hands touching just about every inch of my body, even my crusty toes. And the whole-body massage he gave me afterward lasted even longer than he did. He finished and yet he kept going, taking cuddling to a whole new level, whispering to the parts of my body. At first, it was creepy. I mean, how many men have conversations with an elbow? But after a while, I wanted him to talk to my stuff again, and he was oh so willing.

Roger is an *excellent* conversationalist.

And we didn't use the bed until our fifth date.

On our fourth date, a plastic tarp covered the linoleum, and in the corner was a can of black paint and a paintbrush. I didn't ask what they were for. I just got naked.

He first painted my booty (that shit tickled!) and pressed me up against the wall that hid the bed. We stepped back, and he admired my booty print. I painted his ass and did the same to him, putting his booty next to mine.

His booty was much smaller.

"Paint my girls," I whispered. He did, and now there's a strange set of breasts hanging above my booty, like somehow I was able to twist my upper body completely around. You know I painted his stuff extra carefully, and I used his stuff to sign our names on the wall.

Twice.

In big block letters.

We have been using the wall bed exclusively since then but sometimes we put it up and make love and more art at the same time.

Dangerous. The boy is dangerous, and I like it.

We made a list of all the places where we *might* like to do it, not that we ever would. The list includes the movie theater (back row), the movie theater (front row), a phone booth (unlighted), a phone booth (lighted), a city bus (at night), a city bus (during the day), a taxi (anytime), a restaurant (crowded), a restaurant (no crowd), the men's room, the ladies' room, and right up against the big window of his apartment behind the gauze. We've done that last one twice, and the second time I popped my head out to smile at a stranger walking by who actually smiled back.

That was a rush.

And afterward, we always eat something: popcorn, chips, ice cream, Easy Cheese, cake frosting, pudding, or anything else he has in his fridge. I brought over some freezer pops one night, and let's just say that I will never have something that cold against my skin—or inside me—again. Though it did keep Roger down there a long time. Roger likes the taste of, um, freezer pops.

While we eat, we watch old black-and-white movies with the sound turned off. Then we "nasty them up" by playing the different parts. We were watching an ancient version of *Frankenstein* one night with Roger playing the monster and me playing the sweet little girl by the pond . . .

"Hello, little girl. You look so hot," Roger said.

"Thank you. What do you use those bolts in your neck for, Mister?"

"Would you like to find out, little girl?"

"I don't know. You're awfully big. Oh, here's a flower for you."

"I like flowers."

I giggled. "Would you like to deflower me?"

"Let's throw some rocks first."

I giggled. "So you can get your rocks off?"

"Of course."

The monster throws a few rocks, then throws the little girl into the pond.

"You made me all wet," I said.

"Can I come in for a little dip?" Roger said. "You can hold onto me using my bolts . . ."

And I never used to like black-and-white films.

Yeah, Roger's a little kinky, but deep down *I'm* a little kinky. We tried to do it like normal people once. I got in on my side of the bed in a T-shirt and shorts. He got in on his side of the bed in his boxers. We kissed and traded hands for a bit, he got on top missionary style, and he went to work.

We ended up laughing too much for him to stay inside me.

That's when we went to Kmart to get a couple helium balloons so we could have "chipmunk sex."

It . . . was . . . a . . . gas!

Overall, Roger is really nice. I know "nice" is not necessarily a "nice" thing to say about a man, but he is truly nice to me. He *likes* to spoon. He *likes* to give massages. He *likes* to hold my hand before, during, and after. He *likes* to hold my face with those big ol' hands of his, and it always gives me chills.

Of course, I didn't tell him about Karl or Juan Carlos. Why ruin heaven with reality? Instead, when we talk, we talk mainly about . . . me.

"You really play football?" he asked while massaging my booty that first night on the floor.

"Knead it harder," I panted.

"I can't need it any more than I do," he said, adding a kiss to my left cheek.

"No, I mean, knead my booty like bread dough."

"Oh."

He's so good I could rent him out, but I'll never do that, though

I bet I could retire pretty young if I did. He's that good. You haven't lived until you've had an hour-long booty rub with some baby oil.

"Yeah, I really play football."

"What's your position?"

"Tight end."

He squeezed harder. "Tell me about it."

We talk while he works on me for hours, and what *don't* we talk about? We talk sports, we talk politics, we talk family, we talk music, we talk jobs, we talk food, we talk movies, and then we talk dreams.

"I want to open up a dance club here in Roanoke and call it 'The Spot,'" I told him that reckless night I waved at a stranger from his window.

"Yeah?"

"I'll have to have someplace with lots of parking and lots of space inside."

"Like the Big Lots building over on Peters Creek."

I hadn't thought of that. The store had been out of business for a while. "Yeah. I wonder what a place like that rents for."

"It wouldn't take but one phone call." He smiled. "What kind of a dance club would it be?"

I was about to say "a club for black folks," but instead I said, "Well, first I'd need some big burly men for security."

"Or off-duty cops."

He always has good ideas. "That could work. And I'd need a DJ who only played my club."

"Don't most DJs like to travel to where the money is?"

I sighed. "Yeah. Hmm. Well, I'd only be open, say, Thursday through Saturday, so I'd only need him for three nights a week."

"What would you do Sunday through Wednesday?"

"I don't know. Sleep probably."

"With anyone in particular?"

I didn't answer that question directly. "Oh, I'll probably be a pretty popular girl if I bring a dance club to Roanoke that doesn't have cameras in the girls' bathrooms"—an earlier club in Roanoke failed because of this—"and fights in the parking lot."

"Popular, huh? So . . . I might be part of your harem, huh?"

You already are, I thought at the time. "What night of the week do you want?"

"I'm flexible. Only the nights that end in Y."

That wasn't going to happen.

He chewed on my ear. "Would you serve food?"

"Nope."

"Would you serve alcohol?"

Kids just out of high school are forever complaining that there's nothing to do in Roanoke, and as a result, many of them go away to school or the service and never come back. "I don't think I would. I want to get the eighteen-and-older crowd."

"And all their disposable income."

"Yeah."

"It sounds as if you're building a permanent rave to me."

"Not a rave." That is definitely a white thing. "Just a place to dance all night long."

"How will you make money?"

"I don't know. I'll charge a cover, overcharge for soft drinks, and maybe even have lock-ins. For the ladies, of course."

"Of course."

"Then I'd get some male exotic dancers in, and all the old ladies in the valley would show up to watch the banana hammocks flip, flop, and fly. I'd have an ambulance on standby, just in case."

"But of course." He started nibbling on one of my pepperoni. "Would you ever have lock-ins for the guys?"

"Guys can be such pigs," I said.

"Yeah." He squeezed my girls and started moving down . . . down. . . .

"We have our moments, though."

Yeah, Roger can talk, and most of our dates have mirrored our first night together. I've been worried that we'd run out of things to talk about in between kinky sweat sessions, but we haven't. While Karl and Juan Carlos talk mostly to my body, Roger talks mostly to my mind. All three are lusty, don't get me wrong, but Roger is caring. Roger is . . . loving.

And that scares the shit out of me.

Love just can't be a part of this "love square," or whatever it is I have going. If this thing is to last, the only L-word I can stomach is "lust."

And what have I learned from my three lusty men? I've learned that sometimes knowing exactly what's going to happen in bed is comforting. The expected always makes me feel safe and secure. I know what to expect from Karl and Juan Carlos—hard, fast, and continuous loving where they are in control of me for the most part. And when the expected becomes boring, I call on Roger and his unexpected thrills and my chance to *take* chances. I have learned that I like the unknown, I like a little mystery, I like to lose control, and I like the sheer rush of being especially naughty.

These three have taught me that I have a vivid imagination, and that no matter how we do it, it *always* comes out good.

I guess that makes me good at being bad.

At least I'm good at something.

Chapter 10

Izzie brings me a basket full of what she considers "sexy" lotions for a housewarming gift the third Sunday I've lived at the cottage. She also brings me a bucket of fried chicken.

The chicken is a better gift, though it definitely hasn't been cooked nearly enough. Chicken should be crispy, not limp, and it should make a sound when you eat it. The lotions, though, are just plain nasty. I can't stand the scent of wheat orange marmalade, kiwi eggplant, and cherry avocado. Who comes up with these messed-up mixtures? I put lotion on to keep my skin soft, not to feed my skin food combinations that would never hit my lips. I have a feeling I'll be using this basket—unwrapped—as Mama's gift on Mother's Day.

Izzie is, in most ways, my opposite. She is a classic dark beauty with a perfect smile, slender nose, impeccable hair, cute dimples, and short, thin legs. She's a dark Dorothy Dandridge, physically blessed but also repressed as hell. Men hit on her all the time, and she just brushes them off. She's prettier than I am, smarter than I am, more educated than I will ever be, and more cultured than I'll ever dream to be. Yet, she and I are friends and have been since I started working at Patrick Henry, where she's a guidance counselor. I can't explain our friendship.

It just . . . is.

I suspect most friendships are like this.

They just . . . *are*.

I first met Izzie in the faculty lounge of McQuilkin Hall. She was on her lunch break, microwaving a vile Healthy Choice meal she really doesn't have to eat. She asked me and my bologna, mayo, and cheese sandwich, corn chips, and Pepsi to join her, and we started talking. Eventually, we stopped talking and started ranting about Patrick Henry High School, but only when we were alone in that little room. Whenever any white folks came in, we kept our fire on hold, playing our little "happy Negro" roles. There aren't many people of color working at PH, where forty percent of the student body is a minority. If I ever quit, they'd lose at least a full five percent of their African-American workforce. We fuss about the lack of black people, the new black superintendent who isn't from Roanoke (we have some decent "home-grown" folks, but we rarely hire them), the new building going up on our campus, the bell schedule, the students, white folks, Roanoke—you name it. But as soon as someone white comes in, we chat about the weather, church, shoes, food, and weight loss, usually in that order. They're safe topics for a faculty lounge, and they even allow the white folks to join in on our conversations if they want to.

"It's so strange seeing you out here," she says, picking daintily at a drumstick while I tear into a wing. She wears a dark blue skirt, matching blouse, hose, and reasonably high heels.

"It is kind of strange, but I like it. How was church?"

"Good. You should come with me sometime."

I misquote some poetry to her: "I keep the Sabbath staying at home."

She rolls her eyes and dabs at her lips with a napkin. "But you need Jesus, Lana."

"I don't need another man in my life right now."

She rolls her eyes. "Uh-huh. Jesus should be the only man you'll ever need."

I roll my eyes.

"This is quite a love shack you have here, Lana," she says with a smile. "Does each of your men get his own room?"

"No."

"You must wash your sheets often, then."

Oh yeah. I'll have to do that. I didn't have this problem before. Maybe I'll get two more sets of sheets.

"You are planning to wash the sheets, aren't you, Lana?"

"Of course," I say, nodding.

"You should get some satin sheets. I hear they're the sexiest."

Right. As if I can afford them.

"Are there lots of . . . critters out here?"

Izzie has trouble with the "wildlife" at PH, bees and yellow jackets mostly. "Just a few bullfrogs, a bunch of bats, some mice. Oh, and a ground squirrel that lives in the attic."

She smiles. "At least you have a man to 'go check' when you hear a noise."

"Yes." Though because our lovemaking can get loud, I don't hear the squirrel much anymore. Maybe it's listening? How perverted!

"Which one of your three gentlemen is most likely to go check without giving you any attitude?" Izzie asks.

Izzie likes asking questions like these. Her other favorite is to play "what if?" with me. "All three would go check eventually," I say, "but . . . Karl would check the fastest."

"Karl is the mighty hunter, huh?"

"Something like that." The fact is, Karl has the smallest bladder on Earth and has to pee every ten minutes.

"So, have they all spent the night here since you moved in?"

"No. None of them ever spends the night, and none of them will ever spend the night. I don't go for that."

She blinks. "There's not much you *don't* go for, Lana."

Sometimes I think Izzie judges me, and other times I can't tell. She seems to admire what I'm trying to do one moment and acts like my mama the next.

"But they've all been here with you, um, in bed since you moved in, right?" she asks.

"All but Karl."

"He's still AWOL?"

"No, he's in New York." I think.

"Same thing. What if, say, you're with one of your men and another man happens to show up unannounced?"

I shudder. "I hope that never happens, and it's less likely to happen since I moved out here."

"Well, what if it *did* happen? Would you sneak one out the back or . . ."

"I don't have a back door." Why don't I have a back door? Mama's little house has a front door, two side doors, and a back door. I wonder if it's legal for a house not to have a back door. I have a front door and a side door, both within thirty feet of each other.

"Okay, would you sneak one out a window, or would you invite the other one to *join* the two of you for some interesting fun?"

I don't answer that one, instead growling, clearing the table, and washing my hands. When I lived in Roanoke, I thought the only way all three might actually meet one day was if Karl's Blazer broke down at Fairview Cemetery while he was there selling his Coach bags (for whatever reason) during a funeral Roger was presiding over, and Berglund Auto World sent Juan Carlos to fix it. Stuff like that happens only in bad dreams, worse sitcoms, and the worst movies.

Though I do have this one recurring nightmare, and I will never tell Izzie about it. I'm getting busy with one of them in some generic bed in a hotel. At least I think it's a hotel because there's a Gideons Bible on the nightstand and a really awful watercolor of some ducks hanging above the bed. Anyway, I'm getting busy when either there's a knock on the door or the phone rings. As soon as I hear the knock or the phone, the man in the bed disappears, but there's always a wet spot for some reason. When I get to the door or pick up the phone, there's no one there. For the rest of that dream, I wander the halls of some spooky hotel completely naked looking for my men, only no one at the front desk has seen them . . . and no one notices I'm naked.

"You have thought about having a threesome, haven't you?"

"Hmm?"

"I know you've thought about having a threesome, Lana," she says.

"I haven't thought about it, but I know *you* have."

Though Izzie never acts on her fantasies, she sure has a ton of them. Most of them involve two men, each man "servicing her" (her phrase) while at the same time she "services" them. Izzie even says she has "toys" at home that feel *almost* like the real thing. "You have dildos and vibrators?" I had asked, and she said, "No, they're toys." She has a different name for each, um, "member" of her single-woman's drawer, and from what she reveals during our Sunday talks, she has a lot more members in her "club" than I do, some long, some thick, some that vibrate, and some that even thrust.

"It's a nice fantasy, Lana. You should imagine it sometime." She looks out the kitchen window at the pond. "But if you *had* to have two of them at the same time, which two would you choose?"

"Come on, Izzie. That's not going to happen, so why should I answer?"

"Why won't it happen?"

"Because I'm extremely careful, that's why."

She turns from the window. "Well, what if one day you aren't so careful?"

If I don't answer her perverted questions, she'll keep asking—in different ways—until I do. "Okay, okay. Uh, Karl and . . . Juan Carlos."

And the two of them would probably put my stuff in traction for a week. I should have said Juan Carlos and Roger. They'd be gentler. Karl and Roger? Man, it'd be like making love to a saltshaker and a pepper shaker. Though the contrasts—one fast, one slow, one fierce, one tender—might be nice. Mmm . . . If I had Karl working it down there and Roger licking—

"They're the freakiest, huh?"

"Hmm?"

"You were just thinking about it, weren't you?"

I nod. "It was pretty hot."

She smiles. "I knew it."

"Roger is actually the freakiest," I say quickly.

"The white boy?"

I hate it when she calls him that, though "freaky" is not quite the right word for Roger. "Roger just happens to be the most adventurous."

Izzie leans closer. "How so?"

I know this will make her church drawers moist. "Well, he has this thin gauze instead of curtains in front of this great big window at his apartment, and sometimes we do it behind it, and other times . . ."

"What?" She scoots forward on her chair.

"Other times we leave it completely open, and we don't care who might walk by and see us." Okay, I haven't been bold enough to do that yet, but Izzie won't know.

"You nasty girl!"

"It isn't nasty. And the next time we're there, we might just leave the door open a few inches, you know, just in case anyone walking by might want to . . . join us."

"Whoo."

I always get a "whoo" out of her. "One time Roger attacked me in his kitchenette, doing me right there on the counter while I kept on eating."

"Oh, my God!"

"Trust me, Izzie, *never* try to eat hot soup and make love at the same time." Though slurping chicken noodle soup while a man is slurping *you* is kind of nice.

She fans the air in front of her face. "It's getting hot in here. Let's go upstairs."

We go upstairs, curling up at either end of the couch, me in some ratty sweats, Izzie looking like an advertisement for *Church Women's Wear Daily*.

"Would you *ever* let two of your men service you at the same time?" she asks.

"No." Not unless they tag-teamed me or something. One would have to finish before the other began. I could never do both of them at the same time. I want to live to see forty. "And anyway, why so many perverted questions today? Didn't you just come from church?"

Izzie laughs softly. "Yes. But come on, Lana, you're living one of my main fantasies. You're living a fantasy that a lot of women have. How many women have the services of *three* men? You're the only one I know, and I'm naturally curious."

"And horny."

"I can't help it."

"And nosy."

She looks away, but she's still smiling.

"Can you ask less perverted questions?"

"Okay, okay." She thinks a moment.

"Don't think too long, now."

She looks at her hands. "I only seem to have perverted thoughts today. Oh, I know. Let's say that your friend arrived and you were out of tampons. Who would go out and get them for you?"

Izzie's non-perverted questions are often pretty dumb. "I would never ask them to do that."

"Just suppose, then."

I sigh. "Hmm. Karl would say, 'You trippin',' or something like that."

"He wouldn't go?"

I shake my head. "Probably not. And Juan Carlos *would* go, but he'd come back without them, telling me they were sold out."

"So Juan Carlos would lie to you?"

"Not lie, exactly. He'd just be too embarrassed to buy them." Juan Carlos even seems to have trouble handing me my underwear and bra when we're through.

"What about the white boy?"

"Roger—that's his *name*, Izzie—Roger would go, but I'd have to write it down in detail. He would probably U-Scan it and bring me the wrong size or brand."

She rises and looks at my CDs in a little case on top of the TV. "What a strange collection of music. Do you listen to all of these?"

"It's their music, not mine."

"And you leave it out in the open like this?"

I roll my eyes. "I listen to it, too."

She blinks. "You mean . . . that this is the music you do it to."

"Sometimes. I also listen to it when they're not here."

"Interesting." She holds up *Power Rock of the '70s*. "This *has* to be for the white boy. White boys like that rock 'n' roll stuff."

Not Roger. "No. Guess again."

"Oh, please don't tell me Karl. I would lose so much respect for him."

"It isn't Karl."

"So it's the Mexican. But . . . power rock?"

I giggle. "Girl, you haven't lived until you've had a Mexican playing power air guitar to some Led Zeppelin while jumping up and down on your bed wearing only a smile. It gets him going . . . and going."

She pulls out a CD Karl had a guy make for me. "Hmm. Bessie Smith, John Coltrane, and Muddy Waters. This has to be the white boy trying to get in touch with the black experience."

"Nope."

"Karl?"

"He's older than old school, and trust me, doing it to some stomp music is the bomb." Muddy Waters's "Mannish Boy" makes my waters muddy every time.

She runs her fingers over the rest of my collection. "That means that the white boy likes Keith Sweat, Al B. Sure, and Babyface?"

"Yep."

"Hmm."

"He has good taste, doesn't he?"

She shrugs. "These are all right."

She's impressed. She just doesn't want to show it. "Roger even sings 'Reasons' to me."

"No." She sits on the couch again.

I wince. "It isn't pretty, though he does know all the words. I make him whisper it to me now, and it is *très* erotic."

"So he's one of those white boys who tries to act black."

"No. He's himself all the damn time. He's too busy being Roger to be anyone else."

"Uh-huh." She sits and straightens her skirt. "He's just like all those wiggers walking around PH."

"He isn't a wigger, Izzie." Roger dresses like any other white man, I guess, and he doesn't sling the slang, as most wiggers do.

"Uh-huh. He sounds like one."

"He isn't."

She sighs and shakes her head. "Whatever. Anyway, I believe that all this revolving lust is going to end badly. I just know it."

In addition to being the most perverted church person I know, Izzie thinks she's psychic. She makes goofy predictions all the time, like the time she predicted a white man would win the presidential election. "Hillary Clinton could have run, right?" she had said. She also thinks she can predict the weather, saying vague things like "We're going to be having some weather today." I guess she has nothing better to do . . . until she gets home to her single-woman's drawer, that is.

"I see nothing but trouble from all this," she adds.

"So far so good," I say.

"*Too* good," she says. "And you know what they say about good things. All good things must come to an end."

She's so quotable. She must read *Reader's Digest.* "They also say, whoever 'they' are, that you can never have too much of a good thing, and I intend to have as much of a good thing as my booty can stand."

She tsk-tsks me. "You're playing with fire, girl, and you know it."

"At least I'm warm." And sweaty most nights. Unlike Izzie, who, by her own admission, hasn't had a date since Clinton was in office and hasn't had sex with a living person since her senior prom.

She looks off into space, which means she's probably thinking up a perverted question. "If you had to part with two of them, or if two of them suddenly wised up and dumped you, who would you want to stay with you?"

That's a depressing thought. "As I've been telling you, I need them all."

"Oh, can't you just choose one and leave me the two leftovers?"

"So they can fulfill your fantasy, huh?"

"Yes. And I'll save so much money on double-A and C batteries."

I have to laugh at that one. "Look, Izzie, I'm not parting with any of them if I can help it."

"I didn't realize you were so needy."

I scowl. "I'm not needy. It's just that none of them could support me by himself, not that I take any money from them."

"Just their fluids."

Izzie can't say the word "sperm" for some reason. "Right."

She cocks her head to the side. "Couldn't the white boy support you?"

He could, but . . . "His name is Roger, Izzie. Say it."

She refuses.

She'll never understand. "Roger could support me, but then I'd be the wife of the assistant director of interment of a cemetery until his daddy retires."

"You're right. Not only would it be difficult to be seen in public with him, but it would be hard to tell people at dinner parties that your husband buries dead people for a living." She looks hard at me. This will be a serious question. "What if . . ." She nods her head slowly. "What would happen if one of them got you pregnant?"

She's so tangential. "What? How'd you go from who can support me to one of them getting me pregnant?"

"If you got pregnant, you'd need some of their money, right?"

"That's not going to happen." My men are keeping the Trojan condom people in business. There is going to be a two-condom minimum for entrance into this house. Hmm. Karl might need three, since he's been gone so long.

"Well," she says, looking away, "it doesn't have to happen for real, does it? You know, just *tell* them you're pregnant and see what happens."

I get this vision of a zebra-striped baby with red hair and a Spanish accent. Is it possible for three sperm from three different men to hit the egg at the same time? I bet it happens all the time in the movies.

"By the way, what do you do with their, um, fluids?" she asks.

"Their what?" I want to make her say "sperm."

"Their fluids, you know."

I squint and shake my head. "No. I'm not sure what you mean, Izzie."

She sighs. "Their . . . sperm. What do you do with their sperm?"

I smile. I made her say it! "Oh. That. They take care of that." With a simple flush of the toilet.

"So you don't collect their, um, fluids?"

I can't think of a nastier thing to do. "No."

"Well, I heard about this woman who collected all of her man's fluids, and without his knowledge, she impregnated herself."

I've just thought of a nastier thing. Izzie's good for bringing nasty into the house.

"And now," she continues, "he has to pay eight hundred a month in child support, almost ten thousand dollars a year!"

Hmm. Calling that fluid-collecting woman a "pavement princess" would be too nice. "Why would any woman want to do all that?"

"Maybe her man was cute, and she wanted a cute baby."

I shake my head. "She wanted the money, Izzie, plain and simple. She wanted to own him."

She shakes her head. "Then she didn't ask for enough money. I read that it costs eighteen thousand dollars a year to raise a child."

D-damn! That much? I *can't* be having a child with my measly hourly pay. "Where'd you read that?"

"*Parenting* magazine."

I blink. "You read that?"

"I'm a counselor, remember? I'm a surrogate parent to a lot of kids."

That is a *very* scary thought.

"And that woman's man got off easy," Izzie says. "He only has to give her eight hundred dollars a month."

I roll my eyes. "But it's all so wrong for *him,* Izzie. He wore a condom. He didn't want to get her pregnant. He didn't want to start a family. He was practicing safe sex. He had an expectation of no impregnation." My legal-assistant training sometimes comes in handy. "Hey, that rhymed."

"But possession is nine-tenths of the law," Izzie says, "and he *gave* his fluids to her, so it was rightfully her property to do with whatever she wanted to do."

I get a vision of a woman lying in bed getting busy. She's saying, "You through, boo? Did it all come out? Have you been eating all your vegetables and wearing your boxers so your sperm can get some exercise? Good, good. No, no, I'll take care of it. You just rest now, boo." I see her going into the bathroom and reversing the condom, urging the sperm to swim and be free inside of her.

I now have new definitions for "trifling" and "nastiest."

"I would never do that, Izzie. I'm not ready to have any children, and none of my men seems ready, either."

"Well, just mention that your friend is late to each of them to see which one is still your friend."

"I don't want to test them."

"Come on. I know you like drama."

She's right about that. "I could, I guess."

"It's kind of a relationship check," she says. "My money is on Juan Carlos."

"Why?"

"He's Catholic, right?"

"So?"

"So he'll do right by you—family honor, religion, and all that."

Izzie lives in a world filled with stereotypes.

She looks away. "What about Karl?"

This is getting depressing. "I don't know." There's so much I don't know about that man, and I've been seeing him the longest. "But Roger might."

"Really?"

Izzie has been fundamentally opposed to my seeing Roger since the very beginning, and her only reason is that he's white and therefore wrong for me.

"Really. He's a good man, Izzie."

"So you keep saying. Would he marry you?"

The "M-word" always makes me shudder. "They would all marry me if I gave them the chance." But I am not giving them the chance. Not until I'm . . . fifty. Wait. Oprah's over fifty now, and she's still not married. Can I wait that long?

"They would all marry you?"

"Yes." I think.

"So you think. But think of what might happen. If you married Juan Carlos, he would convert you into a Catholic, and you'd be spitting out a child a year until you're forty."

"Right." Ouch. A child a year? That would make . . . fifteen kids? Hmm. I'd have a football team and four subs . . . and yards and yards of stretch marks.

"If you married Karl, he would disappear on you just as he does now."

I have to stick up for Karl. "Or, a baby would make him stay put."

"You really think that?"

No, not really. "You never know."

"And if you married the white boy, he would come home every night smelling like death. Just think, Lana. He would come through the door and say, 'Hi, honey, I buried five people today, what's for dinner?' every single night."

I blink. I have hooked up with three men who are not exactly marriage material. "None of that matters, Izzie, because I am not getting married." And I hope none of my men ever asks me to marry him. I have no idea what I might say. "Did you ever think that maybe I hooked up with these three guys because I *knew* they'd never pop the question?"

"Which would force you to make a decision, right?" She stood. "I predict that one day either you will have to make a choice or . . ."

"Or what?"

"Or the choice will be made for you, and it may not be the choice you want."

I drop off the couch to my knees. "Oh, great psychic Isabel, your words are so wise and could apply to anyone at any time anywhere." I stand. "You're a walking horoscope."

She checks her little fashion watch, which naturally matches her shoes. "Speaking of walking, I have to go."

"You're going walking now?"

"Yes. This is the Sunday the church goes out and witnesses to the heathen in the community."

I laugh. "You're such a hypocrite."

She smiles. "Maybe, but I'm not the one with three men in my bed."

"*I* don't have a drawer full of men like you do, Izzie."

"At least my men are always at home." She smiles. "Hmm. You're a heathen. Maybe I should witness to you, too."

"Before or after you ask your nasty questions?"

She frowns. "Oh, definitely before." She smiles. "Same time next week?"

I roll my eyes. "If you insist. Hey, are you coming to my game Saturday?"

"Will any of your men be there? You know I've been dying to meet Karl."

Izzie sees only one color of man in her world. "Roger never misses a game."

She shakes her head. "I'll probably be busy, then."

She pisses me off so much sometimes! "Why do you hate Roger so much? You haven't even met him."

She moves to the doorway. "I don't have to meet the white boy to know him. If he's a white boy who grew up in Roanoke, you're only an experiment." She stops in the doorway and turns. "Take care of yourself, Lana. Wait. That's right. You don't have to take care of yourself anymore, do you?"

I smile. "Nope."

Izzie sighs. "Some women have all the luck."

I nod. "Ain't that the truth."

Chapter 11

I feel lucky most days.

I get up with the ducks and drink a mug of instant hot coffee mixed with instant hot chocolate while Sheila starts "percolating." The walk out to the barn is cold, the ground usually covered with dew, but it wakes me up just fine, especially since I'm naked under my robe. In the shower, I flash the pond with my girls, and later I walk through my house *au naturel.* It is so cool to be able to walk around your own house naked, and when it warms up more, I plan to streak to the barn and back, girls a-flopping. Back inside the kitchen, I sometimes watch my footprints evaporate on the linoleum while I drink my "mocha coffee."

It's something we country girls do for fun when we're naked at six in the morning.

After my morning ritual, I dress in my standard teacher's-aide outfit—sweat suit, T-shirt, footie socks, and sneakers. Then it's off to work, from country roads to Route 460, from hilly Bedford County to asphalt-flat City of Roanoke. I'm usually at the Roanoke County line by the time Mama calls me, and she has been calling every weekday morning since I moved away.

My cell phone rings. "Hello, Mama."

"This is your wake-up call."

"I've been up for over an hour, Mama. I'm almost to work now."

"I'm just making sure. How are things going?"

"Fine." The same answer I gave her yesterday and the day before and the day before. . . .

In a few seconds, she'll ask if she can come for a visit.

"I was thinking, Erlana, that maybe we could get together this weekend."

I smile. "Yeah, I have lots of laundry to do."

"No, I meant that I would come out there. I've been dying to give you this housewarming gift and—"

"Like I told you, Mama," I interrupt, "you can always drop it by the main office at the school."

"I'd rather give it to you in person."

"Mama, I have practice all week, we have a game this Saturday, I have plans Saturday night"—though I'm not sure with whom—"and Izzie's coming over Sunday." How did I get so busy?

"It doesn't have to be for long. I could make us some liver and onions, and bring it—"

"Mama," I interrupt again, "you know I hate liver and onions."

A pause. "Okay, then, you tell *me* when I can visit."

"I'll let you know. Have a good day, Mama."

And this has happened just about every morning since I moved away. Mama must be going through withdrawal or something.

I work at the construction site known as Patrick Henry High School. We are the only school system in the state that is building a new school on the same site as the old school. Yeah, it's dusty, loud, and muddy just about every day. Walking from staff parking past the construction workers, many of them Hispanic, is kind of fun. I sometimes get a whistle or two. And once I get past the main-office trailer, I usually get hit-on by freshmen no taller than my hip. "Hey, how ya doin'?" they say, and "Lookin' good, yo." At first, it boosted my self-esteem. Now that April is here and their little hormones are in high gear, it's just plain annoying.

Most of my "job" involves pushing Bobby Swisher in his wheel-chair around the trailer park and the parts of campus that are still standing. Oh, they don't call them "trailers." They call them "learning cottages." But everyone here knows they're triple-wide trailers with low ceilings, leaky windows, and ants coming up through the floor. At least they have actual watercoolers, heat, and air-conditioning.

But let me tell you about Bobby whom I've nicknamed "Bobby Fischer" because he can whip my tail in chess. He is the sweetest child in the world. Unfortunately, he has Duchenne muscular dystrophy, which is so sad. I can't imagine being Bobby, who suddenly couldn't walk, get off the floor, or climb stairs when he was only four. And instead of getting stronger as they got larger, his calves, buttocks, and thighs grew weaker. Bobby has a brilliant mind, but he has been imprisoned in his own body for ten years. Bobby is mainstreamed in his core subjects—math, science, English, and history—and I either take notes for him or add to the notes his teachers print out for him. They say he used to be able to write, draw, and paint, but now he can barely move the chess pieces around, which is fine by me. It takes him at least a minute to move a piece, and that gives me more time to make the wrong move. I will beat him one day.

Nah. I don't have the patience for chess, though Bobby is a great teacher. He sits across from me, watching my fingers touch the pieces, humming when I try to move the wrong piece, nodding as best he can when I choose the right piece.

Bobby hums a *lot.*

I need to learn how to play better so he'll keep moving his head, because one day he will stop moving almost entirely and die from heart failure or respiratory complications.

I don't want to think about it.

In the afternoon while Bobby is at physical therapy or in the resource room doing his homework or taking a test or quiz orally—and he *always* knows the answers—I make copies. *Lots* of copies, usually one copy at a time, praying over the machine the entire time, since it seems to jam up on me whenever I'm in a hurry. And since I'm in a hurry most days, the machine jams on me most days. I copy mainly legal forms dealing with special-services compliance with Public Law 94-142 or the stacks and stacks of IEPs (Individual

Education Programs) for our kids, but occasionally I have to make one or two copies of every page of a fifty-page workbook. That gets old quickly. I get plenty of evil looks from "real" teachers waiting to copy, and I even get some flirty looks, mainly from coaches who think I should get my education degree and teach gym. "When are you going to join the football staff?" they ask.

I will never be a teacher. That's not going to happen, and not because I don't think I could do it. It's because of Bobby. He's only a freshman, and I want to be there for him until he graduates . . . or until he dies. He's already lived three years longer than the doctors said he would thanks to a rigidly monitored diet, physical therapy, and a whole bunch of meds he takes daily.

As for coaching, well, it would be so cool to coach the defensive line for the boys' team. They need all the help they can get! I might even be the first woman in the state to do it. We did have an interpreter join the football staff to interpret for a hearing-impaired player, but she wasn't an official coach. I want to be the first!

But teaching gym or health class—no. I don't want to own the "lesbian" label kids apply to all unmarried, athletic women who teach gym. And I know I'd get bored with what they do for exercise now: ping-pong, basketball games that look more like soccer with everyone chasing the ball, and walks around a track while they gossip. I'd probably pull out the tackling dummies on the second day of school and rough them up.

And as for teaching health class, well, I might like to teach that. We have so many overweight kids here, and you really can't blame the school lunches. Those haven't changed—the kids have. They are so damn lazy! They're not-so-little couch spuds who probably chain themselves in front of the TV or a computer screen and use their fingers only to play games or surf the Internet after school. The school is even ordering wider-bottomed chairs for the new building because of the students' collective girth. It's such a shame that it's almost a disgrace. Young folks are not supposed to get their second chin before they hit puberty. If I taught health class, they would be getting a heavy dose of diet and exercise information.

And I think I'd actually like teaching sex education, and I wouldn't teach them the way I was taught, with diagrams and charts and that stupid condom on the banana. I'd tell them the real deal, including lessons on foreplay, "play," and "after-play."

And I'd probably get my ass fired.

Today is a typical day, and it starts with picking up Bobby at the curb in front of the main office. His mama—who looks as if she could cry at all times—has a van with a chairlift, so Bobby rolls out in style, bundled up as if it's twenty below. Bobby can't even get the simplest cold without it threatening his life.

"Good morning, Miss Cole," Bobby says with a smile, his long eyelashes fluttering onto his chubby cheeks.

I know he has a crush on me.

"How is Bobby Fischer this morning?" I say, and then I wink.

"Just fine, Miss Cole."

He always blushes when I wink, and no, it isn't wrong to flirt with a dying child. I treat him like the man he'll never have the opportunity to be, and if he makes it to his junior year, I'm going to let this polite young man call me by my first name. I may even let him take me to the prom. For a Christmas present, I bought him a book on chess strategy, which I should have read myself. His mama told me that he already had the book, and I felt so dumb. "No," she said. "It's his favorite book in the world. He reads it every night."

It's so sad to think this, but Bobby may actually be in love with me. I intend to return that love as long as he's around.

I push Bobby through crowds of young kids (I know I have *shoes* older than most of them) to the elevator. Once inside with the doors shut, Bobby watches the number one change to number two.

"How was your weekend, Miss Cole?"

"Busy." I do not tell him the details nor mention my friends with benefits. "And yours?"

"I was pretty busy, too."

"Good." The busier he is, the more he moves, and the more he *can* move, the longer he'll live. "What did you do?"

"I played chess mostly."

I smile. "With Sunny?"

He blushes again. "Yeah."

Sunny (not her real name, I'm sure) is a girl somewhere in the world who plays online chess with Bobby. The Web site they use allows them to "chat" while they play, and it seems that Sunny and Bobby have become an item.

"Did you beat her again?"

"Not this time."

Such a gentleman. "Did you let her win?"

"No," he says, looking away.

Yeah, he let her win. "How's your typing?"

"Too slow."

I squeeze his shoulder. "That's okay. You just keep typing slowly. You'll never say something wrong to Sunny if you take your time."

"My mom's getting me some voice-recognition software so all I'll have to do is talk."

Damn. I know his mama means well. She's just trying to make Bobby's last days easy. Muscular dystrophy is hereditary, so everything she does seems to be done out of guilt. "Well, you keep typing. Keep those fingers moving. How else are you going to beat me at chess?"

We get to his first class, history, which is pretty much like all of his other classes. The students are loud, crude, and obnoxious. Somehow, Bobby can focus through all that bedlam and hear the teacher, who is teaching her guts out. I feel like standing up and screaming, "Listen, y'all hoodlums, this boy here is dying, yet he is dying to learn! What the hell is wrong with y'all? Shut the hell up and learn something, damn."

I'll never say all that, but I think it loudly in my head every single day.

Every class has its nerds (in the front row, with notebooks open), jocks (in the back row, with shoelaces untied), immigrants (along the sides, squinting most of the time), and "beautiful people" (in the middle of the room so everyone can admire their beauty). I used to be able to tell who was rich, but not anymore. When I was growing up, the rich girls always wore more clothing with labels that didn't come from Wal-Mart, like Versace, Dior,

Abercrombie & Fitch, and the ever-popular L.L. Bean. Now? It is so hard to tell, since there are so many hoochies wearing as little as possible. I *can* tell which girls *are* hoochies and which girls are shy, and I'm willing to bet that the shy girls put out more than the hoochies do on the weekend.

How do I know? *I* was shy in high school, that's why. While all the other girls were showing every square inch of their anatomies, wearing thongs and other pants that showed off their "camel toes" and tops that showed off their pierced belly buttons, tattooed lower backs, and cleavage, I wore jock clothes: sweat suits, T-shirts, and high-tops. And trust me—I got more play than any of those hoochies because I was approachable. *Any* boy could talk to me. While the hoochies had their noses, tails, and hair in the air, I was firmly on the ground, where boys could find me. I was athletic for the jocks, street for the roughnecks, and just smart enough to talk to any intelligent boy. And I didn't have as bad a rep as you might think. Unlike some of these hoochies who tell their business to the world, I kept things quiet.

I have been sneaky a *long* time, ever since my earliest sexual conquests in middle school. No, I didn't have sex in middle school. I just conquered quite a few boys sexually. I didn't know what I was doing—at first. Mama didn't school me. Daddy wasn't around to school me. I learned through experience. My first boyfriend was a ninth grader two years older than I was. He didn't know what the hell he was doing, but he was willing to try anything. I ruined that boy's drawers so often, his mama caught on and . . . that was that. With him. There was always some other boy willing to try anything in middle school. So I guess I've had boys who were friends with benefits since the seventh grade. And because I was so "advanced" sexually, no boy was actually inside me long enough during his fifteen seconds of fame to break my hymen until I was seventeen.

After his last class, I leave Bobby in the resource room, and he thanks me for helping him. "Have a good day, Miss Cole," he says.

"You, too, Bobby Fischer," I say.

"See you tomorrow," he says.

I *hope* so, I think just about every day. "See you tomorrow."

After work (which really isn't much work), I go to football practice on the field at East Salem Elementary. I get out of my car and
pop the trunk. It's kind of a turn-on putting on all those pads as
cars whiz by. A few of my teammates come fully dressed, but most
do as I do and dress in the parking lot, and occasionally we nearly
cause traffic accidents because most of us wear only sports bras or
tight T-shirts underneath our pads. I nod at my teammates dressing
behind the trunks of their cars or the tailgates of their SUVs, and
they nod back.

Hell, I just play ball with them. I mean, it's hard to be friends
with people you knock heads with five days a week.

I'm just through applying a little greasepaint under my eyes
when it starts to rain.

Hard.

Shit.

We *never* practice when it rains so we won't mess up the pre-
cious field. This, of course, is pure bullshit. It might rain like this
during the game, right? Are we just going to stop playing to save the
field? I start taking off my jersey and shoulder pads as our quarterback, Cherry Zane (her real name, I kid you not), walks by unsnap-
ping her flak jacket and flashing me her tattooed stomach.

"I hear it's supposed to rain like this all week," she says.

"Shit."

I like practice. I like the crunch, the sound, the pain, and the
sheer fun of putting all the knowledge Daddy gave me to good use.
In a depraved corner of my mind, I actually like hurting people.
Hmm. I also hurt myself when I hurt them. In fact, most of the
bruises I earn are self-inflicted. Oh sure, I could just grab my oppo-
nents and throw them down with my hands, but where would the
fun be in that?

"You have any plans?" Cherry asks.

She's still here talking to me? And what is that tattoo, a little
demon face? "What?"

"Do you have any plans?"

"No."

"A bunch of us are going to O'Charlie's."

Good for you! Drink lots of beer! That's what professional athletes do instead of practice! Go on, get drunk. "I might see you there." Not.

I dump my gear into the trunk and get into my car as the rain thunders down. I page Karl. He doesn't hit me back immediately, which means either "not tonight" or he still isn't back from New York. Figures. I call Berglund, and a few minutes later, Juan Carlos is on the phone.

"Hello?"

"It's Lahhh-na," I say, mimicking him.

"Oh. Hello." There's that sexy voice I love. I love to hear him whisper my name on my earlobe. Mmm, that really gets me going.

"Are you busy?"

"You have heard about the recall?"

Not again! "Another one?"

"Yes. Brake lines this time. Over three hundred thousand cars and trucks."

Shit! GM is ruining my sex life. "So you'll be working late."

"Yes. Until we are done, the boss says."

Shit! He's already working double shifts, and now this. "Maybe after you finish?"

"It will be so late."

"It's only twenty miles, and I promise you won't regret it."

"I would, but Mama is not feeling well."

That woman! I'll bet she's a hypochondriac using her phantom illnesses to keep her boy at home.

"Well," I say, "at least come to my game Saturday."

"I am covering for Darren all day Saturday. I can see you Saturday night."

I'm hoping Roger can soothe my bruises Saturday night, since he's the best masseur. "I'll be all worn out by then." And in another man's more capable hands.

"I am sorry."

So am I. I wanted Juan Carlos *tonight.* Damn. I'm not in the mood for the three Rs: reading, relaxing, and reliving. Whenever one of them isn't around, I read, relax, and relive our more intimate moments, and it isn't the same as the real thing. "Get back to work."

"Call me."

Maybe. "I will."

Then I call Roger, and he answers on the first ring.

"Hey, Lana," he says. "No practice today?"

Such a soft voice. "Nope. No cutting grass today?"

"I was about half-done before the rain started."

Hmm. A little afternoon delight at his place, perhaps? "So, can I meet you at your apartment?"

"I wish I could, but we have two more interments later, and this weather is going to . . ."

I tune Roger out. Now dead people are ruining my sex life.

"What about later tonight?" I ask. I have all this energy. I need to channel it somehow.

"It might be late, and I'll be stank."

"We could . . ." I then whisper something so filthy that I hear him breathing hard. I'm good at pushing Roger's kinky buttons—once he taught me how to do it, of course.

"I'll be there as soon as I can," he says.

I hang up. Hmm. Dinner at Mickie D's, or at O'Charlie's to watch lesbians do nasty things with Jell-O shooters.

Decisions, decisions.

I stop by the Mickie D's drive-through, get a couple double cheeseburgers and some fries, and head for home to rest up for the filth to come. I first soak my bum left ankle in some Epsom salts, then doze off in my rocker watching screen snow on the TV as the rain continues to pour down. I get no reception whatsoever when it rains like this, though NBC sometimes blows in and out.

The phone wakes me a little after nine. "Hello, Mama." Like clockwork. She still has to "tuck me in."

"How was your day?" she asks.

"Fine."

"Just . . . fine?"

"Yeah. How was your day?"

I let the phone rest on my shoulder and listen to Mama spew out her day. I know it's tough to be a manager, but why do I have to hear her vent about it? And it all starts to sound the same. Wendy this and Joe-Bob that, and the regional VP said this and Booger said that. I'm about tired of it.

"Mama," I say, interrupting something about someone named Prentice who is always out on family leave (which is strange, since Prentice is a man), "I'm really tired, so . . ."

"It's only nine o'clock, Erlana."

I have plans. "So I'm going to bed early." Which is kind of true.

"You aren't sick, are you?"

"No. I just had a long day."

"Oh, I scheduled your yearly for you."

I groan. There's nothing fun about having your legs up in icy cold stirrups, showing your stuff to an old male doctor and his equally ancient nurse. "Mama, you don't have to schedule things for me anymore." Especially "dates" with Dr. Cold Finger and Nurse Moustache with the Icy Stare.

"You're still on my health plan, and it will only cost you the fifteen-dollar co-payment."

It costs me more than that. I mean, I actually have to shave my legs closely and tidy up the nest down there with some scissors. Oh, and I have to put up with the humiliation of answering his nosy questions, like "Have you been sexually active?" and "Have you noticed any lumps in your breasts?" One day I will ask him if *he's* been sexually active and if *he* has noticed any lumps in his balls—and I won't answer his questions until he answers mine.

"Look, Mama, you can take me off your health plan."

"Do you have health insurance now?"

"No, but I'll look into it." I'm sure the Roanoke City School District offers something I *can't* afford.

"Erlana, I'd be a fool to take you off my plan now. It's football season."

She has a point, but I have to make mine. "Mama, I have moved away from you. I am on my own. I make my own plans now, and if I don't feel like going for a checkup, I'm not going."

"What about the dentist?"

Grr. "Did you already schedule me for Dr. Fumble?" It's actually Dr. Comfort—how ironic—but the man drops metal objects often.

"You know I have, and don't call him that. He's been your dentist for fifteen years."

I do have some nice teeth, but one day that man will stick me with something, I just know it.

"And anyway, it's been on the calendar in the kitchen for months, and he charges when you don't show up."

Time to set her straight. "Mama, don't schedule me for anything anymore, okay? You don't know my schedule." Not that I know my schedule any better. "You don't know what I may have planned."

"Well, at least do these two things for me."

It's only one trip to the doctor and one trip to the dentist, but it's more than that. I can't have her controlling even my body anymore. "Mama, you know I love you, right?"

"I love you, too."

"But you've got to let me go, okay?" I'm trying to be as gentle as I can, but I have a man about to show up any minute for some rough stuff.

"But I'm your mama, Erlana. I'll never let you go completely."

"You have to, Mama. How else am I going to grow up?"

Silence. Then . . . "I'm your mama forever, Erlana. Nothing you can say or do will ever change that. Nothing will ever change that."

If she only knew. Hmm. I'll bet I can think of something. "Look, Mama, I've survived on my own for a couple weeks now. I'm doing fine on my own."

"As long as you can use my washer and dryer."

I hate it when she's right. "So I'll stop using them, damn. I'll find a Laundromat out here."

Longer silence. "You don't have to do that."

Aha! The last binding tie to break is your mama's washer and dryer. "Well, from now on, I'll be doing my laundry elsewhere." But not in the pond. Even Jenny would agree with me there.

"But . . . but when will I see you?"

"When *I* want you to." Damn, I feel powerful.

"Oh. Well, I guess this . . . I guess this is normal."

Mama needs an explanation for everything. So sad. "And Mama, I'll call *you* if I need anything from now on, okay? You don't have to call to check up on me anymore." In a way, I am telling Mama that I don't need her.

"I won't . . . I won't call you anymore."

Silence from both of us. What has just changed?

"Um, you get some rest. Goodbye." *Click.*

It's what I want, right? I want complete freedom, right? I think I've just gotten it, and it makes me feel kind of light-headed. Wow. I think I've finally broken away. I'm free!

Hmm. I'm going to need some quarters for the Laundromat.

A little after eleven, I see headlights flashing through the woods.

Time to get down and dirty.

I throw on an old pair of sweats and an oversized T-shirt, peel off my socks, and get my football. I step out into the rain, and my pepperoni immediately come to life. Roger leaves his headlights on, illuminating our "football field," which tonight is puddly and muddy and just plain gross.

And therefore cool as a place for a free woman to play one-on-one football with one of her friends with benefits.

Roger takes off most of his clothes, leaving me only a T-shirt and some plaid boxers to grab.

I toss the football to him. "I'm on defense first."

"You horny devil, you," he says. "First one to ten wins?"

Though I know we're both about to win, I agree. "Your, um, stuff is hanging out."

He looks down. "We're playing touch, right?"

I shake my head. "Tackle."

He puts his stuff back inside his boxers and tucks the ball under his arm. "Let's get it on, then."

He fakes left, then attempts to go right—the same tired move he always tries—and I hit him hip-high, driving him into the muddy grass. And after that . . .

We end up in a tie for, oh, about an hour.

Roger isn't my earth brother for nothing.

Chapter 12

Luckily for me and Roger, but not for the team, it rains all week, and Roger and I, um, *practice* together in the mud. After that first night, I decide against wearing anything at all, since the weather is so mild, and all Roger wears is a condom. We even turn off the headlights to save the battery in Roger's truck. Roger is so easy to see, even in pitch darkness, and the last night, I made him wear a glow-in-the-dark condom I bought at Spencer Gifts. It was a hypnotizing experience, let me tell you.

I was just following the bouncing balls!

I know. I'm as big a perv as Izzie sometimes.

Cleaning up afterward is . . . different. I hope we don't clog up the drains. We both have so many nooks and crannies!

The morning of the Baltimore Burn game, I go through my pre-game routine. At IHOP, I have to eat three eggs over easy and a stack of pancakes drowning in real butter and blueberry syrup, all of it washed down with a glass of freshly squeezed OJ. I once overslept before a Passion game, wolfed down a stale blueberry Pop-Tart and some Hawaiian Punch, and had the worst game of my life, making only one tackle all day. After breakfast, I go home and take a nap until noon, swing by Mickie D's for a double cheeseburger, and eat it on the way to the stadium in Salem. I try not to drink *any* liquids until after the first hit, and I definitely put my right shoe on before my left.

And no, I am not superstitious. I've just always done it that way.

During the pre-game warm-up, I speak to no one, and no one speaks to me. You can't have a game face if you're running your mouth. Number 39 of the Burn talks her usual stuff across the field, saying she's going to kick my black ass and make me cry for my mama.

Number 39 needs a life, and when I get the chance, I'm going to knock the life out of her.

I feel a hum deep inside me during the national anthem, and it sure isn't from our fans. The class A baseball team next door, the Salem Avalanche, is also having a game, and they have a nice crowd that is actually singing the national anthem. Not ours. I don't look at the crowd and don't take my eyes off the flag because it symbolizes the *white*-wench quarterback I'm going to be sacking, the *blue* welts I'm going to put on anyone who tries to block me, and the *red* blood of number 39 that will be flowing out of her steel-toothed mouth. Those can't be gold caps.

When we win the coin toss and elect to receive, the crowd behind me cheers. Figures. This may be the only thing we win all day. I want to tell them that we've won *every* opening toss this year *except* for that of the game we won.

Deron Lee, our one and only coach, steps up to me. "Feel like returning the kickoff?"

Son of a bitch! He knows no one is supposed to talk to me before a game! He's messing with my mojo!

"Lana?"

Maybe I can nod. That's not talking, right? I nod, and tear off to the ten-yard line. Now I feel the hum, now I feel the energy, now I feel the power from my crusty toes to the top of my peanut head.

Let's get it *on.*

A whistle blows, I see a leg swing, and I lock in on the ball fluttering through the air. "Ball first, ball first," I whisper. I run to where I think I can catch it with my hands and—

Oh, it's on now!

Ground's slippery, run north and south, the Super Sugar Crisp bear says in my head, and I take off, cutting right, staying right, waiting for the block, waiting for it—

"Move your fat ass!" I yell.

My teammate crumples to the ground, I step around, and I'm in the clear down the sidelines with nothing but daylight and—

Oof.

Tweet.

D-damn! That was a *helluva* hit! I have got to get me some more of that and return the favor!

I look up at the legs of some Burn players on the sidelines, a heckling voice saying something about my mama again. I'm sure number 39 is up there somewhere. I toss the ball up to the ref, lean on my left hand, and get to my feet. I take two steps—

Oh shit! Ow!

I fall to the ground holding my ankle. What the hell? Shit. It's already swelling.

"You all right?" our trainer, Tina, asks once she gets her fat ass across the field.

I pull off my helmet. "What do you think?"

She straightens out my leg and holds my heel in her hands. "This hurt?"

Oh damn. "A little." Flames of pain shoot up my leg.

She turns it from side to side, and I bite my lip. Damn, this shit hurts!

A ref comes over to us. "Can she continue?"

"Can I continue? This ain't no boxing match, ref! Shit, Tina, get me a little ice and I'll be just fine, just fine. . . ."

I'm not fine. I've really gone and hurt myself this time.

I thought I'd be in great shape for today's game after a long week of night practice with Roger, and I was more than ready to knock some damn heads today. But here I am in the locker room with ice bags on both sides of my right ankle from a vicious but legal hit by number 39 of the Baltimore Burn. So now, I have a tricky left ankle and a bruised right ankle. They had to carry me off the field on a stretcher—my only standing ovation so far in my ca-reer! And now I'm waiting for—

There he is.

"I brought your car around," Roger says. "Are you sure you don't want to go to the emergency room?"

I swivel off the bench and grab some crutches. "I'm sure. It's just a bruise." A bruise the size of a damn grapefruit on steroids. I am going to have stretch marks from this injury for sure.

"I can drive you home."

I start to the locker room door, one swing of the crutches at a time. "I'll be fine. Just follow behind me. Oh, and get my equip-ment." I point at the pile on the floor.

"I'm glad you don't wear all this when *we* play," he says, gather-ing my gear.

"You're the one who needs it more."

And when we finally get to Jenny's dollhouse, I realize some-thing: If I didn't have three men in my life, I would have no one to take care of me tonight, when I really, really need it. With Karl who knows where and Juan Carlos working all the damn time, at least I have Roger.

And that scares me even more! If Roger is the only one I can count on in the clutch, what does that say about Juan Carlos and Karl? And what does that say about me for picking those two?

Roger practically carries me up the stairs to the bathroom. "This could be an interesting bath," he says.

And it is, in the most painfully erotic way.

After giving me four Motrin, Roger runs the water and adds some bath oil beads.

"No funny stuff," I say.

He winks.

"I'm serious, man. This shit hurts."

Roger helps me into the tub, pulling my right leg out of the tub so I can keep it propped up. This, of course, gives him an excellent view of my stuff. And then he bathes me. Slowly. Carefully. Sensuously, lingering a long time where my hands *keep* him lingering. Without me asking, he joins me, oh so careful to keep my right leg in the air . . . then my left leg is in the air . . . and then . . .

Then we need another bath, and I need four more Motrin.

Though I can limp just fine, I let Roger carry me to the bed. I even let him dress me in some shorts and a T-shirt. Then I let him lie next to me until I fall asleep, dreaming, of all things, of little milk chocolate babies . . .

And in the morning when I wake up, my ankle throbbing like a drum, Roger's gone. I feel his side of the bed, and it's still warm. I sniff the air. Is that coffee I smell? And what's that rumbling outside?

I slide on my booty across the bed to the window. Outside, on a little yellow tractor, sits Roger, cutting my grass. He spent the night?

Damn.

He spent the night.

The first man to ever spend the night with me, and I wasn't awake for it? He cuddled with me all night long?

This is serious.

I slide open the window, waving my hand. Roger sees me and waves. No, fool, I want you to turn that thing off. I mimic turning a key, and he gets the idea.

"Good morning," he says.

"Where'd that come from?"

"Mr. Wilson dropped it off."

Cool. Jenny must have told him. Thanks, Jenny. Maybe with all that grass cut down, the bugs will find somewhere else to live. If I had a bug light, the bugs would have overwhelmed it by now, their sheer weight dropping the bug light to the ground.

"Your coffee's ready," Roger says. "Want me to bring it up?"

"I can get it." I think.

"Okay. I should be through soon."

I close the window as the rumbling begins again. He spent the night, and now he's cutting my grass because the ghost of the lady who used to sleep in this room told her husband to drop off a tractor.

I'm sure shit like this happens all the time.

Luckily, the upstairs hallway in the cottage is narrow enough that I can press my hands on the walls for support. I make it halfway down the stairs when I hear my cell phone ringing somewhere in the house.

I bounce down the stairs to the kitchen, where I find the phone on the table. "Hello?"

"Where you at?"

It's Karl.

Shit.

After nearly a month, it's Karl.

Which means he's back in Roanoke.

"Where am *I* at? Where *you* at?" I ask with attitude. "I've been paging you for a damn month, man. Why didn't you hit me back?"

"It would have been a long-distance call."

Cheap ass.

"What you want?" I always get Ebonic with Karl. We from the 'hood and shit. I can't speak Ebonically to Juan Carlos or he'll learn English wrong.

"What you think I want, girl? I want you, Peanut. I'm driving around town looking for your ass. Didn't you get my message? I left you one last night."

Shit. Well, eight Motrin and splashing water will keep anyone from hearing a phone. "I didn't get it, and how come you just decide to call me last night?"

And why now?

Why now, when I have a man I need to reward just outside my house on a tractor delivered by a man who still talks to his dead wife?

"I'm back from doing my thing. You miss me?"

I hop over to the counter and drink some coffee. No adding hot chocolate mix this time. I need the real stuff. "I don't know. Did you miss me?"

"You know I did, Peanut. So, where the hell are you?"

Hmm. Roger's almost done. . . . Izzie's coming over around two. . . . It's only ten or so now. . . . "I moved."

"I could figure that out. I drove by your crib and didn't see your car on a Sunday morning, and we both know you aren't a church girl, heh-heh."

Heh-heh. I hate that laugh. "I'm in Bedford County, Karl."

"What?"

"I've gone country while waiting on your ass."

"No shit?"

"Yeah."

"Where in Bedford County?"

I give him the directions and purposely tell him to turn left at the big oak tree, just in case he makes good time. "Take your time," I add. "I need to take a shower first."

"So do I," Karl says. "See you in a few."

I finish my coffee and pour another mug, my ankle throbbing worse, my head spinning. This is going to be a close call.

Roger comes in smelling like all outdoors. "How's your ankle?" he asks, kissing me on the nose.

"It hurts."

"Want to ice it?"

Karl drives like a maniac. Even with the wrong turn, he'll be here in thirty minutes or less. Shit. "Maybe later. Uh, listen, Roger, thanks for taking care of me last night."

"I enjoyed it."

So did I. I should get injured more often. I fake a long yawn. "But I'm still really sleepy, and I'm sure you have things to do." Take the hint.

"Not really."

Now what? "Well, um, I think my, um, friend is on her way, you know?"

He doesn't get it at first, and then . . . "Oh. *That* friend." He looks at the ground. "I could stay and rub your back."

Which would be heavenly! "It's okay. She's feeling pretty vicious today." Take *that* hint.

"I understand. I'll call you later." He kisses my cheek. "Should I put the tractor in the barn?"

"Yeah. Oh, and could you turn on the generator? I'm sure we used up all the hot water last night." And Karl wants a shower.

"Sure." He kisses my lips. "I hope your ankle feels better."

"Thanks."

As soon as the door shuts, I take stock of the situation. We did it in the tub, so the sheets are clean. But my stuff is kind of sore. Maybe Karl won't want to . . .

Of course he will. It's been almost a month.

Shit.

Maybe he'll look at my ankle and take pity on me.

Well, Roger didn't take pity on me, but I didn't *let* him take pity on me, so . . .

Shit.

The phone rings. "Peanut, I'm lost."

Unlike most men, Karl admits this—often. "Did you turn right at the tree?"

"You told me left, not right."

"Sorry. Go back to the tree and turn right this time."

"All right."

I look out the window and see Roger's car *still* parked outside. What's taking him so long? Oh shit! He's having trouble with Sheila.

I crawl up the stairs, get my crutches, bounce down the stairs on my booty, and hit the door, crutches clawing the air in front of me. When I get to the barn, I see Roger shaking his head.

"Is there an on button in here somewhere?"

I slide around him as best as I can and flick the correct switch, which for some reason Mr. Wilson mounted on a piece of wood under a bench. Sheila starts up, noxious smoke filling the barn. Both of us leave, hacking and coughing.

"Does that happen every time?"

"Just about. Um, drive safely." Just leave!

He kisses me again, this time with tongue, which I'd really like under normal circumstances. "Get well soon. It's supposed to rain some next week."

I look at my ankle.

"Oh. Yeah. I forgot about that. Sorry."

"It's okay. Maybe we can just play catch." I lower my voice. "You know, you pitch and I catch."

"I'd like that."

Now get on! My first friend with benefits is coming!

"Bye."

I watch him go to his car . . . he starts it up . . . he waves . . . he backs out . . . he's leaving . . . he's gone.

Whew.

What? He's coming back. I crutch my way to his window. "What's wrong?"

"I just realized that I'm going cowboy. I must have left my boxers in the bathroom."

Think fast! "I'll, uh, I'll wash them for you."

"Okay. Just don't wear them."

I smile. "I might."

He winks. "Bye."

"Bye."

I hear a car approaching.

Think fast, Lana! "Oh, um, is that my brother? You better go."

"You have a brother?"

I should have said "cousin." Damn. "Um, he's my half brother, and, uh, he doesn't know about you, and he has this thing against white people, so . . ."

"I understand."

Roger leaves again, and my heart sinks. Their cars will pass each other, and Karl will say something and . . .

Shit.

This wasn't supposed to happen.

I moved out here so that what's happening would never happen!

But here it is . . . happening.

Chapter 13

I'm still standing there on my crutches when Karl rolls up.
Here we go.

Smile pretty.

Show a little of your good leg.

Lick your lower lip.

Act as if you haven't had any in a long time.

And stop sweating so damn much!

As soon as he gets out of the car, I say, "Hey, boo."

"What the hell happened to you?"

I try to raise my leg but fail. "My ankle."

He squats and looks at it. "Damn. Is it broken?"

"Feels like it."

"You been to the doctor?"

Just Roger and his gentle bedside manner. "No. It'll be okay in a few days."

He stands and looks past me to the house. "This your house, huh?"

"Yeah." And thanks for sounding so concerned about my ankle. Geez.

"You been cutting grass?"

"What you think?" Oh yeah. "The, uh, the owner, Mr. Wilson—"

"The guy I passed?"

Well . . . It'll have to do. "Um, yeah." It's just a little lie.

"He makes you call him 'Mr. Wilson'?"

"Uh, no, but anyway, he just came out here this morning—"

"And on a Sunday morning?" Karl interrupts.

"Yeah. He woke me up." Damn, I just told the truth and shit.

He grabs my booty and releases it slowly. "I been thinking about this a long time, Peanut."

Whew. I'm so glad he didn't press me about Roger, but as soon as Karl gets his mind off something and onto booty, there's no turning back.

Shit.

My stuff is going to hate me.

Should my friend arrive for Karl, too? That would be so mean. Maybe I can delay him just long enough—

"I got you something," he says, and he rushes to his car, coming back with two little fake Coach bags and a stack of DVDs, including Denzel Washington's latest, one I've already seen with Juan Carlos *and* Roger at the movie theater.

"So," I say as we go inside, "how's business?"

Thankfully, Karl is content to talk about his trip to New York while I prop up my leg on a kitchen chair and rest my stuff.

"It won't be long, Peanut, it won't be long," he says, holding my hand in his.

"For what?"

"For when I can stop traveling and just be a distributor or even open up a store down here. I've been trying to make some connections up there that will keep me in one place."

Which *is* what I've always wanted, but things have changed. What would one of those white actresses in the movies say to this? "This is all so sudden, dear." Something like that.

"I got it all worked out. I know a few truckers who go up and down the East Coast all the time, and we've been talking about forming a partnership, you know? They go up, get the stuff, I pay them wholesale, and charge retail. It's a perfect setup."

"Perfect."

Shit. And it actually makes sense.

"So, you'll be seeing a lot more of me, Peanut."

"Yeah."

Shit.

"And, you know, maybe I can use that barn back there to store some of my merchandise."

He thinks he's going to store fake Coach bags and bootleg DVDs next to Sheila? "The barn gets pretty smoky when the generator's running."

He points to the storage room door. "What's back there?"

I can't tell him "storage." Shit. He'll look anyway. "It's a storage room."

He gets up and goes in, coming back a few minutes later. "You got plenty of room in there. It's perfect."

Perfect.

Gee, Juan Carlos, I don't know how all those fake Coach bags and bootleg DVDs got back there. One morning I woke up, and there they were. Maybe, Roger, maybe Mr. Wilson has a business on the side, and I'm sure he'll have some explanation.

Because *I* sure as hell won't have an explanation!

Think! You can't have a man leave his shit and not leave himself! It isn't right! "But it's so far from your customers, boo. Aren't most of your regular customers in Roanoke?"

He nods. "Yeah. You're right, Peanut. But at least I know I *could* use your place if I needed to, right?"

That makes sense, too. "Right."

He smiles. "And if my shit was here, I'd visit a *lot* more."

This isn't happening.

The one who I've *always* thought was *least* likely to settle down is using "settle-down" language. But maybe "a lot more" means "twice a month" to Karl.

I have to test him.

"Would that mean that . . ." What the hell else *could* that mean? No. He doesn't want to do that . . . does he? "Would that mean that you might want to move in with me?"

"Huh?"

Well, at least it doesn't mean that. Time to throw a bigger scare into Karl. "I mean, if you're going to be around more, why not make it permanent?"

"Like marriage?"

"Maybe."

He paces around a little. "But . . ." He looks at me. "You serious?"

Hell no! I'm having my beefcake and eating it twice more. I'm getting seconds and thirds. Why would I want that to end? "I'm serious, boo. As serious as I've ever been."

He smiles that smile that seduced me the first time I ever saw him sitting on the hood of his Blazer at Washington Park. "Nah, Peanut, you're just playin'."

My face is a mask, but my mind is doing somersaults. "I'm not playin'."

"You're serious?"

Hell no! Back out, man! "Yes, I'm serious."

"Nah, you playin'. Getting all serious and shit. That ain't like you. I mean all this"—he waves his hands around the kitchen—"this is serious. Your own place and shit. You didn't decorate it, did you?"

I think the moment has passed. "No."

"It sure is countrified, like Andy Griffith and shit." He starts whistling the theme music from that show.

"Boo, you know I'm still a city girl inside."

"Yeah?" He starts massaging my shoulders, pulling up my T-shirt and rubbing my bare skin with his hot hands.

Why did I have to say "inside"? Karl can take the most innocent word and turn it into something sexual. I once told him, "I wish you'd shave more," and in a matter of seconds, he was shaving me down there. And my coochie was cold for weeks! And when the hair grew back, it itched terribly.

"You feel like a city girl on the outside, too." He slides his hands around to my girls, squeezing them tightly.

Oh damn.

"You got a nice bed upstairs?"

"Yes," I whisper.

He scoops me out of my chair. "Give me better directions to your bedroom, all right?"

"All right."

Just as we reach the bedroom, I remember Roger's boxers. I see them out of the corner of my eye lying in the bathroom sink. The nerve!

"Put me down, boo. I need to use the bathroom."

He sets me down, and I'm in that bathroom in a stumbling flash, the door closed behind me. Now, where do you hide a man's—I pick them up—*used* boxers when another man is behind the door waiting to get into your drawers?

The window over the shower. Thanks, Jenny.

I hobble to the tub, step in, and open the window. After balling up Roger's boxers, I drop them, hoping they'll go straight down to get lost among my three trash cans.

They don't.

They get hung up on the bricks on the side of the house!

Shit!

Naturally, they're too far up the side of the house to reach from either here or the ground. Maybe the wind will blow them off. But with my luck today, they'll blow around until they get stuck on the antenna of Karl's Blazer. What would I tell him? That they're mine? That might work.

"C'mon, Peanut, don't keep me waiting."

"Keep *you* waiting? You've kept *me* waiting for almost a month."

Which is . . . sort of true. At least in Karl's case.

"I got somethin' for you, girl."

I know, I know.

I take a deep breath.

Here comes some pain.

And once we're in bed, damn if my ankle doesn't start to scream in pain while he's hitting my booty from behind.

"Damn, girl, you really missed me, huh? Screaming like that and shit. Get as loud as you want, now, cuz daddy's home. . . ."

When he's through ten minutes later, he jumps into the shower, still whistling that damn song, and the only thing going through my head is: *If Juan Carlos calls me, I am not answering. If Roger calls me, I am not answering.*

"Peanut, the water's nice and hot!"

I am not answering. Maybe I can fake being asleep—

He appears dripping in the doorway in all of his African-warrior manliness, every little nook and cranny of him sculpted to perfection. "See anything you like?"

"Give me a second." Damn, I shouldn't have said—

"You want you some seconds, don't you?"

Why didn't I say, "Give me a minute"? He couldn't have done a damn thing with "minute"! Wait. He might have said, "I'll be in it in a minute."

"I'll be right there, okay?"

"I'll be waiting. Oh, and what's up with the window in there?"

Shit!

Did he look out?

"It, uh, keeps the bathroom from steaming up too much."

"Oh."

I watch him turn around. The man is an African god.

"Sorry, Jenny," I say, and I hop into the bathroom lusting for a god, and the first thing I do is look out the window.

"Damn, girl, you lookin' good!"

Roger's boxers are waving at me. They're actually blowing in the breeze like a damn flag! I close the window.

"Oh, you wanna get steamy, don't you?"

I smile and turn to him. "Yeah. I wanna get steamy." I turn and face the water. "Wash my back."

"Yeah, I'm watching it. . . ."

Ouch . . . ouch . . . ouch . . . "I said 'wash,' not 'watch'!"

"Don't worry, girl, I'll soap you up something *good*. . . ."

And after the initial shock, he does soap me up something good. While Roger's boxers wave at the world outside.

Chapter 14

I never thought all this good loving would kill me, but damn! Karl, as usual, gives me more than my booty can handle. I'm still drying off when he says, "I got some people I need to see."

Normally, I'd give him attitude, but today . . . today, I don't have a whole lot left to give of attitude or anything else. "You're leaving so soon?" I ask.

"I'll be back, girl."

"Tonight?" And please don't say yes. Now my ankle, my booty, *and* my stuff hurt.

He looks away. "I'll try, but you know. . . ." He shrugs. "It may not happen."

Which really means it won't happen. "That's okay. I need to rest."

He kisses me with more tenderness than usual. "I *have* missed you, Peanut."

I hug him to me. "I've missed you, too."

"Later."

Just ten minutes after Karl leaves, Izzie shows up.

I am so glad Izzie's not a lesbian. I couldn't possibly do another person today.

"Well," she says once she sees what's left of me on my bed. I didn't even get out of the bed to meet her at the door. "You look worn out."

"I am." I adjust some ice bags on both my ankles, and I almost want to put another bag on my booty and my stuff.

"Lana, do you know you have a pair of men's boxers waving in the wind on the side of your house? Is that some sort of signal?"

"No." I explain how they got there.

"So, was one of your other men just here?"

I nod.

She smiles. "I thought so. Was that Karl I saw on the road?"

I nod.

"He was . . . handsome."

I frown. "Did you expect him to be pug-ugly?"

"Well . . . I didn't expect him to be so fine." She looks at my ankles. "Are you going to explain why you're icing your ankles, or should I imagine the nastiest?"

I tell her about the game, Roger's visit, and then Karl's . . . abilities.

She fans herself. "I have just added Karl to my fantasy with Shemar Moore. Whoo! And I may even let Karl go first."

I sigh. "You can have him."

"Can I?"

Damn, she's eager! I lean back on the headboard. "You can have him, but for your fantasy only, Izzie. *Only* for your fantasy."

"You're no fun."

"I was last night, and that's why I'm no fun today."

She starts to sit at the foot of the bed but stops. "You haven't changed the sheets yet, have you?"

"I haven't had the time."

She sniffs the air. "Or used air freshener. Where is it?"

"In the closet in the bathroom."

She gets the Oust and sprays the room so much that we both start coughing.

"Was it that bad?" I ask.

"Yes."

I point to the foot of the bed. "Take a load off, Izzie."

"I'll stand." She laughs. "So, how was it?"

"How was what?"

"You know, having two men kind of at the same time."

I count in my head. "I had them more than twelve hours apart, Izzie."

"Who was better?"

I shake my head. "They were both good." Though with Roger, it was definitely more intimate and erotic, since we were facing each other.

"Uh-huh." She smiles. "And you thought this kind of thing would- n't happen, since you moved out here. Have you ever wondered what might happen if any of them caught on?"

"They won't."

"You have some white boy's boxers waving in the wind, some nasty sheets on your bed because of Karl, and this room smells of hot and nasty sex. If they keep their eyes open and just go around sniffing the air, they're bound to figure it out, and then you're liable to get dumped three times."

I know it could happen, but . . . "Maybe only two will dump me, leaving me one man to play with."

"Bad things come in threes, you know."

I sigh. That little statement sometimes does come true. "I guess . . . I guess I could handle losing one of them, or even two of them, but losing all three? That would be hard." And something I *never* want to think about happening.

"Do you ever wonder if they're being faithful to you?"

I shrug. "Not really."

"They're men, Lana. It's not in their genes to be faithful."

"I know. I just don't think about it."

She wipes a wrinkle from the bedspread, sitting lightly on the edge. "Well, maybe you *should* think about it."

"Why?"

She shrugs. "They're good in bed, or so you tell me. They must be practicing somewhere."

I roll my eyes. "You're the only one I know who practices having sex, Izzie. Did you have a little threesome last night?"

She shakes her head. "I tried a foursome."

I blink.

"It wasn't that good."

I don't even want to imagine how she did it.

She sighs. "Have you at least tested them lately?"

"Like an AIDS test?"

"No." She laughs. "You know, tested them. Played with them a little. Put them on the spot."

"I don't do that, Izzie. It's not nice."

"Nice or not, I know the very test you should give them."

I hate humoring her, but at least my stuff is getting a rest. "Okay, what's the test?"

"I call it 'The Next Step' test."

"What's that?" Although I think I already know, and I think I already played it with Karl this morning. Izzie probably read about this particular test in some women's magazine.

"Well, for Juan Carlos, the next step is to demand to meet his mama."

That *would* be a major step for Juan Carlos. "And when he says no, and I know he will, what will that prove?"

"That he can't possibly ever make a commitment to you. And since he can't commit *just* to you, that means maybe he has a *chica* on the side he *can* commit to. Understand?"

"That makes absolutely no sense, Izzie. Just because he doesn't want me to meet his mama does *not* mean he has a *chica* on the side."

"There's only one way to be sure. . . ." She looks at my cell phone. "Give him a call."

"Okay." I have to prove her wrong. Since it's Sunday and he isn't working, I dial Juan Carlos's house, and he answers on the first ring.

"Juan Carlos, it's Lana."

"Is anything wrong?"

Yeah, it is kind of weird for me to call him on a Sunday, when I know he's home all day with his mama. "No. Um, I just wanted to ask if I could meet your mama today."

A long pause. "What are you saying?" he whispers.

He whispers only when his mama is nearby.

"I have been thinking that maybe it's time we took the next step in our relationship, and I haven't even met a single person in your family."

Izzie nods and mouths the word "perfect."

"What is this next step?" he asks.

Juan Carlos sounds afraid. I've never heard fear in his voice before. Maybe I should ask to meet some of his second cousins first.

"What is this next step, Lana?"

I need to let him off the hook before he freaks out. "Oh, Juan Carlos, I'm just joking with you."

Heavy sigh. "I knew it. You are always kidding with me, Lana."

"Yeah. I'm such a kidder."

Izzie is shaking her head. I hate it when she's right.

"Lana, are you free tonight? I can get away late."

Three men inside me in less than twenty-four hours? Never! Though just to see if I could survive it might be worth it. . . . No. Two men will have to be my limit. I decide to be mean. "You can get out here tonight?"

"Yes."

"You mean that you'll have to *sneak* away later."

"You have never complained before."

True, but that was before last night in the tub with Roger, and today with Karl in the bed and in the shower. Hmm. "Well, I hurt my ankle at my game yesterday." He never asks about my games.

And then . . . he laughs! He actually laughs! "Oh, so no more dancing for you for a while. Ha!"

Prick. "I gotta go. Bye."

I hang up.

Izzie can't contain herself. "I'll bet he's got a hot little Panamanian mama stashed somewhere."

"He's Mexican."

"Whatever. He doesn't want you to meet his family because *maybe* he already has one. Did you ever think of that?"

"No." I don't like this doubt creeping into my mind. It's not . . . natural.

"Well, call the white boy."

"His *name* is Roger."

"Whatever."

I call Roger's cell phone and get an "out of range" message. Then I call his apartment.

"How's your ankle?" he asks instead of saying hello first.

"It still hurts, but I'll manage. Are you busy?"

"Just recovering."

"Me, too."

Izzie keeps leaning closer to me, and I wave her back.

"Roger, I had a dream about you last night."

"Yeah? Were we covered in mud?"

I smile inside. "No. We weren't covered in mud."

Izzie's mouth drops. Good.

"In chocolate syrup, then," Roger says.

That sounds like fun! The bugs would have a field day, but . . . "And caramel syrup, too," I add.

"And whipped cream," Roger adds. "With a couple of cherries."

This guy is making me hungry and horny at the same time.

"Were we, uh, in my apartment?"

I normally love to play this game with him, and since I don't want to disappoint Izzie and her fantasies . . . "Yeah, we were in your apartment with the drapes all the way open and five people watching us."

He doesn't respond. Izzie seems to stop breathing.

"Roger? You there?"

"Yeah."

I have to calm us all down. "Let me get back to my dream."

"Just when I was getting excited." He sighs. "Tell me about your dream."

"In my dream, we made us a milk chocolate baby."

Izzie's mouth drops open further, and I put my finger to my lips.

"Yeah?" Roger says. "Was it a boy or a girl?"

"It was a dream, Roger. I didn't check if the child had a package."

"Oh."

CAN'T GET ENOUGH OF YOUR LOVE 121

After some silence, I ask, "Does the baby's sex matter that much to you?"

"Well, I was just curious."

He doesn't sound upset about my strange dream. Maybe this is a good sign, and though I know he'd rather continue talking about our "show" in front of his window, I ask him, "Tell me, truthfully, what do you think about my playing football?"

"From doing it with an audience to milk chocolate babies to football, huh?"

Even Izzie looks puzzled. I love tangents. They keep men on their toes.

"We'll get back to our show, I promise. So, what do you think about my playing football?"

"Well, honestly, Lana, I worry about you."

The man's knocking on my heart again. "You worry about little ol' me?"

"Well, some of those women are huge, and number thirty-nine had it in for you yesterday."

"Tell me about it."

"And when I'm not worrying, I am simply amazed."

There's that knocking again. "Yeah?"

"As you've figured out, I'm not very athletic."

I smile. "You're athletic enough, man. And limber. I don't know how we did it in the tub last night."

Izzie grabs her chest. Good.

"You were the limber one, not me. I didn't know your legs could do that."

Neither did I. "Now what were you saying about being amazed at my football-playing abilities?"

"Well, it amazes me how you can gracefully sack the quarterback."

"Gracefully?"

He laughs. "You have awesome moves, Lana. And you're so smooth. I wish you didn't have to get so bruised up, though."

"Would you still take care of me, even if I didn't play football?"

"You know I would."

Okay. Time to put Izzie in her place. It's time for *the* question. "What if . . ." No, that's not the right way to start. "Would you ever consider . . ." Damn. Why can't I ask him?

"What?"

Here we go. "Roger, why haven't you asked me to marry you yet?"

Izzie gasps, my heart skips, and Roger doesn't even hesitate.

"I have thought about asking you, Lana, I really have, but I didn't think you'd have me like that."

Huh? "Why wouldn't I have you?"

"You're . . . free. You have this life in you, this glow."

Talk poetically to me, man. Keep on knocking on my heart.

"I'm going to be interment director at a cemetery one day. You're all about life, and I'm . . . I'm not."

"That is a bald-faced lie, Roger, and you know it."

"It's how I feel, Lana."

"But Roger, you brought me back to life." And Karl put me here in this bed. Hmm. I need to lighten the mood. "So it has nothing to do with you being so white that deer freeze whenever they see you?"

"I've noticed that," Roger says, laughing, "especially on the drive to your place. I *am* getting more freckles, though."

"Yeah? Where?"

"In, um, interesting places."

"How interesting?"

"You'll just have to find them all the next time we, uh, I mean, the next time we play football."

"We're playing catch, remember?"

"Oh yeah. I promise to kiss all your bruises. I think I missed a few last night."

Karl made up for it. And this makes me feel . . . guilty? Damn. I had better get a hold of myself. "So, what do you really think of my dream?"

"I like it."

"You'd like to make milk chocolate babies with me?"

"I would love to make milk chocolate babies with you."

I stick my tongue out at Izzie. "Well, that's all I wanted to know. See you soon."

"Can we talk later tonight about our little show?"

I think my stuff could handle a little phone sex. "Sure." I lick my lower lip and smile at Izzie. "And maybe one or more of those people watching us will join us this time."

"Oh . . . boy," Roger says. "Are they, um, women or men?"

"I'll tell you later. Bye now."

I click off my cell.

Izzie's face looks flushed. "My my," she says.

"It's getting hot in here, huh?"

She nods. "You've just added a few more fantasies to my brain."

I nod. "Glad I could help you."

"Whoo."

"Roger would marry me in a heartbeat." A tiny little lie. "He says he would love to make milk chocolate babies with me." Who would have flaming red hair. Hmm. I guess we can dye their hair. Maybe their hair will come out orange. Brown clown children?

"Are you going to call Karl now?" Izzie asks.

"I already know Karl's answer. He'll say I'm trippin'. I already asked him this morning if he wanted to move in, and he said no."

She raises her eyebrows. "Sounds like there's trouble in paradise."

"There isn't."

"Sounds like two of your three men don't want you all that much."

True, but . . . "You're just jealous, Izzie, and I bet if I talked to Juan Carlos and Karl one-on-one, I could convince them of anything."

"Do you want to bet?"

Geez! The humoring continues. "Sure, Izzie. What's the bet?"

"I bet . . . that if you were *pregnant* . . ."

"What?"

"Come on, girl, you've had three men in a matter of, what, a week or two? It could happen. You could be with child at this very moment."

I sit up. "We use a condom every time."

"So one of the condoms breaks. I hear it happens all the time."

Oh God, I hope not. "You want me to tell each of them that I may be pregnant?"

"Right."

"I can't lie to them about something like that."

"You lie about everything else."

True.

"And it's not really lying to tell them you're late. Just tell them you're late and see how they react. If all three of them react positively, you win the bet . . . and I'll bring you Sunday lunch for the rest of the year."

"Can you bring something other than chicken sometimes?"

"Yes." She smiles. "And if even just *one* of them reacts negatively, you have to give me Karl's pager number."

The hoochie! "No!"

"It sounds to me as if you aren't sure of your men."

"I am, it's just . . . You want Karl's pager number?"

"Yes."

"Why?"

"I like what I saw."

And she hasn't seen Juan Carlos or Roger. She might like Juan Carlos, but Roger . . . a definite no. "And all you want is a pager number?"

"That's all I'll need."

She's too sure of herself. But am I sure enough about my men? I can't show any fear in front of Izzie. "It's a bet." I remove the bags of ice, now turned to cold water. "You really want Karl?"

"He would be the only one I'd want."

At least Juan Carlos is safe now. "Karl is hard to pin down."

"That's okay, as long as he's down with me."

I laugh. Izzie doesn't normally sling the slang. "He's hard to find,

Izzie. Do you want a man who shows up out of the blue, knocks your boots, and leaves?"

"Yes."

I sigh. "It's no picnic having a man with little conception of the time or the calendar."

"So we'll be spontaneous."

Izzie and Karl? Church and Street? Gospel and Hip-Hop? The Lady and the Warrior? The Woman Who Loves God and the African God? "Why not Juan Carlos?"

"He's too much of a mama's boy."

Too true. "What about Roger?" I ask just to ask. I already know her answer.

She snorts the kind of laugh that makes her look ugly. "Never."

I shake my head, my blood pressure rising. "You know what, Izzie? We don't have to have a bet."

"Are you afraid you'll lose?"

"No. In fact, I'm going to give you Karl's pager number right now."

Izzie blinks. "Right now?"

"You know a better time? Get some paper."

She rushes out and comes back with a black book. "It's my address book."

I'll bet it's empty. I give her the number. "He may not ever call you back, and if he does, I promise that he won't give you the time of day."

"He will. I'm psychic, remember?"

"Right."

She whips out her cell phone.

"What are you doing?"

"Paging your man."

I watch her punch in some numbers, wait a few seconds, and hang up.

"He won't—"

Her phone rings.

The son of a bitch!

"Hello?" She winks at me. "Hi, Karl. I'm a friend of Lana's."

The bitch! Throwing my name in it like that will help!

"Yes, I understand that you have some Coach bags for sale."

Ho! Tramp! Pavement princess!

"Yes, I would love to see them tonight. Your place or mine?"

I cannot believe—

"Your place?" She raises her eyebrows. "Wonderful." She writes down his address. "I'll see you then. Bye." She presses the END button on her phone with sculpted nails I'll never have.

"You . . . witch!" I shout.

She starts for the door. "I have to go now. I hope you don't mind. I have to get ready for my date."

"And you're meeting him—"

"Yes, at his place. He gave me the address."

The . . . snake! The dog!

"And you thought he wouldn't give me the time of day, Lana. How sad you must feel."

As she walks out of my room, I yell, "It's all about business to him. You ain't nothing but a customer."

"I may surprise you, Lana," she calls out. "After all, I've learned from the best, right? See you next Sunday."

"Don't bother."

She returns to my room. "Well, I have to visit you, and this time, *I* will have a story to tell *you.*"

"Izzie, you're not going to tell him about the other two, are you?"

"If I have to."

Oh damn. "You wouldn't."

She shakes her head. "Lana, I won't have to resort to something as low as that to get his interest. Besides, I am your best friend, right? Just consider this another test."

After the front door closes, I start to worry. What have I just done? I've declared open season on one of my men! Karl won't . . . will he? Didn't I just give him some good lovin'? Won't he be too tired?

Wait.

Karl has amazing powers of recuperation. "Gimme fifteen minutes, and I'll be ready," he tells me.

Shit.

I call Izzie's cell phone. "Izzie," I say before she can respond, "I don't want you to—"

"You don't trust Karl? My my, I thought you had everything handled."

"I do, but . . ."

"Bye, Lana."

"You ain't nothin' but a—"

Click.

"Pavement princess," I say to Jenny's yellow walls.

I sit and stew for a bit. She wouldn't. She's a church girl, a member of polite society, a high school guidance counselor, and Karl's, well, Karl, tattooed, streetwise, roughneck Karl. That would never work . . . would it? But she's so beautiful, and he's a man, and—

I call Karl's pager. I need to warn him about Crazy Izzie, the man-eating, Christian perv. I need to remind him of where he was this morning, whom he was with, what he did, how well he did it, how often he did it, and where he can get some more.

My cell phone isn't ringing.

I page him again. He calls a new number *immediately*, but he can't call me! He calls an unknown number before a known number! I need to tell him that he can store his fake shit here. I need to tell him he can visit as often as he wants and that I won't bring up the M-word ever.

My cell phone isn't ringing.

"C'mon, Karl, call me back!"

I page him off and on for the rest of the day and into the evening.

My cell phone doesn't ring once before I fall asleep.

I hate Karl.

But I hate Izzie more.

Chapter 15

Karl finally calls back after midnight.

"What?" I say with attitude.

"Got your page, girl. What's up?"

I have been practicing what to say all day, and I can't get "I want you to spend the night with me" from my brain to my mouth. "I paged you all day, man. Why didn't you call back?"

"I been busy, you know, doing my thing."

"Or doing someone."

A pause. "You know I'm not like that, girl."

"Then why didn't you call me back immediately?"

"We just saw each other, Peanut."

Now what the hell kind of answer is that? "What if I needed you, Karl?"

"Did you need me?"

Not really. His going away made my booty like me again. "Of course I did, Karl. I ran out of Motrin, and I needed you to get me some more."

"You did?"

No. I'm trying to make you feel guilty, fool. "Yeah. Didn't you notice how swollen my ankle was?"

"I just figured, you know, it must have been all right. It didn't seem to bother you when we were getting busy."

Those were screams of pain, not pleasure! "Look, if I page you, it means I have something important to tell you, all right?"

"All right, all right."

"So call me back immediately next time, all right?"

"I said all right."

Time to check on Izzie. "So, did you see my friend Izzie tonight?"

"Who?"

I roll my eyes. "Isabel."

"Oh, yeah. She came over and bought some bags. Thanks for sending her my way."

I don't say, "You're welcome."

"I didn't know you had friends like her."

What's that supposed to mean? Pretty friends? Shit. "Did you charge her full price?"

"Sure did, but she didn't have enough cash on her, so she's out at an ATM getting some more."

Sure. She just conveniently didn't have enough money. But if she's out, then he's not *in* her. That's good. Time to ruin Izzie. "Look, Karl, Izzie's not the person you think she is."

"Huh?"

"She's, well, how do I say this? She's not quite all there, you know?"

"How do you mean?"

"Well . . ." I need to lay it on thick. "I mean, she's sort of attractive, right?"

"Yeah."

Damn. He was supposed to disagree and say she wasn't his type or something. "Well, would you believe that she's really pushing fifty and has four grandchildren?"

"No shit?"

"No shit, and all five of her kids have different daddies, so watch out. She has been known to use sex instead of cash to buy things."

Some silence. "And she's a friend of yours?"

Hmm. This is starting to look bad for me. "Well, she visits me every Sunday to witness to me." Sort of true.

"She's all that *and* she's a church lady?"

"Hard to believe, but it's true."

"But she can't possibly be pushing fifty, Peanut. How you know that?"

Oh shit. He has *really* been checking her out. "Um, I didn't believe it either when she first told me." That ought to be enough. I mean, if she said it to me, he has to believe it.

"Well, she sure likes Coach bags. If she buys all the ones she's picked out, I may have to go back to New York soon."

Nuh-uh! So *that's* her plan. She figures that if she buys him out . . . "You just make sure she pays you in cash, understand?"

"Oh, I will."

I hear a knocking in the background. "Is that her?"

"Yeah."

"Call me back after she's gone."

"All right." *Click.*

And then, I wait.

And wait.

My phone rings after two. It's Roger.

"How are you feeling?" he asks.

Pissed. "Okay."

"I, uh, I hope I didn't wake you."

"I'm having trouble sleeping," I say.

"Me, too. I keep thinking about what you said."

Oh yeah. I'm supposed to be having phone sex with Roger. "Uh, me, too."

"Would you *really* let our spectators join us?"

I sigh. "No. You're all I need, Roger." Oh God, another damn lie. "Though it might be . . . interesting to let one or more of them inside, you know, let them get closer to us." And it might be. Shit. They might just stand there and watch, or raid Roger's refrigerator, I don't know.

"What if they . . ." His voice trails off.

"What if they do what?"

He sighs. "What if she—or he—"

"Or them," I interrupt.

"Yeah. What if they try to, you know, get between us?"

Whoo, I'm warming up. "Are you inside me?"

"Yes," he whispers.

"And are you grabbing my ass tightly?"

"Yes."

"Then there's no way anyone can get between us—" I hear a beep. "I have a call on my other line. Can you hold?"

"Damn," Roger says. "Just when it was getting good! Sure, I'll hold."

"Hold it tight," I say, and click over to Karl.

"Hey, Peanut," he says.

"Don't you 'hey, Peanut' me. It doesn't take two hours to complete a sale."

A pause. "She had to go out and get more money, and, um—"

"Did you fuck her?" I am *really* tired. I hardly ever use the F-word, even in my mind. I might use it with Roger in a few minutes, though. . . .

"No, girl, I didn't. Shit! Is that what you think?"

I don't answer.

"Girl, she bought every last one of the bags, and that was all. You really think I'd do that to you?"

A glimmer of hope. "I don't know, Karl. I mean, what am I supposed to think when you're gone for a month and take two hours to call me back after I just asked you to call me right back?"

"Isabel can't count, yo. Every time she came back, she had the wrong amount."

Izzie's persistent, I'll give her that. "And what did she say or do when she kept coming up short?"

"Well, like you said. She was all up on me."

Sundays with Izzie have just ended. "And do you *swear* that you didn't do anything with her?"

"Girl, I swear on my grandma's grave. You wore me the hell out today."

Hmm. "And that's the only reason you didn't mess with her?"

"Damn, Peanut. You're my girl. What would I want with some-one's grandma when I have you?"

Yes. Good. I can breathe easier. "So, nothing happened?"

"I swear."

Time to reorganize a bit. "You have enough DVDs to keep you in town for a while?"

"Maybe a day or so."

Shit. "Well, I'm not going in to work today, and I want to see you before you go back to New York, all right?"

"All right. I'll bring you lunch."

I smile. "Thank you. Good night."

I click back to Roger, letting my fingers work their way to my thigh. "So, where were we?"

"I was . . . inside you, grabbing your ass."

Good thing I'm not wearing any drawers. "So you were fucking me while two other people were with us?"

"Yes."

He's panting, and so am I. "Who are they?"

"It's . . . it's a man and a woman."

Yeah, I'm getting wet. "What do they look like?"

"She's, um, she's . . . short with long black hair."

He's leaving out a few details. "Is she white?"

"Do you want her to be white?"

"Sure. Does she have a nice shape?"

More panting. "Nice tits, nice firm tits."

Holy shit! Roger is just busting it all out tonight. "What about him?"

"He's, uh, he's black."

Jesus. If he only knew how close to the truth he is. "Yeah? What's he doing?"

"He's . . . he's kissing the back of your neck."

Whoo. "Is he . . . is he hard?"

"Yeah."

Whoo. "And what's she doing?"

"She's . . . she's trying to get between us. . . ."

Don't stop.

"She's kissing on your nipples. . . ."

Oh, don't stop.

"Her tongue is going lower—"

I hear another damn beep. Shit! "Roger, hold that thought. I have another call." I click over. "Hello?"

"Checking up on me, Lana?"

Izzie.

"Huh?"

"I know you called Karl while I was there."

Time to break bad on Izzie. "Yes, I did, and I'm wondering how you could have ever become a guidance counselor if you can't count."

A pause.

"Karl told me everything y'all *didn't* do."

"Oh, did he?"

"Yeah. And all you got were some fake Coach bags, Grandma."

Another pause. "He told you about that?"

"You bought them all, right?"

"No, not about that. He kept calling me 'Grandma,' and I wondered why in the world . . ."

"By the way," I interrupt, "you got *four* grandchildren and *five* kids by *five* different daddies."

"You *witch!*"

"Isn't that one of your fantasies?"

I hear a low growling sound. Does Izzie have a dog?

"Oh," I add, "and don't bother coming over next Sunday."

"Why?"

"Because you *won't* have a story to tell. Good night, Izzie."

Click.

Now, what am I *ever* going to do on Sunday afternoons without Izzie? Hmm. I may just have to do nothing all day.

Or have more phone sex with Roger. I click back to him. "Is she licking me down there yet?"

"Uh-huh."

This has never been my fantasy, but I can't help but get more excited. "What's the . . . what's the man doing?"

"He's, um, he's fucking her, hard. . . ."

Damn.

"And he wants to fuck you next. . . ."

Oh . . . shit . . . damn . . . Oh yes, here come the rainbows. "Roger?"

"Yeah?"

"I came."

"Yeah?"

Oh shit, oh shit. "Yeah. Did you?"

"Yeah."

"Um, I'll talk to you later."

"Okay. Good night, Lana."

"Yeah. Good night."

I look around my room, at the crumpled sheets, at all that yellow.

Yeah. It has been a good night.

Chapter 16

After a nice nap and a phone call to PH to tell the secretary that I'm "under the weather"—and after having a difficult time getting Roger's boxers off the side of my house using a step stool and a long stick—I sit in the reading room and think.

Another woman, a so-called friend of mine, tried to steal away one of my men today. And this gets me to thinking about other women I don't know out there who might be trying to do the exact same thing with Juan Carlos or Roger. I can't let my men lose interest in me. Should I put them on a schedule? Hmm. A timetable of lust. Yes.

Nah. It wouldn't work. Whenever my friend comes, no one can see me—

Or should I continue to test them?

I can't live my life full of doubt. I can't sit here wondering what each of them might be doing. I didn't have these thoughts when I was living in the city, but the same as when I was there, I can't just sit here by the phone. If Roger can talk me into an orgasm, what's to stop him from calling someone else? His fantasies are so detailed, almost as if maybe he's already done them.

I need another test.

I pat my stomach. It's mostly flat with a little roll just under my belly button. I never could get rid of that little jelly roll no matter how many sit-ups I did. Must be genetic—

A test, yes. But this time, it will be a test of their friendship.

Yes.

I pat my stomach again. "I think I'm going to be late," I say.

When Karl arrives with lunch, I get right to the point. "I'm late, Karl. I think I may be pregnant." I dig into the Hardee's Thickburger he brought me, ketchup and mayonnaise oozing out of the sides of my mouth.

Karl doesn't seem to be breathing.

"You hear what I said?" Damn, this is a sloppy burger.

"I heard you. Are you sure?"

"Of course I'm sure. My friend has been faithful since I was thirteen. I was going to tell you yesterday, but I didn't want to ruin the moment. So, what do you think?"

Karl fiddles with a curly fry. "I think it's great."

I smile. "Yeah?"

"Yeah."

And then he, um (sorry, Roger!), puts me right up on that kitchen table and starts to get busy with me while I finish my burger. But then I realize—

"You got a condom?" I say, sitting up.

"I don't need one anymore, right?"

Shit.

Why didn't I think of this? They all *hate* to wear condoms, and now I've just given Karl the chance for his stuff to be free!

"I'm late, boo. That doesn't mean I'm pregnant. You still need to wear a condom."

He steps back. "You don't want to be pregnant with my child?"

Huh? "I was just saying that you need to use a condom like always."

"I heard you. You're saying I need to use a condom because you don't want to be pregnant, right?"

Karl is just full of surprises today. He's actually thinking something through. "I didn't say it that way. It's just . . ."

"Well, what *are* you saying, Lana?"

And suddenly I'm not Peanut. "I'm just saying that now is not the time for us to have a baby, with you on the road so much."

"But I just told you about being a distributor or opening my own store down here." He sits in a chair as he shrivels up and my stuff dries up. "What was all that stuff you were talking about yesterday?" He pulls up his pants, zipping his zipper.

Oh yeah. I was pushing him about hooking up long-term. "Baby, my hormones are all out of whack right now. I know I'm not making much sense, so—"

His pager starts vibrating on the table.

"Don't answer that," I say, but it's too late.

He snatches up his pager, snatches my cell phone, and goes outside to make his call. If I'm lucky, he won't be able to get a clear signal.

I limp to the window and see him talking on the phone using that salesman's smile of his. Shit. He sees me and mouths "business." Ten minutes later, he comes back inside.

"I have to go meet with one of those truckers, the ones I told you about. He's over at the truck stop in Troutville."

"You're just going to leave me like that? Karl, I may be pregnant."

He sighs. "And this deal, if it works out, will keep me home with you *and* our baby. I have to go."

"But I need you" escapes before I can stop it.

He nods. "And I need you, too, Peanut. I'll come right back when I'm done. I promise." He kisses my cheek. "I'll be back."

"How long are you going to be?"

He shrugs.

Thirty minutes pass. Then thirty more. I toy with paging him but don't. I even think of calling Izzie, just to make sure the two of them aren't scamming me. There's no scam. There can't be a scam. I believe in Karl, and I'm even beginning to believe he's about to become my one-and-only boo. He's trying to put down roots around me. Maybe it's time I simplified my life. Karl seems sincere, and with that smile and body, he'll be a great salesman. It will take me a good long while to control my jealousy of other women checking out my African god, but I think I can handle it.

Am I making a choice here or what?

I think I am.

I think . . . I'm about to become a one-man woman.

Then it's time to weed out Juan Carlos.

I call Berglund, and the service manager gets him for me. "Hello, Lahhh-na."

"Hi." For some reason, his saying my name that way didn't make me tingle today. I'm doing the right thing. "Juan Carlos, I want to meet your mama today, and I *won't* take no for an answer." That ought to do it. That ought to weed him out.

"But Lana, I am not ready—"

"It's now or never," I interrupt.

"But Lana, it is impossible today, you see. She is at—"

"I thought you loved me," I interrupt. This is going so much better than I had hoped! Almost done.

"I do, I do, Lana, but I cannot—"

"Then it's goodbye, Juan Carlos. We're through." I should hang up now, but I owe him the last word. After all, he did bring some passion into my life when passion was missing in my life.

But he doesn't give me the last word. "I am coming to see you." *Click.*

Oh shit! I call back, but the service manager says Juan Carlos is "gone in a flash."

Shit shit *shit!*

Karl's coming back.

Juan Carlos is on his way.

Should I just . . . vacate? Is the sun starting to go down? It is. I could just roll on out of here, go for a drive until, oh, midnight. That's what I'll do. I know the country roads around here by now. I don't even have to turn on my headlights. I'll just take a long drive without my cell phone—

No, Karl might worry if he tries to call me and I don't answer. I mean, I may be "having his child," and he'd worry. What if Roger calls? He'd worry, too. And what about Roger? I've been sitting here clearing the way for Karl, and I've completely forgotten about the man who made me see rainbows without even being in the room!

I should have stayed in the city.

Okay, okay, calm down. That Bonneville can barely get over forty without shaking. That gives me at least half an hour to—

To do what?

Page Karl. Tell him . . . tell him I'm going to my mama's to do laundry. That might work. Yeah. I'll meet Karl at my mama's.

But that will leave Juan Carlos hanging, and knowing his temper, he might wait here for me until I get back.

Damn.

I thought I was perfectly clear on the phone with him. "Then it's goodbye, we're through" should have been enough! What's there left to talk about?

I page Karl and wait, staring hard at my phone. "Ring, damn you," I whisper.

Hmm. I'll need laundry. The sheets! I get up the stairs with some difficulty, and as soon as I get the sheets off, my cell phone rings.

"Karl, thank you for calling back so soon."

Silence. "Lana, it's Roger."

Oops. "Hi, Roger. I was expecting a call from . . . from my brother."

"Oh. You sound out of breath."

Has it been forty minutes? Of course not. Juan Carlos is still miles away from here, and why doesn't Juan Carlos have a cell phone so I can tell him not to come? Everyone on this *freaking* planet has a cell phone, but *no,* I have to hook up with a man—

"Lana, are you all right?"

"Uh, well, it's been kind of hard getting around with this bum ankle."

"I suppose so. You need some help? It's been a slow day at the cemetery. Our customers aren't dying to see us today."

Normally I'd laugh, but today, I can't. "Uh, no, I can manage."

"Well, um," Roger says, "I'm already . . . here."

Every blood cell in my body freezes.

I can't move.

"You're . . . here?"

"I wanted to surprise you."

Surprise.

Damn.

I usually like surprises, but today . . .

Breathe, Lana, breathe.

"Well, uh, Roger, I was just about to do some laundry down at my mama's." God, I hope Juan Carlos hits every light and stops at every stop sign. Maybe he'll be pulled over for going too slow!

"I can help you. Is the front door open?"

"Um, yeah. I'll be upstairs."

Freaking out.

Yes.

I'll be upstairs freaking out.

I click off my phone and hear the front door open. I look at the sheets in my arms, and they all smell like Karl! I drag my bad leg behind me to the closet and stuff the sheets inside. Just as I close the closet door, Roger is standing in the doorway.

"Hi," he says. "What can I carry?"

New plan. "Oh, just some towels from the bathroom"—oh shit, and *three* of them are wet!—"and some dish towels from downstairs. The rest of my laundry is already at Mama's. I just need to pick it all up."

I watch Roger collect the towels, and he comes out smiling. "I can't believe they're still wet from last night."

Believe it.

"Um, where are my boxers?"

Oh yeah. Them. "Um, I put them out in the barn."

He blinks.

"They were wet, and I thought they'd dry off more quickly out there. You wouldn't want me to hang them out on a tree or something for everyone to see, would you?" Please believe me!

"Boxers blowing in the breeze," he says. "Kinda kinky."

"I, uh, must have known you were coming back, huh?"

In my sickest, most twisted thoughts, I *never* would have thought up this scenario. Three men are trying to visit in one day, and, it seems, simultaneously. No freaking way.

"I'll take these downstairs."

·He walks down the hall, and I follow behind him—praying. *Oh God, what is about to happen? If You just let me get out of this house, I will owe You big-time. I'll even go to church. I'll even—*

"Oops," Roger says, stopping at the bottom of the stairs. "I dropped something."

He stoops over and comes up with . . . a fuzzy black ring box. Is that—

"Now, how did that get into my pocket?" He turns to me. "Lana, I didn't go to work at all today."

"You . . . didn't?" I can't take my eyes off that box. Please be earrings inside, or a brooch. Brooches are nice. Maybe a charm for a charm bracelet. Or the bracelet itself.

Anything but a ring!

"No. I spent all morning picking this out for you." He opens the box. . . .

A ring. A diamond ring. A diamond engagement ring.

Oh shit.

"I've been thinking about this moment for a long time, and, well, you practically asked me to ask you to marry you yesterday, and this might not be the right time, but . . ." He drops to one knee. "Will you marry me, Lana Cole?"

Before I can answer, I hear shouting outside.

And it isn't Mr. Wilson.

Unless Mr. Wilson has suddenly learned to speak Spanish.

And city slang.

Oh . . . no.

Chapter 17

Roger goes to the door. "Is that your brother?"
Oh God!

I can't move.

Why didn't I hear a car pull up? I should have heard *two* cars pull up!

I look past Roger's head and see Karl and Juan Carlos walking toward the house. Well, they're not exactly walking. More like running. No, more like racing to see who can get to the door first.

Please, please, please, God, wake me up from this nightmare!

Roger turns to me. "What's going on, Lana?"

Find your voice, girl. "Roger, I want you to know that no matter what happens—"

The shouting begins again.

"Your brother sounds pissed. Should I leave?"

"Um, Roger, he's not my—"

I can hear what they're shouting now. Karl is yelling "bitch," and Juan Carlos is running off in Spanish, and—

Yep.

I'm a bunta.

Roger turns to me, repeating, "What's going on?" When I don't answer, Roger puts the ring box back into his pocket.

Is this where I'm supposed to faint? Maybe I can break a leg and get some sympathy before they arrive. They wouldn't dump me if I'm lying in a heap on the floor, would they? If I had a back door, I'd be stumbling out of here right now!

They're at the door, pounding away, Karl yelling, "Let me in, Peanut!" and Juan Carlos screaming, "Lahhh-na!"

"Should I let them in?" Roger asks.

Only if I can go out. They can stay, though. That's right. I'll just go for a walk. Y'all just stay here and work this thing out without me.

"Lana?"

"Yeah."

Oh God!

"Lana?"

Damn, I'm beginning to hate my name. "Let them in." Maybe they'll understand. Maybe they'll be okay with it. Maybe—

I sit in the closest chair. They are all going to be pissed.

So this is how it ends.

This is how paradise crumbles.

The door opens. So much noise, so much shouting. I'm the only one sitting. Suddenly this kitchen isn't as big as it once was.

I need to take control. "Why don't"—my voice is so small!—"why don't y'all sit?"

"What's Mr. Wilson doing here?" Karl shouts, pointing at Roger. Oh no. Karl's upper lip is touching his nose. He's most definitely pissed.

"His name," I say feebly, "his name is Roger."

"This is the guy who cuts your grass, right?" Karl demands.

I nod.

"Are you're doing him, too?" Karl shouts.

I have trouble looking any of them in the eye. I hear a chair move. At least Roger is sitting down now, his big ol' goofy feet tapping out a beat on the linoleum.

"I can explain," I say, my voice shaking. "I can explain everything."

"Yes," Juan Carlos hisses, "explain everything." Juan Carlos's nostrils are flaring. Shit. He's angry, too. "Explain!"

What's to explain that isn't already obvious? I look at Karl. "Karl, what took you so long?"

"What?" Karl says. "You said you were going to explain."

"Just . . . just answer my question." I have to know exactly how badly I've messed all this up.

"Well," Karl begins, "after meeting with that trucker, I came right back, but I took a wrong turn at that damn tree."

"I have done that, too," Juan Carlos says. "She should put a light out there or a sign pointing the right way to her house."

"Let me finish, all right?" Karl says to Juan Carlos. "So I nearly end up in the pond again, I back up, and by the time I get to that big tree, there's this guy under the hood of his car."

Right on top of Mr. Wilson's granddaddy.

"The alternator in the Bonneville is bad," Juan Carlos says.

"It wasn't the alternator, fool," Karl says. "It's the distributor. My mama had a Bonneville just like that."

"I am the mechanic here," Juan Carlos says, "and I know."

"Whatever, man," Karl says. "So, we start talking, and I'm like, What are you doing out here, anyway, man? And he tells me about his future *wife* named Lahhh-na who he's taking to meet his mama today. And I tell him, No, her name is Lana, no *ahh,* and she's *my* girlfriend, who might be about to have my baby."

Roger hasn't spoken. I wish he'd say something. Oh. His ears are wiggling. He's pissed, too. Everybody's mad at me today.

"Anyway, while we're standing there fussing back and forth," Karl says, "white boy over here rolls by without stopping."

"I didn't see you," Roger says. At least he can speak.

"Cuz you were doing sixty at least, yo!"

Roger was in a hurry. He was in a hurry to ask me to marry him, and now he'll be in a hurry to leave.

Karl steps closer to me, and I don't dare look up at him. "So Juan and I decided to go for a walk to see what the hell is going on."

Silence.

"So, Peanut, what the hell is going on? You pregnant or not?"

"No," I say.

I hear more than one sigh. Oh, that's comforting.

"And," Juan Carlos says, his voice filling with rage, "you have been seeing these two . . . these two men when you have not been seeing me?"

"Yes." I raise my eyes to look at Roger briefly. He's in that chair, but he's already gone, his jaw set, his eyes glazed over, those ears of his wiggling.

"How long has this been going on, Peanut?" Karl asks.

"What did you call her?" Juan Carlos asks.

"It's her nickname, Juan," Karl says. "She must not have told you that, either. Evidently, she only tells a man what he wants to hear." Karl squats in front of me. "How long, Lana?"

I stare at his chin. "About five months . . . with Juan Carlos, and about two months with Roger."

Karl sighs and drops his chin to his chest. "Damn! Shit! You're good. You played us all." He stands. "I never would have believed it." He turns to Juan Carlos. "It's the quiet ones every damn time, yo. Never hook up with a shy girl, damn."

"I would not believe it, either," Juan Carlos says. "And Lana is not so shy."

Roger says nothing.

Karl whistles "MF" under his breath. "And I'm almost out of gas."

So am I. I've been running on empty for the past five minutes.

"I can't even escape this fucking nightmare," Karl whispers. "Peanut, you got any gas left in that barn?"

I nod.

"I'm out." In two steps, he's out of the house, the door slamming behind him.

One down, two to go.

Roger rises from his chair. "You need a ride, Juan?" His voice is so gravelly.

I hear Juan Carlos breathing rapidly. "Yes. Yes, I need a ride to my car."

"I can take you," Roger says.

"Bunta," Juan Carlos spits at me, and the two of them leave together, this time without a slam.

I'm alone.

Shit.

Eight months' work gone in five miserable minutes.

A moment later, I hear shouting again and stumble to the door, expecting to see three men beating the shit out of each other. Instead, I see Roger leaning out of his window waving Karl to his truck. Karl waves my gas can in the air. He wants no part of them. I can't blame any of them for not wanting any part of me. Juan gets out and puts his hand on Karl's shoulder. Karl shrugs it off and steps back. Roger gets out. He's saying something . . . they're nodding . . . they all look my way.

It's not one of the best moments in my life.

Karl puts the gas can on the bed of Roger's truck and climbs in after it. Juan gets in the front passenger seat, and Roger is the only one standing and looking my way.

"Go on," I say, and the tears start to fall. "Go on."

Roger gets in, the truck rolls forward, and the red glow of the taillights vanish into the darkness.

They're gone.

Gone.

No friends.

No benefits.

I'm alone.

In five freaking minutes.

Chapter 18

I need more toilet paper.

I've already finished off my only box of Kleenex, and I'm down to one roll of Angel Soft. My pillow has become a sponge. It's just me and Jenny sitting on a bed without sheets in a yellow room while Roger's boxers get "smoked" in the barn.

I guess this is as bad as bad gets.

My phone rings. It's Izzie.

No. I was wrong.

This is as bad as bad gets.

The hits just keep coming.

I let it ring five times before answering. "Yes?"

"Why weren't you at work today, Lana?"

This will teach me to ditch work for three men and a bad ankle. "I hurt my ankle, remember?"

"That's all? No man or men involved?"

I don't need this. Not now. And from the happy tone of her voice, I'll bet Izzie already knows something went terribly wrong. "Izzie, I don't want any more drama tonight, okay?"

"Did something happen?"

Do I tell her? Do I tell anybody? Would anyone believe it? I can't tell the witch who tried to take my man . . . the man who is no longer mine. Hmm. "Remember what you were saying about how it could all end?"

"Yes?"

"Well, it all ended in just five minutes."

Silence.

"All three of them were just here, Izzie."

"All at once?"

"Yeah."

More silence. I bet she's doing a church-lady dance or something.

"And they're all gone now?" she asks.

"Yeah."

"Oh, Lana, are you all right?"

More tears and not nearly enough toilet paper. I need more pillows on this bed. "Of course I'm not all right, Izzie." I may never be all right again.

"How bad was it?"

I do my best to describe the mess, but I know I'm leaving something out. Oh yeah. "Girl, Roger even asked me to marry him tonight."

"He didn't!"

"He had the box and had just proposed when all hell broke loose."

"You didn't give him an answer, did you?"

"I didn't have time!"

"Well, it's lucky it all ended when it did, then."

A few of my tears dry up quickly. "Lucky? How am I lucky? I've just gotten dumped by three men at the same time."

"It was bound to happen. You can't have too much of a good thing. What goes around comes around."

I ignore her and her stupid sayings. "I had all three of them in the palm of my hand, and they all slipped through my fingers. I never should have listened to you."

"Hey now, don't blame me. It was a disaster *you* created, not me."

She's right, of course, but I have to be pissed at someone. "But I took *your* advice. I forced the issue. I backed them all into a corner with those damn tests of yours. . . ."

And they all showed up at my door swinging.

Wait a minute.

They all showed up.

They all came to me.

I didn't scare them away.

Karl came to tell me about a deal that would keep him home with me. Juan Carlos came to take me to see his mama. Roger came to ask me to marry him.

They all came to me.

Oh, this is messed up! In solidifying our "love square" by forcing the issue, I ruined it!

And I'm out of toilet paper except for several partial rolls in the bathroom closet. I hope I have some paper towels downstairs, just in case.

"Maybe all this is for the best," Izzie says.

What the hell? "How? How is *any* of this for the best?"

She sighs. "You know I tried to seduce Karl last night, and he wouldn't budge. I tried everything short of doing a striptease. That man loved you, Lana."

Time to get those paper towels.

"And at that moment, I hated you, Lana. I've been looking for a man who would love me that much, and you had *three* men who loved you like that. It wasn't fair. And I envied you for that. Girl, you know exactly what you want in a man."

Which doesn't make sense, but then again it does.

"I've never been able to make up my mind," Izzie says. "Not many women know what you know about men."

Or know and feel what I'm feeling right now.

"It's so weird, though. I just finished reading an article about breakups."

Oh joy.

"They say it takes half as long as the relationship lasted for a person to fully recover."

Who measures this shit? What, do they (whoever "they" are) go around talking to the newly heartbroken and ask them, "Let us know when you're over so-and-so. We're crunching some numbers for our next article." As if any woman knows when she's finally over a man.

"Are you doing the math, Lana?"

"No. Why?"

"I just want to know how long I should avoid you."

"Why?"

"Because you are going to be a bitch."

"Ha, ha." But she's right again. "Let's see . . . I should be over Roger by the end of next month, Juan Carlos by the end of July, and Karl by the middle of September."

"Have a nice summer," Izzie says.

I groan.

"Just kidding. Can I ask you one question?"

"Sure."

"What if one or more of them wants you back anyway? They may have all left tonight, but one or more of them might come back."

Only in my dreams. "None of them will want me, Izzie. Not after what just happened."

"I don't know. That kind of love doesn't evaporate overnight."

"It might."

"You can always stalk them."

She's pissing me off! "I'm on crutches, Izzie! How am I going to stalk them?"

"Stalk slowly, then." She giggles.

I giggle, too. It *was* kind of funny.

"Well, let's say all the love you have for these men is still there. Will you take him or *them* back?"

I wipe my face with my free hand. "They're not coming back."

"But what if just one came back? Who would you want him to be?"

I don't want to think about this. If I couldn't choose which one man to be with, I sure as hell can't choose which one man I want to have come back. "I don't know, Izzie."

"Oh!" she shouts.

"What is it?"

"I have a call on my other line. What do I do?"

"What?"

"I've never had this happen before."

Geez. Izzie needs to get a life. "Hit the flash button."

"The flash button . . . Oh, okay."

And Izzie disappears without saying "Can you hold, please?"

Sure. Whatever. I can hold. I'll be holding myself for a while, right? I can hold.

Five minutes later, she comes back on. "Um, Lana, I really feel badly for you, but I have to go. I'll call you soon, okay?"

"Okay."

"And did you mean what you said about Sunday?"

I don't want to see anyone, and I don't want anyone to see me. "Let's hold off on that for a while, okay? I need some time alone to think." About all that went wrong.

"I understand. Take care." *Click.*

How do I "take care"? About all I want to do is take more Motrin, take a month-long nap, and take some time to cry.

This house is so quiet. I wonder if I can stand myself. Yesterday, I had three men wanting me, and today . . .

Today I have only me, myself, and I.

I am such lousy company.

Chapter 19

There's no denying it.

Izzie has to be right.

They *will* be back.

That phone will ring off the hook all day, and I'll be giving *my* flash button a workout. And in a little while, I'll be flashing my girls and my good leg at probably all three of them—one at a time, of course.

Oh sure, they will be angry for a spell, but then they *will* be at my door in no time at all, maybe soon.

I ease out of bed, blinking at the sunrise. I had better get ready for all my gentlemen callers.

I shower for a long time, shaving my legs closer than I've ever shaved them before. I bathe in lotion, drowning my girls with some of my "good" cologne. I call in sick to Patrick Henry ("bad cramps this time," I tell the secretary) and hobble down to the kitchen to make some Chex mix. All three of my men—who'll be here first?—*love* this stuff because I use real butter, never margarine. I'll have to make more than I've ever made before.

They're all going to be hungry.

While the Chex mix is warming in the oven, I call Dial-a-

Horoscope to find out how their days will go, something I do from time to time. Karl, a Libra, is supposed to "pursue love and romance." Here I am, Karl! Come and get your love! I'll be here all day! Juan Carlos is an Aries, and as long as he doesn't use "aggression" today, he's supposed to be able to "charm anyone" into seeing things his way. Juan Carlos, come charm me, you Mexican Prince Charming, you! I'm ready to be charmed, and if you want to get aggressive, I'll be ready! I don't like the sound of Roger's horoscope at all. He's a Taurus. It says, "The less time spent dealing with personal matters today, the better."

Well, I am not a "personal matter"—I'm his boo.

I bet they all feel guilty for leaving me. I know that *I* would feel guilty for leaving someone with a swollen ankle in her time of need.

Karl will feel guilty for not paying close enough attention to me all these months. He'll get down on his knees and beg me to take him back. I'll let him stew a bit, of course, and then tell him, "Only if you're good to me, boo, and only if you stay in town." He will cry tears of joy and say, "I promise, Peanut."

Hmm. But do I want Karl to come back to me? He actually wanted to use my place for a fake-shit depository. I may have to let Karl stew for a couple *days.*

Juan Carlos will feel guilty about not letting me meet his sainted mama sooner. He'll be back with a rose and a song, begging for one more chance. I'll let him wait outside a while (and I hope it rains!) before telling him, "Only if you let me be me, Juan Carlos." He'll promise, of course, and make mad, passionate love to me until I say stop.

Hmm. But do I want Juan Carlos to come back to me? He probably still doesn't think I'm good enough to meet his mama. I may have to turn Juan Carlos away for at least a week or two.

Roger . . . hmm. Roger will feel guilty about not saying anything, for not fighting for me, for withdrawing that ring from its rightful place on my finger. He'll be back with that ring, begging me to take it. "Only if you take my last name, Roger," I will say with authority, because "Lana Joy McDowell" does not have a nice ring to it. "I promise," he, the future Roger *Cole*, will say. And we'll just have to have a long engagement so I can ease away from the other two. Maybe . . . a four-year engagement. That would work.

Hmm. But do I want Roger to come back? He's an Indian giver! He offers marital bliss, then steals it away! I may have to tell Roger to take a long hike for at least a month.

Yeah, they'll be back.

I check my phone for the one hundred ninety-ninth time in the past hour.

I had better charge up my phone. It's going to have a busy night.

Yep, they'll be back.

There's no denying it.

Chapter 20

Iam so pissed!

They didn't call me at *all* yesterday, and I've had to take another day off, another *unpaid* day off "with the cramps" to wait for them to come to their senses.

What are they thinking? *Are* they thinking? Do they think I'm made of money or something? Why haven't they called? What could they possibly be doing that's more important than I am?

And why is my lower leg so shiny and blue?

Pain is shooting up my leg.

Shit.

Did I break it?

Nah. It's just a sprain from hell.

I'll deal with that later. That's not important.

I have another ankle.

I look out the window for the fiftieth time in the past hour, but nothing stirs the dusty driveway.

Why me, God? I was just doing what men have been doing to women since the world began. If it's okay for them, why can't it be okay for me? Men, the pigs, have been catting around like dogs since you made them, slithering around like snakes and howling like wolves.

Would a city girl use all those animals to describe men? I bet she wouldn't. We country girls know our animals, and we definitely know our men.

So what gives, God? Aren't we all supposed to be equal in your sight? Aren't we all your children? Why are you treating me like an unwanted stepchild, then? Why are men your favorites when we are so much prettier? Oh sure, you created Adam first, big deal. You had to create Adam first because he would have been late or gotten lost being second! And you had to create Eve because you knew Adam was going to mess things up. That's all women are to you: fixers of the problems men create. We're the long-suffering ones. We're the deprived ones. We're the abused, used, and discarded ones. Not men, no. They're allowed to drop their fluids whenever, wherever, and with whomever they want! It's so unfair!

God is a jerk because he's a man.

I open the window and shout, "You jerk!"

Hmm. It's not wise to challenge God by calling him a jerk.

I lean out and look up into the sky. "Sorry."

I close the window.

"But you're still a jerk," I whisper.

Who else can I blame for this mess?

Who else *can't* I blame for this mess?

Hmm. I can blame society for being such a prude. Yeah. It's society's fault. A woman is allowed to be happy, a woman is allowed to feel pleasure, but society says, "No way, sister, you just lie there, take it, and be miserable." Society sucks. Society can kiss my black ass.

What's left of my black ass. I'm losing weight? Oh yeah, I haven't eaten in a while.

Now what was I saying? Oh yeah. Society. Society says a woman is to go through school quietly, not take math and science seriously, not play sports but be girly, not do anything but stand by her man and make babies. Society says a woman must look gorgeous at all times, yet as soon as we do something "man-like," like Martha Stewart, they use our gender and our beauty against us. A woman, dressing as provocatively as all those ads scream for us to dress, gets raped, and all the damn lawyers can say is that "she was dressed provocatively, and she was asking for it." We're damned if we do, and we're damned if we don't. A man screws two thousand women, and we put him in the Basketball Hall of Fame. A woman screws two thousand men, and society calls her a "ho."

Who else, who else . . .

Oh yeah. Number 39, the bitch. You can kiss my black ass, too. If you hadn't tackled me with your big, fat head inside that helmet, Roger wouldn't have even been here taking care of me. We would have had some fun after the game, but he would not have spent the night, instead leaving long before Karl came over. I would have been better rested, I wouldn't have let Karl go see his trucker, and I wouldn't have weeded out Juan Carlos at all.

Damn, that ankle's misshapen. And I can't afford getting an X-ray! Why did I tell Mama to take me off her health plan?

Shit.

Ooh, I am going to hurt number 39 next year, you wait and see. She's going to have a torn knee ligament from me—for *both* her knees. The only thing she'll be able to do is crawl. Yeah. I'll use her to wipe off my cleats. I'll use her as a footstool. I'll make sure she never says anything about anybody's mama again!

Juan Carlos, why did you hang up on me? Why didn't you let me finish breaking up with you? You didn't have to come all the way out here. It wouldn't have come out any differently in person. If you hadn't run your Mexican ass out in your mama's broken-ass car, I could have saved the day. I could have gotten Roger out of the house by saying "my half brother Karl" doesn't like white people. I would have told Karl that "Mr. Wilson" was fixing my sink or something. I could have played it all off! I *know* I could have pulled that off. But no, Juan Carlos, you had to come up in my yard cussing in Spanish and fussing about the damn alternator in your mama's broken-ass car.

And Roger, why the hell did you take the day off? People get buried on Mondays, don't they? I'm sure several dead people didn't get planted because you were here. I was managing my affairs just fine. I have lived twenty-five years without you. Why would I suddenly need you just a few hours after you left me swimming in my own juices after that erotic phone call?

And Karl, why do you suddenly reappear at the wrong damn time? Who or what told you to come back from New York City to ruin not just my life, but four lives. Four lives, Karl! *Four* lives you ruined because you wanted to come home and get a leg up.

I could also blame Mama, for not fighting to keep me at her house. If I had stayed home, none of this would have happened.

No, moving out here was all my idea. And she did try to stop me. I just wasn't listening.

I could even blame Daddy, for teaching me how to play football. If I hadn't been playing in a football game, I wouldn't have been injured, Roger wouldn't have been here, and . . .

No, I can't blame Daddy. Teaching me football was one of the only gifts he ever gave me. I wouldn't be who I am without football in my life.

I'm still pissed.

I need to break some shit.

After taking a full twenty minutes to get out of bed, down the hall, down the stairs, and out of the house, I collect rocks, stacking them on the dock. Then, I go frog hunting, whizzing rocks into the reeds, throwing them high and watching them splash, choosing ones with sharp edges to cut the heads off cattails.

And all this reminds me of Roger. Damn. This reminds me of *Frankenstein* and the little girl who the monster made wet.

Owww!

Damn, my lower leg is the same size as my upper leg. That's not supposed to happen. I had better go to the emergency room.

I drive to the emergency room at Roanoke Memorial, talking and cussing all the way. Drivers around me must think I'm crazy, but I don't care. I'm just working it out, y'all, that's all.

In the emergency room, the intake nurse, or whatever they call her, can't believe I waited five days to come in.

"I've had plenty of ankle injuries before," I say, "and most of them were just sprains. I've been icing it, and the swelling just didn't go down this time."

"You could have a blood clot," she says.

Oh, I feel *so* much better. "Look, I, uh, I don't have health insurance."

She frowns. "You're not under your mother's policy with Aetna anymore? Our records show that you are."

Yes! Thank you, Mama! "I meant, I don't have"—think fast—"I don't have the fifteen-dollar co-payment."

"That's okay, dear," she says. "We'll just add it to the bill."

Which will arrive at Mama's house at the end of the month. Shit. She'll find out, she'll worry, she'll start calling again—

Damn you, number 39!

Two hours and some nifty black-and-white pictures later, I find out that I have fractured my ankle.

Fractured.

Yep, that about sums up the last few days.

They put me in a plaster walking cast, load me up with prescriptions for painkillers, and roll me to my car in a wheelchair.

How in the *hell* am I supposed to drive? I'm not left-footed! I have to do a split to put my right leg on the passenger seat, and I'm not wearing clean drawers.

Luckily, the nearest pharmacy has a drive-through, and even more luckily, I have to pay only a buck forty-nine for three bags of generic painkillers, and luckiest, I don't get a perverted person helping me while I'm spread-eagled in my own car.

I'm glad Mama didn't drop me from her coverage. I'm glad she doesn't listen to me.

But when I get home, I get the urge to break shit again. They *still* haven't called me, those assholes! I open a few kitchen cabinets and look long and hard at Jenny's many china plates. I pick one up. This is a hefty thing. Nice balance. I could throw it like a discus against the trees outside. But then I notice little chips on the edges and lots of skinny lines etched into the china. Hmm. Lots of forks have hit these plates. There's a lot of history in my hands. I'll spare them.

For now.

I wish I had some pictures to burn, but I have no pictures to speak of. None. They don't have any pictures of me, and I didn't dare have any pictures of them around the house. I have nothing but memories, nothing but memories that are fading fast because of these painkillers. I have nothing, and I'm feeling nothing.

All I have is a pair of boxers and some bling to remember them by.

Oh, and the nasty sheets in the closet. I still have them.

I could burn them, and the colors would be so pretty. . . .

Chapter 21

It's Wednesday. I've already missed two days of work. Why not make it three? These painkillers are kicking my ass, and at least I can call in with the truth this time.

"I won't be coming in today. . . ." Hmm. "Or tomorrow," I add.

"Why?"

All secretaries are nosy by nature, I guess. "I broke my ankle."

"You poor dear!"

All secretaries are also sympathetic by nature. "Yeah."

"When did this happen?"

"Saturday, at my game."

Silence.

"I thought it was just a bad sprain, but it turns out I fractured it."

"You could have had a blood clot."

What's up with all this blood-clot nonsense? "Well, it's in a cast, and I'm heavily medicated, so . . ."

"So you'll be out tomorrow, too?"

"Yes."

"What about Friday?"

What about it? Damn. Get all in my business. "I'll let you know."

"Hope you feel better."

"Thanks."

What to do, what to do . . .

There's not much you can do in a bed with your leg encased in plaster. The damn thing made it nearly impossible to turn over last night. I have never had a fractured or broken anything before—besides my heart, that is. And this cast is supposed to help it heal? How? How is not moving something going to help it heal? I should be in physical therapy or something, icing it or something . . . something . . .

Damn. I have to stop taking so many painkillers. What time is it? Two o'clock? I need to wake the hell up.

I'm sure one of my men will return to me today, maybe all three of them. I have to be conscious in case that happens. And when they take a long (and hopefully hard) look at me, they'll get much more than they bargained for. They'll see me in my pain, feel even worse for leaving me, and beg for my forgiveness.

Speaking of forgiveness . . .

Hey, God, um, sorry for calling you a jerk yesterday, but, well, I was pretty pissed at you. You understand, right? I'm sure you have lots of people pissed off at you, and I'm willing to bet that more women are pissed at you than men are. It's just a guess, God. I mean, when you've been coming in second as long as we have, you just have to channel your aggression, pain, and suffering somewhere.

Anyway, I'm here all alone with this broken ankle, and, well, could you maybe kick one of my guys in the ass and get him out here? Just one would do, that's all. Just one of them, and I really don't care which one right now. Just give me one, God, and I promise I'll be faithful to him. That's right. I promise to get on the straight and narrow, shape up, and fly right. I'll get married and stop being such a hoochie.

I even promise to go to Izzie's church (although it doesn't seem to be doing her any good). And when my ankle gets better, I'll go witnessing with her.

Just one, now, God. That's all I need. Just one man out of the billions of men on this earth. Just, you know, whisper in his ear, something like, "Lana needs you." Oh, you'll have to whisper,

"Peanut needs you" to Karl and "Lahhh-na" to Juan Carlos. Otherwise, they may not understand.

And I, um, I promise to let Mama come visit me. She wants to visit so badly. It would be a shame to keep her away any longer. I'll call her right up just as soon as one of my men comes back to me. And as I said, it doesn't matter which one. Really.

Okay, I like Roger's bedside manner best and at least he can cook a little. I am kind of hungry. Though Juan Carlos has the warmest hands. I'm, uh, I'm feeling kind of cold these days, you know. Kind of lonely, too. And if you should send Karl, so be it. I sure could use Karl to give me one more night of pleasure—

Hmm. I might be asking for a bit too much here.

And four hours later, I have to put another bug in God's ear.

Listen up there, God. I know I was asking a bit much from the original inventor of abstinence, but what's it to you? What does my sex life have to do with the grand scheme of things? Don't you have a quota of good deeds you have to do every day? Well, get with the program. I mean, you invented sex, right? You invented it so it feels good, and it feels so good that we humans miss it when we aren't having it, you know? You don't know. That's right. Damn. How could you invent something you didn't ever try out first? Well, you sort of had a fling with Mary, but I'll never understand that one. I'll bet she didn't fully understand it, either. "Honestly, Joseph," she probably said, "I went to sleep and woke up with child."

Look, I'll settle for just one kiss, just one more kiss, and it doesn't have to be with tongue. You know all about kisses, right? They're sweet, they're innocent, and they're really a sign of friendship.

Oh yeah. Your son was betrayed by a kiss. Well, he wasn't kissed by the right person, okay? Judas wasn't his friend, but then again, you knew that, right? Why didn't you stop it all?

Okay, okay, I'll settle for a kiss on the cheek, then, damn. I just need to know there's some love out there, you know? One kiss on the cheek won't break you. One little peck, and I'll be fine. And I won't complain if his lips are chapped. Honest.

Okay, okay, okay, a visit. He doesn't even have to get out of his car. I can just talk to him from the window or the front door. Yeah, we can talk through the door. I don't have to touch him. We can just talk, okay? And all those promises I made, I promise to keep them. I am promising to keep my promises.

All right already! One stinking phone call. Is that asking too much? Just a one-minute "How ya doin'?" Come on, God, you know I don't normally make promises, so you know this is a great sacrifice! Hell, I'd even be glad to get a hang-up. At least I'd know someone thought enough of me to dial my number.

All right then, a letter. Get one of them to write me a damn letter. It should get here in a couple days, and I'll use my crutches to go out to the mailbox and get it. I'll get off my ass and accomplish something. One letter.

The sun is setting outside.

Anything! A shout-out on the radio! A howl! A wrong number! A scratching at the door! Hell, even a Peeping Tom will do the trick!

The sun has set.

Thanks a lot, God. All I have is a stank foot, crusty toes I can't reach, and a body that will smell like feet for six weeks.

Thanks for more nothing.

Jerk.

Chapter 22

A nd now, I'm sick.
I didn't sleep a wink, keeping my eye on the cell phone on the nightstand. Damn green light kept me up all night, and now I have a sore throat.

"Hello," I say to Jenny's yellow walls. I sound like Barry White. "Hey, baby." Okay, maybe like Barry White when he was going through puberty. It's actually . . . kind of sexy, husky and musky.

No, that's just my body. I have to get in the shower somehow today. The doctor said to use a garbage bag on my cast, sealing it with duct tape, as if I have some handy.

Wait. If I sound like Barry White on the phone, the first man to call will think another man is here! I have to take some cough medicine or something, or—

They aren't calling.

No one will call.

They can't call.

They just found out they were part of a love square.

They won't come running back.

Speaking of running . . .

My nose *isn't*. And that's kind of good. I can't smell the extent of my funk. Ooh, my chest is tight. I need some cough drops or something. No, cough drops make me cough. I must have an ironic body or something.

And why am I thinking "or something" all the time? Whoa, the bed is tilting, and what's that? Sweat? Shit. I bet I have a fever. Is there any vitamin C in the house? Why take that shit? All it does is turn your pee bright yellow. Uh-oh—

Damn, I'm sweating so much I can barely stay on the toilet seat. I had food poisoning once and nearly threw out a hip thanks to the diarrhea. Ooh, this is stinky stank. Where are the matches? Shit, they're downstairs. Oh . . . damn! My body's letting go and flushing itself. I've already flushed four times, and—

My goodness. A flock of ducks just left the pond when I flushed. My shit isn't flowing into the pond, is it?

I will never eat a fish out of that pond.

I stagger out of the bathroom carrying what's left of a partial roll of toilet paper just in case, flopping onto the bed. I have a pounding in my brain, two hammers clocking my temples, and two little birds pecking behind my eyes. I wipe some crusty green goo from my eyelids. I am so colorful. I unravel some of the toilet paper and blow bleu cheese dressing out of my nose. Definitely chunky. Then I cough, and it's as if I'm hocking up a lung, a sour, metallic taste in my mouth.

Hey, God, thanks for letting me know I'm alive. This is just great!

I call the secretary at PH. "Joanie, I'm really sick. I think I have the flu or something." There I go again with "or something."

"What's your temperature?"

I don't have a thermometer in the house. "One-oh-two," I say, though it might be higher than that.

"It might be your medication. Is it a sulfur-based drug?"

Secretaries know just about everything. "I don't think so. It's just some . . ." I pick up the painkiller bottle and shake it. I barely hear anything rattling around in there. I open it. Just one left?

"Lana, are you there?"

"Yeah, um, I'm just taking some painkillers." I read the label to myself: "May be habit forming." Wonderful. But I'm not worried. I was sort of addicted to men, and now look at me. I can quit them any time I want.

"Well, you take care of yourself, and you better stay home again tomorrow, just to be safe."

"Okay."

I hang up and realize that I can't take care of myself at all.

While breezes crisscross through Jenny's bedroom, drying my sweaty face, I feel so numb. I guess I'm being punished. Yep, that's it. I'm being punished. God is punishing me for having too much happiness.

Jerk.

King Solomon had a thousand wives, and I can't have even one man come check up on me. Jezebel was worse than I ever could be. Bathsheba was at least twice as bad as I am. Salome was a million times worse, dancing for her stepdaddy and getting the head of John the Baptist for a present. Whatever happened to her? Did *she* break her ankle and have three men dump her for *her* punishment?

I have to call Mama. She'll take care of me. She'll make me some of her good homemade chicken soup and help me out of this.

But . . . I can't.

I just . . . can't.

Great. Now I'm crying.

Shit.

I can't use the toilet paper for my tears. It's probably the only toilet paper left in the house, and paper towels will be cruel to my booty.

Okay, Lana, now what? You can't call your mama. You're not a child anymore. You don't want her pity, anyway. She'll come over and run the show, ruining all of this solitude. She'll come over and say, "I told you so." I came here to be alone. I came here to be myself *by* myself. I can get through this. I can—

Uh-oh.

My friend *should* be here.

Why isn't my friend here?

I know I'm due.

Oh shit.

But we used condoms every time!

Unless that last time with Karl a little juice got in there? No. That's like a one-in-a-billion shot. No way!

I need to do a little math now.

Okay.

Relax.

Count the days.

It was the Saturday after the second time we played the D.C. Divas. Roger wanted to come over, but I told him my friend was in town. He understood. He was always so understanding. Damn, D.C. Diva bitches ran up the score on us. Seventy points! Twice! We were shut out 140–0 in two games.

I'm supposed to be adding days, not scores.

Okay.

All that was . . . five weeks ago, thirty-five days.

I'm seven days late.

Seven days.

I was with all three of them this past month.

Oh damn, I've just become an episode on *Jerry Springer.*

I sit up and immediately fall back. My head weighs too much.

Think, Lana, think!

What if you're pregnant?

Who do you want your baby's daddy to be?

Well, if it's Karl, the baby will be muscular and tall with a dark 'fro. Karl would want it to get pierced ears and a little henna tattoo. Yeah. It would be a cute baby with dark eyes. But Karl's hairy. So it would be a cute *hairy* baby with dark eyes.

If it's Juan Carlos's baby, it will be shorter, and light-skinned with curly hair. I wonder if it would cry with an accent. Juan Carlos would want to get it baptized, feed it tamales, and teach it Spanish.

And if it's Roger's baby . . . I smile. I've already had this dream. It will be a milk chocolate baby with reddish brown hair and light eyes. And Roger will just . . . he'll just want to hold it as he used to hold me.

I can't believe I might be pregnant. They *always* used a condom, *always.* But just like everything else made in America, our technology has gone to shit. I wonder if there was a condom recall? How would a condom recall work exactly? "Bring your unopened and your used condoms to Kmart for a full refund"?

Damn, I must be sick . . . Condom recalls? Only sick people think of this sick shit.

I wake up a few hours later to the phone ringing.

Finally.

"Hello?" I say in my deep, sultry, sexy new voice.

"Miss Cole?"

It's a child's voice. A little boy's voice. "Who is this?"

"It's Bobby."

I sit up—almost. I slump against the headboard. "Bobby, are you all right?"

"Yes. Are you?"

Hell no, I'm not. "Um, not really."

"I heard you broke your ankle."

"Yeah. Are you calling from school?"

"No. From my house."

Where has the time gone?

"Does it hurt?"

"Some." And I'm not lying. Compared to the pains in the rest of my body, my ankle actually feels pretty good.

"Do you have a cast?"

"Yes, and I want you to sign it."

"When?"

"Oh, I have a nasty cold now, and I shouldn't be around you, but I promise to be back at school early next week, maybe Monday."

"Okay. I hope to see you Monday. Bye."

"Bye, Bobby."

And then I laugh. It's not a giggle, it's not a snort, and it's not even a snicker. I just . . . laugh and look up at the ceiling. "He's a little boy, God, not one of my men," I say. "That doesn't count."

But the more I think about it, the more I know God *has* answered my prayers. Hearing that little boy's voice is the wake-up call I need, so I do the best I can to get well, mainly by sleeping through the rest of the week and the weekend. Eventually, Italian dressing replaces the bleu cheese dressing in my nose, my fever breaks, I bathe . . . I even squirt some baby powder down into the cast to make it smell less funky.

And today—Monday—though I'm sweating rivers pushing Bobby around in his wheelchair, me in a clumping walking cast, at least I'm alive. I let Bobby sign my cast, and I'll bet that was the first time he's had a woman's leg in his lap. I guess he is the only man in my life now. Anyone watching us today would see both of us as cripples, but they'd be wrong.

I'm the only cripple in this tandem.

At least . . . at least I'm alive.

Thanks for . . . something . . . God.

You're not such a jerk after all.

Chapter 23

My friend showed up a full week later. I'm sure it was all the stress of losing all my friends with benefits, having a broken ankle, and getting the chest cold from hell. Then I let the last part of the school year pass me by.

I was just . . . floating through life.

No, that's not right. I had a damn cast on my leg. I was floating through life loudly, only I didn't hear a sound.

So now, it's the middle of June, school's out, I'm still alone, no one has called—not even Mama, who had to have gotten that Aetna statement—and God and I aren't talking anymore.

No more pushing Bobby around. He'll spend the summer inside trying to stay healthy, probably playing chess with Sunny as much as he can.

No more football practice or football games. I couldn't bring myself to even go to any of the remaining games, not that it would have mattered. We still lost, and no one from the team even called to check up on me. I guess they just figured I was done.

No more Sundays with Izzie and her uncooked chicken, edible lotion, and perverted questions. I haven't really missed her presence at all, but it hurts that she hasn't even called. I guess I'm not worthy of her attention now that my fantasy life has ended.

No more sexy Mexicans playing air guitar on my bed. My car needs work. My body needs work. I stare at my cell phone and almost call him at work several times a day.

No more aerobic sex with a tattooed African god. I fight the urge to page him, and I have six of the seven digits of his number lighted up on my phone right now. I can't push that seventh digit.

No more night football in the mud with Roger. I have the most phone numbers for Roger, but I can't even look at them. I really should delete all their numbers, but I just can't.

And Mama? Mama hasn't called me after that day I told her I hated her liver and onions.

And, actually, I could use a whole heaping plate of liver and onions right about now. I haven't been eating. Well, it's sort of hard to eat when you haven't been cooking, and it's hard to cook when you haven't been shopping, and it's hard to shop when you don't want to get out of bed. It's also hard to get out of bed when you have nothing clean to wear. Mr. Wilson brought over a brand-new washer and dryer, and set them up in the storage room, but I haven't used them yet.

I guess I've pretty much put my ass on lockdown at my own damn house.

Oh, I go outside when it's not too hot. I cut the grass even when it doesn't need cutting, taking special care not to run over any of Jenny's flowers. I have put some mileage on that tractor, expanding the lawn around the cottage by at least three or four acres. At least the bugs aren't as bad. After Mr. Wilson brought me a truckload of wood stumps, I split it all with an ax, even though I had nowhere to stack it and I was still in the cast. I spent one morning finding the concrete steps to the dock, which over the years had moved some, now looking more like hopscotch squares than steps. I sometimes just take walks around my property, and one day I discovered an old baseball field with its own chicken-wire backstop, sturdy trees growing up at what used to be home plate. I'll bet the Wilson boys had a high time playing there.

I almost dread when the sun goes down. I'd rather stay outside, since the memories inside the dollhouse are too strong. I hear this "soundtrack" running through my head filled with male voices and the songs we used to listen to, only it skips around like an old eight-track on crack. "Stairway to Heaven" changes abruptly to "Mannish Boy" and skips to "Tender Lover" before getting drowned out by a mean guitar riff, which switches to "Reasons" before morphing into some Bessie Smith blues with a disco backbeat. Just as I start to hum or sing along, the song changes. And I don't dare play "our" CD collection. I look at them sometimes and almost put them in the boom box. I guess that music has just gone out of my life. I don't even listen to the radio in the car anymore.

And whenever I close my eyes, I see this "movie" starring three handsome men and me. It's not always erotic, but when it is, my skin sweats something terrible. I see one of them making love to me as if I'm floating around in the room watching. I watch him go in and out of me, and see the ecstasy on my face, watch my hands grabbing at him, clawing at him, watch my legs wrapped around his back pulling him deeper inside of me. But whenever I want to join in the action instead of watching, the man vanishes, leaving two of me unfulfilled in the room, one on the bed, the other just floating around. And just when I think that I've recaptured a gesture, sigh, moment, or touch with one man, the scene shifts to another man . . . or to me alone, trying to grasp at my thoughts.

One night, after I ate *way* too much chocolate ice cream, I dreamed all three were, um, getting busy with me, and trust me, it was intense. I suppose it was Izzie's fantasy plus one. While Karl and Juan Carlos worked on me, I was kissing and talking to Roger. But no matter how much I try to keep these movie dreams going, they always end with me alone and looking out a window. And when I wake up, all I have are some sweaty sheets and the urge to fall asleep again to go back to the dream, but I can never fall asleep because I'm too excited.

And all this is just plain weird. When I was with them, I rarely had any erotic dreams—just that nightmare of me walking naked through a hotel looking for them. Why is it I dream of them after they're gone? What is my subconscious trying to tell me now?

To keep myself sane, I find myself talking to Jenny, which isn't exactly a sane thing to do. Sane people don't usually talk to ghosts, but she's pretty agreeable as ghosts go. We "talk" mostly about her house and her huge "garden" outside, and I imagine myself sitting where she sat doing her needlepoint. I doubt I will ever have the necessary patience—or skill—to do needlepoint. I've found Jenny's to be, well, priceless, even if they're not professional look-ing. I even found a wildflower pressed inside a Wilson family Bible. I flipped through the Bible and found lots of highlighted passages in Song of Solomon—which is *really* hot stuff. I'm beginning to think that Mr. Wilson and Jenny had a hot thing going on in this dollhouse.

And, of course, I'm sad about that, and the only thing that seems to break through my sadness is a thunderstorm. I sit on my bed looking out over the pond as the lightning flashes, counting to my-self, "One stupid Lana, two stupid Lana, three stupid Lana . . ." until rolls and echoes of thunder shake the house and long fingers of lightning plunge toward the pond.

Speaking of plunging, I need to plunge the tub. The water hasn't drained right since Roger and I had our bath, oh, and Karl and I had our shower—

But I'm not thinking about any of that.

Or them.

So now, I'm Lonely Lana, ten crusty toes in the pond, one foot shriveled and a lighter color than the other because of the cast (which I cut off myself), mosquito bites even on my ass. I'm turning blacker and blacker in the sun, not eating, not sleeping, and not caring. The grass needs cutting again, more wood needs splitting, the laundry needs doing, my hair needs tending, and my stuff—

Nah. I'm not going there. My stuff needs a rest. Maybe I'll have another movie dream tonight. Maybe Roger will make love to me so I can talk to Karl or Juan Carlos.

I want to call Mama and invite her over for a visit, but I just can't. I've been here so long without her help, and I don't want her (or anyone, for that matter) to think I'm weak. They say that whatever doesn't kill us makes us stronger.

I ought to be able to lift Jenny's dollhouse pretty soon, maybe even with one arm.

Damn. Another mosquito bite. I can't have much blood left, y'all. Go suck on a bullfrog or something. Go get yourselves some green blood.

I see a huge yellow truck rolling down the dirt road. I watch it park next to my Rabbit. Who's this?

Mr. Wilson gets out.

He sees me and comes down to the dock.

"Hey," I say.

Wow.

This is the first time I've spoken to anyone since . . . I can't re-member when. Damn. The last time I spoke to anyone was to say goodbye to Bobby on the last day of school.

"Just came to show Jenny my new truck," Mr. Wilson says.

No wonder the truck is so yellow.

He sits next to me. "She also said I needed to do some fishin'. You been fishin' yet?"

Define "fishing." I hooked a few men, and they all got away, even in my dreams. "No."

"Want to go?"

"I don't know." I should go fishing. I mean, I have nothing else to do . . . and no one else *to* do. "Sure."

"I'll be back presently with the canoe."

And then . . . we fish. I learn the finer points of worm tying and bait casting from Mr. Wilson, who has me throwing my line up into the reeds while we float in the middle of the pond in the canoe.

"Up in those reeds is where the fish are, as hot as it is," he whis-pers.

Fishing is a quiet sport.

Oh, I get tangled up and snarled and hooked and every other kind of thing, so much so that Mr. Wilson can barely keep his line in the water. He has to keep reeling in his line to rescue me.

"You aren't doing much fishing, Mr. Wilson," I say, casting to-ward a collection of cattails.

He doesn't speak for a moment. "Maybe I was just supposed to be your guide today. I never did listen to Jenny all the way through. She whispers 'Go fishin', old man' to me, and I go."

Creepy.

For the most part, nothing happens. I might make this nothing part of the nothing I usually do all day. It's relaxing in a sweaty, eye-squinting kind of way. It does give me time to philosophize, ponder, and think. It also gives me time to sweat buckets in a metal canoe roasting the soles of my feet. There's obviously nothing here but mosquitoes, and I doubt they'd fit on the hook. The fish are taking naps or something. Maybe I've infected them with my laziness.

Just then, a bass shoots out from reeds like a shark to take my worm and—bam!

"Keep the rod tip up now," Mr. Wilson says calmly.

How can he be so calm? I've just hooked Moby Dick or something! I fight the hell out of that fish, and the fish fights the hell back, dipping my pole into the water several times and pulling the canoe in circles while I scream and shout.

"Easy . . . easy," Mr. Wilson keeps saying, and it's easy for him to say! My forearms are about to burst off my bones!

I drag the fish to the side of the boat. "Don't you have a net or something?"

Mr. Wilson reaches into the water . . . and pulls up my fish by its mouth. "Don't need one." He holds the fish lengthwise. "Nice bass. Pregnant, too."

Moby Dick is really Moby Jane?

"You might want to put her back."

After what I've been through, that is so true—and weird—on so many levels. "Yeah." Damn, I have goose bumps on a scorching hot day.

He removes the hook carefully and "swims" the fish back and forth in the water before releasing her to the deep. "Hard to catch, easy to put back."

Unlike men, whom I've found are easy to catch and hard to put back.

"You done?" he asks.

I smile.

I'm smiling.

I haven't smiled in . . .

I'm smiling.

Damn. Did I brush my teeth this morning?

"No," I say, "I'm just getting started." I attach another slimy worm to my hook, rigging it Texas-style.

Mr. Wilson nods. "Get to it, then."

I am a casting fool after that. I have been bitten by the thrill of the hunt. I can taste another catch in my mouth. I can almost see the bass lying in the reeds, their orange eyes looking up at my flopping, flying worm, their salivary glands (if they even have any) dripping and—

A whole bunch more nothing happens for about an hour. All I catch are some rays, and I lose another pound of sweat into the bottom of the canoe.

"It's getting pretty hot," I say.

"Nah, this ain't hot," he says, paddling us back to the dock. "It ain't August yet. If we don't get more rain, this pond is liable to dry up again."

Oh no! Not the pond I named "Mine"! "Has it happened before?"

"Sure. Plenty of times." He grabs the side of the dock, holding the canoe steady while I get out. "And trust me, you don't want to be downwind of this pond when it's almost empty."

I hear before I see another vehicle.

"You expecting company?" Mr. Wilson asks.

"No, sir," I say, and I shield the sun from my eyes.

Mama? Is that Mama's car.

I stand.

It's Mama.

I have never been so glad to see her.

Chapter 24

"Pshaw, girl, you smell like all outdoors," Mama says as I hug her in front of her car. "You could use a bath."

"I've been fishing."

She coughs. "And you smell like a fish, girl. Damn."

Mama cussed! I leave for a little while, and Mama lets her hair down. I step away from her. "What brought you all the way out here?"

"I was in the neighborhood." She opens the back door of her car, grabs a casserole dish, turns, and hands it to me. "I've been cooking you a nice Sunday dinner."

Sweet potatoes! Yummy! "It's Sunday?" Where has the time gone?

"Yes, it's Sunday." She shakes her head. "It looks as if I got here in the nick of time, too. Just take that inside and get in the tub."

I sniff myself and don't smell anything vile. "Do I smell that bad?"

"Girl, even the flies are scared to buzz around you. Now go on and take a bath."

I kiss her cheek. "Okay."

Damn. I'm acting as if I'm ten years old or something. I have to get a hold of myself.

But when I walk into the kitchen, I immediately feel shitty. I have let this place go completely to hell. I haven't done dishes since . . .

I can't remember. Plates, dirty clothes, mildewed towels, unopened mail, an overflowing garbage can . . .

Where the hell have I been?

Mama bursts through the door behind me with a Crock-Pot and a hanging plant. I know what she's thinking, and I brace for it, but she acts as if she can't see the dishes, the dirty laundry, or the mess, putting the hanging plant on top of the icebox, clearing off a space on the counter, and plugging in the Crock-Pot.

"Go on, now. You're stinking up the kitchen."

"What's the plant for, Mama?"

She sighs. "To give this room more oxygen. Now go on."

I smile. "Is that my housewarming gift?"

She nods. "Yes, Erlana. Now go on. You stay any longer in this kitchen, the plant will *die.*"

"Is that, um, *the* plant?" Mama has been growing this one hanging plant since the day I was born, somehow keeping it alive.

"Yes, and unless you want to kill a twenty-five-year-old plant, you'll get out of this kitchen."

"Okay, okay," I say, and I limp up the stairs.

I don't even know if I have *any* clean clothes, not even one clean footie sock. I'm afraid to look in the closet, since I have yet to clean *those* sheets, and the only drawers I have are—

Roger's boxers.

I had rescued them from the barn and cleaned the smoky smell out of them with dish soap.

I put them on. Better than nothing. They hang on me some. Damn, where did my hips go? Shit! Have I lost that much of my booty? I have to get that booty back.

I collect a pair of shorts and a T-shirt that smell less funky than the rest and hit the shower.

Without first turning on Sheila and letting her warm up for thirty minutes.

I now know what shock treatment must feel like. Even my teeth get goose bumps, but I scrub, scrub, scrub away about a week's worth of filth, and when I'm done, my ankles look almost the same color again.

I need to take more showers.

The water, though, doesn't go down the drain. Shit. And it kind of looks like the pond, with tiny waves lapping at the sides of the tub. I'll deal with that later.

In front of the bathroom mirror, though, I feel so hideous. My hair is a rat's nest even a rat would avoid. I check the bathroom closet for some Optimum Care shampoo and find an empty bottle. Why'd I put an empty bottle back? Oh sure, I have *plenty* of conditioner. Can you put conditioner on dirty hair? At least it would smell better.

"You need your hair done," Mama says behind me, and I can't help but jump a little.

"Yeah." I turn and see her holding a nearly full garbage bag, green rubber gloves on her hands. "What are you doing?"

"Cleaning up."

I feel so low. "Thank you" is all I can manage to say.

Instead of making me feel worse, she smiles. "I don't mind. It brings back some good memories." She looks past me to the tub. "You got a slow drain?"

"I nod."

"You have a plunger?"

"No."

"We'll get you one."

I nod. "Thanks."

"Dinner should be ready in about twenty minutes."

"Okay."

After she leaves, I realize that she hasn't been judgmental or critical even once. She had every right to be, yet she chose to be nice.

Wait.

My mama, the woman who fussed me up and down and sideways for the last twenty-five years is suddenly . . . nice? How is this possible? Maybe my being away from her has made her nice!

No. Maybe *my* being away from *her* is *allowing* her to be nice. That's probably it. I brought out the worst in her from the day I was born. I turned her mean.

Two carefully tied do-rags later, I'm down the stairs and in . . . a clean kitchen that doesn't smell like mold or sour milk. Even the floor is shiny. I must have been in the shower a long time!

"Mama, you didn't have to—"

"I know." She brings over a glass of iced tea and hands it to me. "I like this place," she says. "It has character." She sits at the table, which is also shiny. "When you first told me about it, I didn't believe it. You have yourself a real home here."

I sit opposite her and take a sip. It's sweet. Damn. She even brought her own sweetened tea for me to drink, and now I'm crying in it.

"Too sweet?" she asks, which is what she always used to ask, and now she's here asking it again and I'm crying and I can't explain why, and suddenly I'm standing and she's holding me and I'm saying, "I'm sorry, Mama, I'm so sorry," and she's just humming something beautiful the whole time in my ear.

She gently pushes me away. "Are you going to tell me about it now?"

And then I tell it all, talking about Karl, my African god, gone away; about Juan Carlos, my romantic stallion, gone away; about Roger, my earth brother, gone away—and she doesn't interrupt me even once.

"That's . . . that's about it, Mama."

She gets us some more iced tea. "I just knew something was wrong, and now I know what." She sits and takes a sip. "Too sweet."

"Just right," I say.

She takes another sip. "Do you miss them?"

I nod.

"*All* of them?"

"Yes."

"Well, you can't have them all, Erlana," Mama says.

"But I did. I did have them all."

She stares me down. "After all you just told me, you have to know that you can't have them all." She looks side to side, raising and lowering her chin. Then she looks under the table. "Because they ain't here no mo'."

And now she's talking all country? Cussing and country. This place seems to get to everyone.

"I know, I know," I say. "I *used* to have them. I have to keep telling myself that."

She sighs. "Oh, you never know. You might still have them, and they're just being stubborn."

"It's been almost two months, Mama. They're not coming back."

"Is that what you think?"

"Yes."

"Hmm. And you thought this little foursome would last, too." She smiles. "I wouldn't put too much stock in any thoughts you have, Erlana."

"Thanks a lot."

"You're welcome." She stares into my eyes. "Which one of them still makes your heart hurt?"

A question out of left field. "They all do."

She shakes her head. "I don't think so. One of them makes your heart hurt the most. Who is it, Erlana?"

All of them make my heart hurt, but if I'm truly honest about it . . . "Roger."

"Because he proposed to you?"

"No. Because we used to talk, really talk."

Mama nods. "And which one excited you the most?"

That's easy. "Karl."

"He's good?"

"What do you know about 'good,' Mama?"

She opens her eyes wide. "Your daddy was *good.*"

I giggle. "Karl was good, then."

She nods. "Just one more question. Which one romanced you the most?"

"Juan Carlos."

"Hmm," she says, a twinkle in her eye. "I'm beginning to understand it all now. Are you?"

Understand what? "No."

"Put them all together, Erlana, and you'll have your daddy."

Gross!

I mean, what?

I've been dating my daddy?

"Your daddy was all of that."

I see Roger, Karl, and Juan Carlos in my head. Jeans. Boots. Long-sleeved shirts for the most part. Working men. Damn, she's kind of right, but . . .

"Mama, I'm not trying to date my daddy."

"It seems that way to me."

"I'm not, Mama. I don't look for my daddy in every man I meet. I mean, for the most part, I met all three of them by coincidence." Romance has lots of coincidences, if you really think it through. "I met Karl at the park while I was on a jog, I met Juan Carlos when my car broke down, and Roger came to my front door. I didn't go looking for any of them. They came to me."

"It makes me envy you," Mama says with a sigh. "I was never that lucky. I had to do all the work." She sighs again. "And I let your daddy get away from me."

"I've never asked, but Mama, why? Why did you really leave Norfolk?"

"All of what your daddy was and probably still is was too much for one man to have and one woman to handle. He was charming, handsome, strong, intelligent, and passionate." Her eyes look far away from this table. "I never married him because I knew I would live in fear of some other, prettier woman taking him away from me. I mean, I'm . . . plain, you know?"

"You're not plain, Mama. I am."

"No, I'm pretty plain, and you . . . you're something else. I never thought I was beautiful enough for him. Oh, I loved him, don't you ever doubt that, but I had to let him go." Her eyes return to me. "Now, which one of these men did you truly love?"

"I think I loved them all."

"I guess it's possible, but there you go thinking again." She leans closer. "Who do you dream about?"

"Roger." I don't mention the milk chocolate baby. Mama seems okay with the idea of Roger so far, and I don't want to ruin it.

"Who do you talk to when no one's around?"

I catch my breath. Besides Jenny? Hmm. "Roger." Again.

"And who do you talk to in your head just before you fall asleep?"

It's true.

I loved Roger the most.

"Roger."

She leans back. "I still talk to your daddy, you know. We have conversations all the time in my mind. I still miss him."

"Do you know where he is?"

She shakes her head. "Your daddy is in the wind or on the sea, where he belongs, where he can be a man. He tried to make a man out of you, right?"

I look at my hands, hands roughened by football, fishing, and chopping wood. "He, um, he sort of did." I sigh. "What am I going to do, Mama?"

"Well, I have a suggestion, and it's only a suggestion, now. I don't want you to think I'm giving you advice, now that you're on your own and don't need me anymore."

Ouch. "I'll always need you, Mama."

"I knew that the second you told me not to call."

Ouch again. "I'll take any advice I can get."

She scrunches up her lips, then relaxes them, the sure sign she has made a decision. "I think you should go talk to each of them."

"What?"

"Try to explain to them what you just explained to me."

No way! "I can't do that."

"Child, look what you've *already* done! If you can date three men at the same time without them catching on for, what, two months, you can do *anything*."

There's too much doubt in my mind for that. "They won't want to see me."

"Maybe. For now. You might want to wait a bit. I'm sure they miss you."

"I doubt it." About all they probably miss is my booty.

"Who do you miss the most?"

That is a loaded question. "Well, when I'm . . . horny"—and I can't believe I'm saying this to my mama!—"I miss Karl. When I'm feeling unappreciated, I miss Juan Carlos. He tries to take care of my every need. And when I'm . . ." I stop.

"When you're what?"

Why am I just now realizing this? "What I was going to say is that . . . all the other times, I miss Roger. What does that mean, Mama?"

"It means . . . what it means, though it might mean . . ." She stops.

"What?"

"It might mean that your love is deeper for Roger than for the others. It might also mean that you love the others for what they can do *for* you, and that you love Roger for what he can do *with* you."

Damn, my mama is wise! "I never looked at it that way before."

"This Roger sounds like the real deal."

"And you're okay with that?"

She shrugs. "I don't have to live with him, right?"

"Right." But then I pout. "But he was all set to marry me, and then I really fucked things up."

I expect her to scold me for cussing, but she doesn't. "I suppose I could buy a plot at Fairview Cemetery."

"What?"

"Well, I have sort of met him. He was in my kitchen once, remember? And he wasn't that unhandsome." Her face clouds over. "But, child, that hair. He could be Lucille Ball's son!"

A laugh escapes from my mouth so loudly that Mama's hair moves. "You'd really do that? You'd call him about a plot?"

"He's a smart man. He'll see right through that. It was just an idea." She touches the back of my hand. "But for your own sake, I think you should speak to all three of them."

I don't know if I can do that. But they went away hating me, and I can't have that. Not after all that good loving.

She stands. "You hungry?"

"Yes."

"You're looking pretty skinny, girl. They may not recognize you. Let's eat, and you better have you some seconds."

And as I eat, I think to myself: She's right. They won't recognize me when they see me again, because for the first time in *their* lives—and mine, too—I'm going to be myself.

Chapter 25

But first I have to get my hair done.

Damaged. My hair is damaged.

But when I walk into Mama's kitchen later that night, I know she'll take care of me. I have memories of her warming up irons on the stove, just sitting on a kitchen chair working on her own hair with an oven mitt, those irons, and a little jar of gel, and she never used a mirror. I have to have a mirror and an arsenal of curling irons.

And it still doesn't come out right.

She hands me a towel and points to the sink.

"I can wash my own hair, Mama."

"I know you can. Just let me do it, for old time's sake."

"Okay." I stand in front of the sink, dipping my head under the faucet.

"You had better let the water warm up first, Erlana."

I twist the cold knob. "I need to wake my head up first."

Cold water on a warm head . . . Mama's strong fingers massaging in the shampoo . . . water warming up . . . rinsing . . . soap in my ears . . . repeating two more times . . . "Surprised there aren't any birds up in this nest" . . . ten years old again with shorter hair . . . Mama humming something slow, sad, and beautiful . . .

"What are you going to do about those ashy knees?"

"Mama, I—"

"I tell you time and time again to use more lotion. And are you getting behind your ears good?"

"I try, Mama, but—"

"Try harder, Erlana, and quit trimming those nails so close. You aren't chewing on them again, are you?"

"No."

"Uh-huh. And wear your good shoes and that skirt all *day tomorrow. I know you put some sweatpants and some sneakers in your book bag. I wasn't born yesterday."*

"But Mama, those shoes hurt my feet."

"They make you look like a lady."

"And that skirt makes my legs cold. And I can't have nails and play ball, too. . . ."

"Relax," Mama says.

I try, but I have too many memories of my head in a kitchen sink. I have stronger neck muscles than most women because I was always trying to get my head up out of that sink. Why couldn't I wear a baseball cap like the boys? It would have been so much easier for Mama. Why did I have to wear skirts and dresses? Most days I was the only girl in my class dressed that way. Why couldn't I just have a ponytail? Why did I have all that pink gooey stuff put in my hair every single day? The smell followed me around all day.

She dries my hair with a towel, then plasters my head with conditioner, setting an egg timer for five minutes. "You sign a lease on that place?"

I sit at the table, drying my face, trying to forget my childhood. "No."

"So it's an open-ended arrangement, then?"

"I guess." I don't ask why she's so interested because I know why. She wants to know how soon I can be home if I wanted to move back.

"Well, I want you to know you can come back anytime."

"Thanks for the offer, but I'm going to try to stick it out."

She turns from the sink. "I knew you'd say that. But if it gets too cold out there, you just come on home, okay? Snow in the country is heavier and deeper than snow in the city because you know they don't plow all those country roads, and that little house probably doesn't have much insulation."

I could argue with her, but it's probably true. Everything seems bigger in the country, and even the smallest breezes flow through that cottage.

"And you can always come home if there's something you want to watch on TV."

I blink. Damn. Football season is coming, and I can barely get any reception! Pre-season NFL and college football start in August, so I am going to need a satellite dish or an antenna quick!

"And I'll make those nachos you like. . . ."

She doesn't play fair. She melts a pound of Velveeta and adds a jar of hot salsa, serving it on some big blue tortilla chips with freshly cut jalapeños.

"I'll keep them in mind."

The timer goes off, I stand, and she rinses the conditioner from my hair. I towel dry my hair while walking to the bathroom, where I fire up the blow-dryer. My hair has gotten so long!

"You need your ends done, girl," Mama says.

They are looking pretty ragged.

"You want me to trim them?"

But my hair is wild and free, and suddenly I don't even want to comb it. "No."

"No?"

"No."

She sighs. "Suit yourself."

Another miracle has just happened. I turn to see her facial expression, but she's already out of the bathroom. Suit myself? She has *never* said that to me. All those years she experimented on my head with straws and extensions and Shirley Temple curls, and she says, "Suit yourself?"

I look at the wild thing in the mirror.

This suits me.

Chapter 26

Once I get my wild self back to Jenny's dollhouse, I ask myself one simple question:

Who the hell am I? Who is Erlana "Lana" "Peanut" Joy Cole?

Okay, two questions. I was never any good at math.

I let my daddy define me until I was eight, and he turned me into a Smurfs-loving, football-playing, tenacious tomboy. Then I came to Roanoke and tried to become what Mama wanted me to be—a girl. At least I let her *think* I was trying to be a girl. I wasn't. I was a tomboy in a dress, still tenacious, replacing the Smurfs with boys but never giving up football. My peers helped redefine me through middle school, mainly with me doing the exact *opposite* of what they were doing, and reverse peer pressure or something made me "me" during high school. But since high school, I have had four crummy breakups, and for nine months, I let three different men define and redefine "me." Does that make the real "me" beyond definition? Is there any hope for "me"?

I have strange thoughts while I fish.

I'm not exactly fishing. I'm just standing on the dock at high noon on a scorching July day casting a sinker into the reeds, probably knocking some poor bass in the head. I had left a container of worms out on the dock after doing a little fishing last night—not a nibble. I think my wild hair scared all the fish away. And by the time I woke up this morning, all the worms were, um, toasted flat from the sun. I know I'm dehydrated, too. My scalp is turning darker black (if that's possible), my wild hair is on fire, and even my eyes are probably sunburned. As for the rest of me, I'm looking pretty damn good—sweaty, but slim and trim.

Damn, I'm lonely.

No, Lana. Don't you sink into the green, mucky, moss-covered pond of despair and think that another person has to define or complete you. Your development has been arrested, you're just incomplete, you're just . . . you're just a damn tadpole that still has its tail. You'll never be a bullfrog if you don't lose your tail.

I look at my own tail. If I come out here every day this month, I'll have a white girl's booty. Where did my booty go? I pull out my shirt to look at my girls. Damn, y'all have shrunk, too.

I'm melting, I'm melting . . .

I think all my pores are draining at once. Maybe this is what withdrawal feels like. Maybe this is the rehab I need to rid me of the memories. Maybe I can just sweat these men out of my mind—

They all made me sweat like this.

They all made me ooze.

Nasty.

I made them ooze, too. . . .

Nastier.

But I didn't collect any of it.

Nastiest.

Change the subject.

I need to get a satellite dish or something. Yeah. Then I'll get all the sports packages, all the NFL and college games. I would be any man's dream girl, though I need a bigger TV, one of those wide-screen ones I'll never be able to afford. Maybe I can rent-to-own one. Yeah. But could they get a wide-screen TV into Jenny's dollhouse? Hmm.

But wait. If I get all that, a man might love me for my TV and not for me. Hmm. Knowing my budget, I'll probably go to Radio Shack and get an antenna. That should be enough. I need to keep things simple. I don't need the Outdoor Channel when the outdoors is right outside my window. I don't need any of those shopping channels. I'll just go shop . . . at Wal-Mart, since my funds are pretty low until the end of September. And why would anyone watch a cooking show? Go cook! No wonder Americans are so obese. We sit and watch what we used to do! We watch what we could be doing! Crazy!

For that matter, why do we pick up a meal to take *home* and then eat it in our *car* on the way home? Why do we have kitchen and dining room tables we never eat on? Why do we buy packaged foods to microwave instead of preparing food from scratch? Are we all that much in a hurry?

And why is there no sinker on my line? Did a bass eat my sinker? My line is just waving in the air. Hmm. It's kind of cool-looking, like an almost-invisible snake striking in the wind.

This next school year, I am taking my lunch every single day. I will prepare food to microwave, and folks will smell it and ask, "What's that wonderful smell?" And I am not eating out ever again. Why am I in such a rush? What's my hurry?

I am going to take my time, enjoy the moment, and live life like a meal that I don't want to end.

I'm even going to stop shaving my eyebrows. Why did I ever start doing that? I could have plucked the stray ones in between, but no, I had to shave them, and that wasn't enough, so I had to shape the eyebrows, and then they grew back thicker, and—

Whoo, I'm getting dizzy. I had better sit. I reel in my waving line, set down my rod, and flop my feet to the pond to cool off my toes and—

Either my legs are getting shorter or the pond is evaporating.

I look at the shoreline. I've never seen that particular rock before. Or that rusty can. Is that an old license plate? Is that a tire? And what's that smell? It's not me, is it?

I smell myself.

Nope. It's not me this time.

The pond is drying up.

I wonder what's at the bottom out there in the middle. Maybe there is no bottom. Maybe there's a huge black hole in the muck, and if I look down it, I'll see China. Maybe . . .

Maybe I had better get what's left of my ass inside for a couple gallons of water so my brain doesn't boil over with ridiculous thoughts.

Hopscotching my way across the steps to the side door, I enter and feel instantly cooler. The floor in this kitchen is always so cool no matter how hot it is outside. I wonder why that is.

Hey, who did the dishes? Oh yeah. I did. I also did the laundry, took the trash to a big green Dumpster at Mr. Wilson's, and dusted off all the books. I even got some Drano and a plunger, and made the tub water rush out. I also own every cleaning "ointment" available—all the spray bottles, scrubs, and powders—and have three different kinds of Brillo pads, two brooms (one for outside only), a squeegee, a cloth mop and bucket, and a vacuum. Whenever I'm especially, um, down, I get down on my hands and knees, and scour Jenny's dollhouse. It's beginning to smell like pine again.

I put my head under the faucet and flip the lever. The coldest water God ever created pours out of this faucet and onto my head, and I turn back into myself.

At least I think I do.

Wait.

Maybe the tub drains into the pond, and the Drano is causing the pond to shrink.

I keep my head under the faucet until I can't feel my earlobes.

Now, what was that about a cup of Drano causing a pond to evaporate? As if that could ever happen. I need a nice, cold shower.

Before I step into the tub, I examine what the sun is doing to my body. I'm black on my scalp, face, neck, shoulders, and arms, and from about my thighs down. The rest of me is so pale I can see my veins. My girls have veins? Gross! I need to lay out in the nude or something. Who's going to know?

Get in the damn shower, Lana.

I get in the shower and brace myself. Every pore in my body is about to snap shut, I'm talking gibberish to myself, and I'm contemplating lying out in the nude to make my black self blacker.

Yeah, I'm getting better.

I don't know who I'm becoming, but it's definitely someone wild and new.

Wait.

Maybe Joy is trying to make an appearance.

Maybe Joy is trying to push Erlana and Lana aside.

I crank the knob, and streams of arctic water sting my body, making me dance in the shower.

I think I might like Joy. She likes to take cold showers and dance.

Erlana, Lana, step aside.

Joy is in the house.

Chapter 27

Joy and I are getting along famously. We even sleep together (don't tell!). She's fun to snuggle up to, and she looks at her hair and just laughs!

She laughs.

She's just about the bestest friend I have, and she's taught me so much about myself. She had me dig out Roger's poem to me from under my mattress and told me to change it from "She Is Beautiful" to "I Am Beautiful," leaving out any stanzas that gave me pain:

When I wake,
I am beautiful,
flashing a little leg
and yawning shyly,
my mouth a delicate O.

When I sing,
I am beautiful,
flashing teeth and singing strong,
my neck arched as my lips
whisper sweetness into the air.

When I bite my lower lip,
I am beautiful,
softening bad news to myself
with wide eyes and a pout.

And when I walk,
Lord God!
I am beautiful,
swaying with hips and legs and back
in time to a rhythm I want
only myself to hear.

I don't need a magazine
to tell me
I am beautiful
because
I am beautiful.

And I am beautiful because I've let Joy back into my life, and Joy sure keeps me busy. She is never bored, and she is never boring.

For one thing, Joy likes to walk.

I have done some cross-country walking around this place as part of my self-imposed physical therapy, and I've discovered a "rose tree." It's the most amazing thing I've ever seen. Wild red and white rose plants twist and turn all over a weeping willow, some of their flowers blooming in the sun above the willow, which has to be fifty or sixty feet high. The willow doesn't seem to mind, even though the thorns scratch its tender bark. Beauty, pain, and life all wrapped up together in the middle of the woods in Bedford County.

Erlana wouldn't have noticed the rose tree. Lana would have taken a rose to put in her hair for some man to take and put in his teeth.

Joy just takes it all in.

Joy also likes nature.

I'm no poet, so I can't always put beauty into words, but . . . this place is beautiful. The sounds around Jenny's dollhouse are so

much purer than anywhere I've ever lived. I listen to cicada sere-
nades every night and see ducks, swans, and even herons chatter to
each other on the pond. Whenever a flock of birds flies over, I actually hear the beating of their wings. Even the wind has more sounds
and flavors as it whips around the house carrying pine as it whines
through the cattails. The sun seems different, too, with more colors
and many more reflections. The clouds seem bigger, the sky bluer,
the night sky clearer, more brilliant, more sparkly.

Erlana would be annoyed with the noise. Lana would smell
something and remember a man.

Joy just puts herself in the middle of it all, sucking it all in.

Joy *thinks* she can write poetry.

On rainy days, I stay inside and try to put my feelings into words.
I'm not very good at it. I barely paid attention in English class whenever we discussed poetry. I thought it was too frilly, too girly. Now, it
gives me an outlet. I don't know if any of it is poetic or not, I don't
title them very well, and all of them are short and probably unfin-
ished, but at least some of my feelings have left my brain and hit
some paper.

1.
They come into my dreams made of darkness
Giving me kisses
Leaving me with whispered echoes
Leaving me to contemplate their flesh
And my devils

2.
They say love lives only in poetry
They say memory has no mercy
They say many things about loss
And they're usually right

3.
I guess I'm an old shoe
Who still dreams of being a glass slipper

4.
I have listened to the echo of my own voice
While lightning flashes and rain licks my window
I have seen darkness echoing
While storms prowl my pond
Echoes of distant thunder mocking me

5.
Even the shadows here whisper of the sun
And summer stars shiver in the sky

6.
If I had a handful of sun
Stolen from skies of blue
I'd give it to you
To still the grumbling in your heart

Taken one at a time, my poems are depressing! Taken all at once, my poems are *clinically* depressing! I hope one day to write a happy poem, but until then, I'll just take in all I see and feel, and flush my system.

Erlana would rather do *anything* than write poetry. Lana would rather write erotic poetry to make people hot.

Joy just puts her mind on paper.

Joy also likes animals.

Something about this place draws every critter you can imagine, and thanks to Mr. Wilson's frequent visits, I now know what I've been seeing. I have at least one mink and a family of muskrats living around the pond, several gray squirrels playing tag on my roof, and an orange cat feasting daily on field mice. The cat leaves me "presents" (field-mice carcasses) on my doorstep just about every morning. I see deer drinking from the pond and hear a woodpecker pecking just about every morning. I see the eyes of a family of opossums, and hear one noisy raccoon playing with my garbage cans every night. And birds—you name it, it has probably flown in for a sip in the pond or a rest in my trees. Mr. Wilson says I should be able to see barn swallows, red-shouldered hawks, and great gray owls, but all I can see are sparrows, crows, and cardinals flashing their colors as they dive in and out of the yard.

Erlana would look for bird poop on her windshield. Lana would collect bird feathers to use in the bedroom.

Joy just marvels at her zoo.

Joy likes to garden.

I have bought every petunia of every color that exists from Home Depot. I don't even park in the parking lot at Home Depot anymore. I just pull right up beside the flats of petunias, turn on my flashers, and get the largest cart I can find, loading it with every petunia I can find. I know I pissed off one lady about to buy some, but that's her loss. She just wasn't quick enough. It all barely fits in the Rabbit, and I get out at Jenny's dollhouse smelling like petunias. The flower boxes under the front windows are bursting with flowers, and I water them daily, even if it rains. Mr. Wilson says he'll need to put up more flower boxes to contain all the unplanted petunias I still have in their little black plastic pots all over the house.

Erlana wouldn't have noticed the petunias at all. Lana would have plucked a petunia and put it in her hair for some man to rub on her booty.

Joy just takes care of them.

Joy also likes to listen.

Whenever Mr. Wilson visits, I ask him about Jenny. We look at old family albums filled with photographs, filled with stories, filled with love. I meet the woman who has been haunting her old house, and she's right plump with a "twinkle in her eye and a story on the tip of her tongue." I meet his sons: Thaddeus, the "best darn swimmer in the county" who "could have swam in the Olympics"; Junius, the "best squirrel hunter in the county" who "does something with bonds or stocks or something like that up in Baltimore"; and Matthias, the "best cowhand I ever had" who has "the cutest children on God's green earth." All it takes is a name, and Mr. Wilson takes me to him or her, and to a kinder, gentler time in the past. He reserves his best thoughts for Jenny.

"I thought she was a cute gal, right young-looking, smoothest skin, brightest smile, darkest eyes in the county. Kind. Jenny was kind. The strays around here, and I'm talking stray dogs, cats, cows, and even horses, they would come to her, and she would tend them. There might be an old bluetick hound visiting you now and then. He was just a pup twelve years ago when we were still living here. He'll tree a few squirrels, maybe dig up a few moles, and then he'll curl up under a tree for a nap. He was quite a stray, that one. I was a stray, too."

He laughs, and I laugh with him.

"She's still here, isn't she?" I ask.

"She'll never leave this place," he says. "Even when we moved to the bigger house, her mind was always out here, raising her boys, tending her flowers, fishing her pond. She could outfish me even on her worst day. I used to think she could coax the bass out of the reeds with just her voice. 'Come an' get it, come an' get it,' she'd whisper to the fish, and they would come an' get it. She had a light in her that just never went off. She glowed."

"How long were you married?"

"Fifty-seven years. We were barely seventeen when we got married, and we spent our honeymoon over in Roanoke, which back then was the big, bad city of dreams. What did we know? I never gave her a proper honeymoon, and I told her so. Know what she said?"

"What?"

"Every single day I've known you, Mr. Wilson, has been a honeymoon."

Every single day I've known you has been a honeymoon.

If anyone ever asks me to define love, I'll tell the story of Jenny and Mr. Wilson.

Erlana wouldn't have cared. Lana might have sighed and even cried.

Joy understands.

Joy likes to get spiritual.

I used to keep the Sabbath at home on Sundays, and now I keep the Sabbath at home *every* day. I can't quite get myself into a church, and there are several just down the road, but I'm afraid folks will know I'm a heathen. But at Jenny's dollhouse, my own church, I'm finding God everywhere, even when I'm only doing the laundry. I see deep green grass stains vanish from my jeans and sweatpants. A miracle! Oh, I'm sure the stain-removing product is partly responsible, but detergent wouldn't work without water— and that's God's doing. A petunia wilted by the heat at noon springs to life the next morning because of an evening shower or a heavy dew. The tiniest birds sing the loudest songs, and even the ravens that come to visit have beauty. There are rainbows in their wings just under the surface of all that black. And music! I almost forgot! God's music plays nightly, his melodies floating off the pond. Bullfrogs play bass, cicadas play percussion, crickets play the strings, and mosquitoes play the harmonica. I had heard the music before, but I never really listened to it. Those bullfrogs can jam! And all this brings me back to what I learned a long time ago in Sunday school: "God is everywhere." And to this, I add: "God is everywhere, so he's always nearby."

Erlana would have shrugged her chip-filled shoulders at all these miracles. Lana might have wondered for a spell.

Joy thanks God for everything.

Last but not least, Joy also likes to travel, taking day trips just to take them.

I drove up to Rockbridge County to see the Natural Bridge, dis-covered by Thomas Jefferson himself, or so the brochure says. I'm sure some Native Americans might have discovered it first. Anyway, I checked out the bridge itself ("One of the Seven Natural Wonders of the World!"), walked the Cedar Creek Nature Trail across the Lost River (all two feet of it) to Lace Falls, ducked inside the Saltpeter Cave and looked at a Native American village, where the Monacan inhabitants don't do their thing until the weekends, when there are bigger crowds. I toyed with the idea of going into the Natural Bridge caverns, but I'm a little claustrophobic, and that cave goes down 350 feet, or ten stories. I could have visited a wax museum and a toy museum (which instantly reminded me of Izzie!), but I decided I had to get back to my little slice of heaven.

I eventually drove down to Dixie Caverns, where I was alone with my blackness (and I was the only black person) in a cave as cool as a glass of lemonade while trying not to frighten the tiny brown bats or step on salamanders no more than an inch long. It surprised me when we climbed *up* a whole bunch of stairs before descending into the cave, and our guide knew just about everything there was to know about the cave. He told us that a dog named Dixie had "discovered" the cave simply by falling in and barking for his master about a hundred years ago. I can't imagine being that dog all alone in that darkness and barking at the light.

Hmm. Actually, I know exactly how that dog felt.

At one point in that tour of the cave, we walked under what our guide called the "Wedding Bell," and the rock formation did look like a big old bell. He told us that over a hundred couples had been married under that bell, and that if one drop of water hit you as you went under it, you'd be married within eight years. "If you get hit by two," he added, "you'll have eighteen children."

I was hit by *three* ice-cold drops of water. I wonder what that means. Maybe I'll be married within eight years *and* have eighteen children.

Speaking of children, I relived a piece of my childhood at the Star City Roller Skating Rink one day. I arrived when it opened on a hot July day expecting it to be crawling with kids. It wasn't. I was the first person through the door, everything was dark inside, and they even asked me if I was some daycare worker when I paid for my skates. "No," I said. "I'm just here by myself." Yeah, they gave me strange looks. I skated by myself for a while to some old school funk until the daycare centers arrived. I became a giantess to a bunch of little kids whizzing by me wearing yellow-and-orange in-line skates. One little light-skinned boy with curly black hair and light brown eyes was having a difficult time staying on his feet, so I took his hand and helped him around. He asked me if I wanted to play some video games, and I said, "Sure." When we got to the first game, called "Football Mayhem" or something like that, he held out his hand. "It takes two quarters to play." That little boy ended up hustling me out of four dollars' worth of quarters while we played the most ridiculous football game ever created. Thirty yards for a first down? Two-minute quarters? No running game whatsoever? Where was Ms. Pac-Man? Still, it was fun hanging out with a milk chocolate boy.

I also visited the National D-Day Memorial, just up the road from me, hanging out with some scruffy, tattooed bikers with jean jackets and some ancient war heroes still wearing their old uniforms. I explored Explore Park, a series of historical buildings on the Blue Ridge Parkway, to watch "living history" reenacted by real folks dressed as folks dressed two hundred years ago. I raced a go-kart at Thunder Valley and lost to a ten-year-old boy who taunted me the entire time. I even played Skee-Ball, earning enough tickets for a sunshine tattoo and a gaudy plastic ring. I did some midnight bowling over in Vinton ("Just one lane, please," I said, not feeling sad at all), and I even made time to feed the ducks from a bridge over the Roanoke River beside where Victory Stadium used to be.

I wasn't on the clock, and I didn't have to be anywhere.

That's freedom.

But something was . . . missing.

And I thought it had something to do with my daddy.

"I'm going to Norfolk to find Daddy," I say to Mama in early August. "Where should I look first?"

"Child, he's probably not in Norfolk anymore. NorShipCo isn't owned by the same family as before, and he might have lost his job because of that. He could be anywhere."

"Where do I look first?"

"Erlana, it's been seventeen years. You should make a few phone calls first, to see if he's even up there anymore. I'll bet if you look him up first in the White Pages on the Internet—"

"Where should I look first?"

Joy is persistent.

With only a full tank of gas, forty dollars, and a water bottle filled with Mama's sweetened sun tea, I drive five hours to Norfolk, taking the scenic route of 460 through towns like Spout Spring, Appomattox, Evergreen, Prospect, Nottoway, Petersburg, Disputanta, and Zuni. I keep my windows open the entire way, the steamy hot air filled with the scents of hottest summer: decaying vegetation, honeysuckle, and kudzu. Everything looks strange, different, and new at the same time. I try to see the scenery and the towns with an eight-year-old's eyes, but I fail, and in the failing, I see the beauty more clearly. An eight-year-old football player missing her daddy couldn't have seen all this beauty, all this greenery tinged with browns and beiges and golds, all this small-town Virginia finery shining in the August sun.

Or all this traffic. Geez. And on a Saturday? "Where'd you learn to drive?" I shout. "In a video game?"

Joy does not like traffic, and Erlana and Lana agree.

I finally find myself on Granby Street on my way to Daddy's old house. I know it's a long shot, but stranger things have happened. I count the numbered streets—26th, 27th, 28th, 29th. Hang a left, and . . .

Either I've gotten huge or all of these houses have shrunk. Damn, they're all packed in here, and no one has a yard to speak of. You could wash your neighbor's windows without leaving *your* house. You could turn on a box fan and suck up your neighbor's mail. I stop in front of 623, where a FOR SALE sign sits in a dirt yard behind a chain-link fence. That fence wasn't there when Daddy lived here, and those trees were much shorter and actually had leaves. The bricks also used to be browner. Now, they're looking gray. Wait. Some fool tried to paint those bricks. They used to be a pretty brown!

I get out to stretch, stepping up to the gate. I notice no drapes on any of the windows and can see inside to a completely empty front room.

No one lives here. Damn. But I can see why. These dead-looking trees give no shade at all, and that yard is mostly sand. A house like this would be at home in Arizona or Nevada. And who paints brown bricks with gray paint?

I squint in the sun up and down the broken sidewalk, hoping to find someone, anyone, outside, walking in my direction. Directly across the street on the remains of a plaid couch on the front porch of a magnificent old Victorian house sits a little gray old man. As far as I can tell, all he's doing is sitting. I wave, and he nods.

Well, I came all this way. I might as well talk to somebody.

Erlana wants to go home. Lana is hungry.

Joy wants to find her daddy.

I cross the street and stop at his gate. "Afternoon."

He nods.

I point across to Daddy's old house. "I'm looking for Earl Davidson."

"Who?" The man stands.

"Earl Davidson."

He wipes his forehead with a blue bandana. "I haven't heard that name in years. Come on up."

Shoot. Daddy's been gone a long time from this place, but in a way, I'm happy. That little house couldn't have contained him. I'm surprised it contained him when he was my daddy.

I open the gate and walk up a brick sidewalk to the bottom step of the porch, shielding my eyes.

"What you lookin' for Pearly for?" he asks, resuming his seat on the couch, a stack of newspapers beside him.

"Pearly?"

His eyes narrow. "You ain't police, are you?"

"No, sir. I'm his daughter, Erlana."

Blink, blink. "Pearly had a daughter, too?"

Too? I have a brother somewhere? I guess that makes sense. I wonder if he also has a peanut head.

"You don't look like Pearly."

I smile. "I take after my mama mostly. How long has he been gone?"

He looks up at the paint peeling from the ceiling of the porch. "Hmm. Going on . . . seven, eight years. He took off for San Francisco to work on the docks out there."

Joy has a sudden need to get in an airplane, but Lana, the eight-fifty-an-hour worker, can't afford it.

Erlana still wants to go home.

"My mama and I moved when I was eight, and I remember playing football at a park around here."

"Probably Lafayette Park." He reaches down for a can of Coke and takes a sip. "You say football?"

"Yeah. My daddy and I played football."

"I believe it. Pearly was built like a linebacker."

He hit like one, too. "Why do you call him Pearly?"

"He had the whitest teeth I ever seen on a black man."

Pearly. I like it. "He used to call me 'E.'"

"Yeah? He was always talking about someone named E, but I thought he was talking about his boy."

Same thing. Wait. I'm the *boy* my daddy told this man about? "What did he say about E?"

"Just that E was gonna be in the NFL some day." He scratches his head. "But if *you're* E, then . . ."

Yes, that's me. My daddy was bragging on me. "I, uh, do play professional football now." I hate saying "semi-pro." It makes me feel so cheap.

"You don't say?"

"I play defensive end for the Roanoke Revenge."

"I heard about y'all having a league." He leans forward. "You look more like a wide receiver."

Not anymore, sighs Lana. Erlana tells Lana to shut up. Erlana wants to play defensive end. Joy just shakes her head at the both of them.

"I may have to play strong safety this next year." If I decide to play at all. It's no fun having no one in the stands to play for.

"Are you a mean girl?"

I smile. "When I play football I am."

He leans back. "Your daddy was mean *all* the time. No one messed with him. Cats from around here would get up in his face, and all he'd do was smile that smile of his and crack those big ol' knuckles without saying a single word. They usually scattered after that." He sighed. "The neighborhood was different then. Used to be a fistfight now and then, maybe a gunshot here and there, but now . . ." He shakes his head. "I don't suppose things are like that over in Roanoke."

"We have our troubles, too."

"Yeah. Too many fools out here with their courage attached to the trigger of a gun. Ain't too many real men like your daddy left." He smiles.

I smile, too.

"You traveled all that way to find him on a hot day, and all you got was a story."

But it was a good story, and I *have* found my daddy.

"You have to be hungry."

"I am." A little. My new body doesn't require as much fuel as it did before.

"Wish I could offer you something, but my wife isn't cooking today. Saturdays are when my wife and I go to Harry's. You ever hear of Harry's?"

I've heard that name before. "The barbecue place?" Mama used to take me there with Grandma Lula.

"Yeah." He checks his watch. "Now would be the time to go so you can find a parking spot. It's downtown on Granby."

"I think I passed it." I stand. "Thanks for taking the time to talk to me."

"I got plenty of time. You drive safe."

"And, um, if you ever see Pearly again, tell him E says hello."

"I will."

I call Mama on my way to Harry's. "Mama, he's out in San Francisco."

"I'm sorry, Erlana."

"It's okay." And it is. Daddy's still out there doing his thing. He's still working on the big ships, and he's still near the water in his sweatshirt, jeans, and boots. "Mama, did you know Daddy had a nickname?"

"You mean 'Pearly?'"

"You knew?"

"Everybody knew. They called him Earl the Pearl after some basketball player."

I'm learning so much today. "So it wasn't because of his teeth?"

"Yeah, he did have him some pearly whites."

"And Daddy played basketball?"

"Well, he played something that kind of looked like basketball. He was pretty physical."

I see my daddy busting through a double team or setting a pick. Boom! "Was he any good?"

"Not particularly."

Good thing he taught me how to play football, then. "Guess where I'm going for dinner?"

"You on Granby?"

Mama's psychic. "Yes."

"You're going to Harry's. Bring me back a sweet potato pie. A whole one, now."

I smile. "I won't be home until late."

"I'll wait up."

"Okay."

I pass Harry's and am two blocks away when I find a parking space. Once inside Harry's, I read a dry erase board full of specials, but once I'm seated, I want only food for my soul. I eat a messy plate of wet ribs, the meat falling off the bone, and some macaroni and cheese good enough to rival Mama's, while an old jukebox plays some old soul. *This* is real food. *This* is how all food should taste. *This* is how all the food I should cook from now on until the end of my days should taste.

Joy is going to get some cooking lessons from Mama.

On the way out, I buy a whole sweet potato pie. They ask if I want a to-go fork. "I couldn't eat another thing," I say, "and I have a long drive, so . . ."

I take the fork.

I have half that pie gone by the time I get to Petersburg.

And it is *good.*

And as I drive, I say a little prayer for Daddy: *Wherever you are Daddy, I hope you're happy. And stay mean. Yeah. Stay mean, Pearly.*

Chapter 28

"But Mama, you're not measuring anything."

She throws another pinch of sage into a boiling pot of chicken breasts on the little stove at Jenny's dollhouse. "I just put in a pinch."

"But how much is a pinch?"

She tilts the jar of sage to the side and squeezes her pointer and thumb together. "This much."

"But my fingers are skinnier than yours."

"Double it, then." She returns to the cutting board, slicing some more celery, while I furiously write it down on a little notepad I'm hiding from her. "And what have I been trying to tell you all day?"

I sigh and slide the notepad under my leg. And this preparation is only for some homemade chicken soup! "That cooking is feeling, not measuring."

"That's right."

I continue to hack away at the carrots on my cutting board. Why we're making chicken soup on a day that's threatening to hit ninety, I don't know. All the windows in the house are open because Mama says this place needs "a good airing out."

She also says Jenny's kitchen is a real kitchen, with lots of space and room for the imagination.

I need to work on my imagination.

"How many carrots should I cut?"

She shrugs. "As many as can fit in the pot."

I peel another carrot. "When will the chicken be ready?"

"Like I said, there's no timer on any of this, Erlana. I usually wait until the meat falls off the bones." She stops slicing the celery and puts something else into the pot.

"What was that?"

"A touch of parsley."

"How much is a touch?"

"Erlana Joy!"

I am no fun in the kitchen. "Well, with the bay leaves you were pretty specific. You said no more than one, two at the most."

She roots around in a drawer for a measuring spoon, dropping in a little parsley. She brings the measuring spoon to me. "This is a touch."

There's not much there. "Oh."

"Soon as you're done with those carrots, get started peeling those potatoes."

"How thin do I slice them?"

She sighs.

I withdraw the question, Your Honor.

She places a huge sweet Vidalia onion on the cutting board, and in four rapid strokes reduces it to eight chunks. She looks at me. "Any questions?"

"No."

"Are you still counting?"

Yes. "No." Eight chunks. I bet they unravel after they've been in the hot water a while. I write it down on my notepad.

She dumps the celery and the onions into the pot. I want to ask why, but I don't. I just write it down.

"You want me to bring over the carrots?" I ask.

She comes and scoops the carrots into her hands. "We'll need two more."

Again, I want to ask how she knows, but I don't. She feels. She doesn't measure. Her hands are the scales. I peel and cut two more carrots and bring them to the pot. There are so many vegetables that I can't see the chicken.

I can't stand it anymore. "Mama, why are we cooking the vegetables before the meat is done?"

"The vegetables take longer to cook."

"Oh." I feel so dumb.

She shakes a little celery salt into the water. One shake, two shakes, three—

"You're counting again."

"Sorry."

She turns me back to my cutting board.

"Are you going to add some pepper?" I ask.

"I might, I might not," she says, scrubbing some huge potatoes in the sink. "Every time I make it, it's different. In fact, I make every meal just a little different so no meal ever gets old. For example, sometimes I add long noodles, and sometimes I use the star-shaped kind instead. Today I'm adding these potatoes. The recipes in my head leave me room to be creative."

In other words, her recipes are vague. I decide to test her. "What if I wanted to add some corn?"

"Add some corn."

"Or lima beans?"

"Add some lima beans."

"Or beets?"

"You have never liked beets."

I smile. "Well, maybe I'm *feeling* like beets, and I promise not to *measure* them. See, I listen to you."

"Then throw away that little pad of paper you've been writing everything down on over there under your legs."

Busted. "What paper?"

"The paper you've been sitting on."

I pull the offending notepad from under me. "I just . . . I just want it to taste like your cooking, that's all."

She shakes her head. "This is your kitchen, Erlana Joy. *Your* cooking should taste like *your* cooking, not mine. It's how you'll make a name for yourself. Someone will say, 'You just *have* to taste

Erlana's jerk chicken. It's the best.' As soon as you hear your name attached to a dish, you've made it."

And slowly but surely, my cooking is tasting much better. I add more salt and oregano to my fried chicken and don't use nearly as much butter to fry it as Mama does. I use a lemon rub mixed with Cajun seasonings for my pork chops, cook my greens overnight in a Crock-Pot with turkey necks, and somehow make my liver and onions taste more like steak and onions. My first attempt at potato salad was a disaster—I used sour relish instead of sweet relish, and *way* too much mustard—but I'm getting better.

And I'm getting a little fatter. I'm still walking, even jogging a little, around the pond, which has filled up along with me after four weeks of steady rain at nearly every sundown. It even has water so clear now that I can see the bass looking out the sides of their heads at me. At night, I'm studying *The Complete Idiot's Guide to Chess* and *Bobby Fischer Teaches Chess* so I can whip Bobby's tail for a change. I even have my own magnetic chessboard, a purchase I made at Wal-Mart.

So, the pond's back, my booty's almost back, and I'm ready to go back to work.

And for a solid month, I haven't thought about Juan Carlos, Karl, or Roger.

Erlana and Lana are amazed.

Joy just hums something beautiful.

Chapter 29

I show up at Patrick Henry in late August tanned, toned, and tuned-in wearing a sky blue skort, matching short-sleeved top, and sandals. Walking my land barefoot has smoothed my feet, and the minerals in the water have healed my toenails, the nine I still have. I have dressed differently today because this is going to be a different year, a better year, an awesome year.

It will be a year to remember, which will erase last year's memories completely.

I smile at everybody. I've never done that before. I am, after all, Pearly's daughter, and I ought to show off what he gave me.

I speak even to people I don't know at the convocation, the big meeting of all the staff from the Roanoke City School District at the Roanoke Civic Center. I sit with Rachel Jones, head of Patrick Henry's Special Services Department and my immediate supervisor, as the lights dim and the show begins. Oh, it's not supposed to be a show, but somehow every year it becomes one. It's really a song-and-dance act for the media. The superintendent reads a list of major accomplishments from the previous school year . . . and ignores the real problems. Still, it's fun to see kids from local schools singing, dancing, and strutting their stuff to entertain us.

"Same song, different year," Rachel says as the superintendent rambles on and on. "I almost didn't recognize you without your sweats."

"It's too hot for sweats."

"You said it. Have a good summer?"

I want to tell her I found myself, but that would sound strange. "Yes. And you?"

"All I can say is that it's over."

Rachel needs to come out to Jenny's dollhouse to get rid of her attitude.

"Did you hear about Isabel?"

I haven't heard from Izzie since that . . . since that night. "No."

"She took a counseling position at Addison Middle."

And Izzie didn't tell me. Now who will listen to me rant and rave during my lunch break?

"Have you heard from Bobby's mother?" she asks.

"No." My heart thuds. "Is he okay?"

She shakes her head. "He'll have to be homeschooled this year."

Which means . . . the end is near. Damn, it's like losing another man. "I need to call him."

"Go on."

I walk out of the Civic Center auditorium into the sun and call Bobby. His mother answers. "Mrs. Swisher, this is Lana Cole."

"Hi, Lana. I guess you've heard."

"Yes, ma'am. Can I talk to Bobby?"

"He's, um, he's having trouble breathing today. His allergies are acting up."

And with Bobby, his allergies can be killers. "Could you tell him something for me?"

"Sure."

"Tell him that I studied chess-strategy books all summer, and that the next time we play, he's going down."

"I will. And if you ever want to visit . . ."

That would be so hard! "I want to, Mrs. Swisher. Just call me when he's able to play some chess."

"I will. Goodbye."

From the sound of her voice, I'm going to have to visit soon. I knew I'd have to say goodbye to him someday, but this is much too soon! Bobby was going to be part of this awesome year, and now . . .

Take care of that boy, God, okay? I pray. *You kept me going all summer, so use some of your power to keep Bobby going, too.*

During our first workweek without the students, I look into getting my education degree, talking to Nancy Knowles, who runs PH's Career Center.

"You could take night classes at Radford, Hollins, or Virginia Tech," she says.

The classes at Hollins University won't be cheap, though the drive won't be so bad. But driving down to Radford or Tech? That's some serious mileage. "That's a lot of driving."

"Some courses are offered downtown at the Higher Learning Center, and some of the basic courses are offered at Virginia Western."

Cool. I'll have to take as many of those as I can. "How long will it be before I have my degree?" I ask.

"If you only take night classes, oh, about four years."

Damn.

"But that depends on what you specialize in and how many classes you take during the summer. As you know, there is a heavy need for special services staff throughout the city now."

And the rest of the country, too. I read that the state of Florida will need close to thirty thousand new teachers in the next few years in its effort to reduce its schools' class sizes. I can't see myself in, say, Palm Beach, but it's nice to know there are so many openings in sunny places.

"I'm not sure I want to stay in special services," I say, because there are plenty of obese kids out there who could use my help, too. I recently read that childhood obesity has tripled since I was born, and there seems no end in sight. "What about health and PE?"

"I'm sure human resources could use you somewhere, maybe even at one of the middle schools."

"Or at an elementary school." Where this rampant obesity starts.

At Star City Roller Skating Rink, I saw a kid who couldn't have been older than nine laboring and throwing his sweat around the rink, and he had to weigh more than me. "What if I take a few courses during the summer? Will I get certified faster?"

She sits back. "If you took, let's say, three classes every summer, you could possibly be certified in less than three years. I'm sure you could work and do your student teaching at the same time, maybe even right here at PH."

Hmm. Three years is a long time, and if summer classes start in June, I probably couldn't play football for the entire season. Still, I could be a real teacher—with real pay and benefits—by the time I'm twenty-eight.

"And if you're really serious about this, the city will help pay for your classes."

I smile. "I like the sound of that."

"We could sure use you."

It's nice to be needed, but it would be so hard to start a season and not be able to finish it. I may have to give up football. Hmm. At least this gives me something to think about and look forward to.

Because there's not much for me to do until the students show up next week, I get online in one of the computer labs and check out Virginia Western's course offerings. Since I've already taken Principles of Psychology, I can take Child Psychology, Educational Psychology, Abnormal Psychology, or Adolescent Psychology. Too many choices. I've heard that Ed Psych is duller than dishwater, but it's a requirement for my teaching certificate. A course called "Health, Safety, and Nutrition Education" jumps out at me.

I sign up for that one, and since it's a distance-learning course mainly on the Internet, I can "take" that class during my free periods at PH.

Erlana says she's sick of school, and Lana would much rather surf the personal-ad sites for a new man. Joy hugs them both and tells them it's a brand-new day.

Every day, I walk by pre-season varsity football practice, and each day I drift closer and closer to the action. While watching some line

CAN'T GET ENOUGH OF YOUR LOVE 217

drills, I see a sorry defensive end getting slammed into the ground on just about every play. He's doing it all wrong!

Erlana, Lana, and Joy all agree that this is something that has to be remedied immediately.

I march right up to the young man, looking down on his sorry self all crumpled up and dirty in the dust. "You have to keep your outside arm free, man. As soon as the blocker has that arm pinned, you're useless."

He stands and looks at his coach.

"I'm talking to you," I say, and he snaps his head back to me. "What's your name?"

"Curtis."

"Okay, Curtis, listen up. You have to go up and under with your inside arm"—I demonstrate on him—"then stick your elbow hard into his back, like a hook move in basketball, only meaner and completely legal."

I elbow him hard and hear a little "oof." Damn, he's bony. Why aren't they feeding these kids? If it weren't for his pads, Curtis would blow away in the wind.

"Up and under with your inside arm, then hook. It's just like swimming, only you're standing up. If you do this every time, you'll be ready for anything coming your way. And keep your feet moving, stay balanced, and work to the outside." I point to a chunky lineman. "Get set." The chunky lineman gets into his three-point stance. "Line up," I tell Curtis, the Bony One, and he gets down in a four-point stance.

I shake my head. "Stand up, Curtis." He stands. "Don't grab the dirt with both of your hands. Use a three-point stance. Grab dirt with your inside hand so you can start with your outside hand free."

He gets into a three-point stance.

"Now as soon as you fire off the line, Curtis, start swimming."

Curtis, the Bony One's, first attempt leaves him once again on the ground, but at least he ruined the lineman's block.

"Again."

His second attempt ends in a stalemate, but at least Curtis has his outside arm free, his feet moving laterally to the outside.

"Better. Again."

His third attempt works like a dream, the chunky lineman spinning behind Curtis, the Bony One. Curtis smiles.

"Do that *every* time, Curtis," I say, tapping his chest, "and I'll be reading about you in the newspaper."

I look at the coach, who is old, gray, and white, shake my head, and walk away. The coach runs up to me, and I've never seen him before. Oh yeah. We have a new head coach, our third new head coach in the last four years.

"They respond to you," he says.

Because I'm cute, *and* because I actually know what I'm doing.

"Where'd you learn all that?" he asks.

I stop. "My daddy. I also play defensive end for the Roanoke Revenge."

He doesn't blink. "They play in the spring, right?"

"Yes."

"So what are you doing this fall?"

I don't answer right away, because I'm not sure how to answer. Is he asking me if I'll help him coach? I look out on the rest of the practice field and see at least six other coaches.

"Look," he says, "I shouldn't be coaching the line, but I have to. I'm short-staffed, and I don't have a paid assistant position left. But I might be able to get you some booster money."

"To do what?" I ask.

"To coach the line."

"You want me to . . . coach?" I like a new man with new ideas, but . . .

"Yes. Defensive ends, tight ends, whatever you feel comfortable with. They need lots of work."

I nod. "They sure do."

"So, will you do it?"

Unpaid work *after* work? And what if I want to take a night class in addition to the distance-learning class? How will that fit into all this?

Erlana loves the idea, but only if she gets to blow a whistle and cuss at bony little boys. Lana doesn't like the idea of hanging out with sweaty boys and taking long bus rides on Friday nights when she could be out on a date. Joy . . . Joy thinks that Erlana is too mean and that Lana is tripping about going on a date.

Joy also thinks the idea is perfect.

"I'll do it," I say. "But I have to look like a coach. I'll need a coach's shirt, sweats, a whistle, and one of those purple satin jackets y'all wear." Those jackets are *so* cool, and I've never seen a woman coach wearing one. "And I will have to be paid as much as the other coaches somehow, some way."

"Okay."

Okay? That was too easy! I should have asked for more! "Have you taken your team picture yet?"

"No. It's scheduled for tomorrow morning."

I smile because . . .

I am *in* that team picture, and I am not in there as the cheerleader sponsor, trainer, or water girl. I am listed in the program as "DE/TE coach Erlana Joy Cole."

Daddy would be proud.

And those boys do respond to me.

Because I know what I'm talking about.

And I'm pretty damn cute, too.

Chapter 30

Rachel has me working this year with Hakeem, a stocky black boy with Down syndrome. He is a sweet child, we spend most of our day in the resource room playing paper football to work on his math skills (the boy can definitely count using threes and sevens), and he likes to hold my hand.

And, he likes football.

Unfortunately, he's a Cowboys fan. "They rock!" he shouts. Hakeem likes to shout, and I like to hear it. Sometimes education is just too darn quiet to be educational.

At least he doesn't like the Washington Redskins or the Carolina Panthers, the teams closest to Roanoke. "What about the Steelers?" I have a thing for wide receiver Heinz Ward. I used to dream that one day I would bear him a child. It's why I wear number 89 for the Revenge. "The Steelers are a good team."

"Nah," Hakeem says. "Steelers are bad. Cowboys are number one!"

"You know, Hakeem, *I* play football."

He widens those big eyes of his. "No, you don't."

"I do."

"Girls can't play football."

"Wanna bet?"

CAN'T GET ENOUGH OF YOUR LOVE 221

He pulls out a quarter. "Yeah."

"You're going to lose that quarter, boy."

I take him out to the practice field between classes and tell him to go out for a pass. A number of other students stop and watch us. "That's Coach Cole," one of them says, and it gives me goose bumps.

Hakeem takes two steps and turns around.

"I can throw the ball farther than that, Hakeem."

He shrugs, takes two more baby steps, and turns.

"Hakeem. Go out for a pass. Start running."

"You can't—"

I cock my arm back. "Start running, boy."

"You can't—"

I step back and launch that football about forty yards downfield. It isn't a perfect spiral, but it looks pretty in a wounded-duck kind of way. My crowd of admirers say, "Wow!" and "Damn, she got an arm and a half."

Hakeem looks at me. He looks at the ball bouncing down the field. He looks back at me, and he smiles. "Hot damn!" he shouts. "Hot damn!"

"Hey now, no cursing."

He frowns. "Sorry."

"It's okay," I say, laughing. He is so cute! "Go get the ball."

His smile returns. "Okay."

I think I have made another friend.

And in mid-September, after coaching the defensive *line* to two straight victories (okay, the offense had a little something to do with it, too), I receive a stray phone call from one of my old friends after an article appears in the *Roanoke Times* about PH's "most unique" football coach.

Juan Carlos calls.

"What's up?" I say, all cool and collected, but underneath, I am *not* cool or collected. I haven't spoken to him since he called me a "bunta." Of the three, I thought Juan Carlos was the least likely to ever speak to me again, and here he is on the phone.

"I am sorry to call you so late."

It's only eight thirty, but that's late for a workingman. "It's okay."

"Um, Lana, my mama died today."

"Oh no!"

"Could you . . . would you come to the wake? It is tomorrow evening at Valley Funeral Service on Peters Creek."

"Sure, sure, I'll be there. Oh, Juan, I'm so sorry."

Silence, then . . . . "I will see you tomorrow." *Click.*

He sounded so devastated! I know I'd be completely overwhelmed without my mama. I wonder what happened. I call Mama. "Mama, would you look in the paper for me?"

"When are you going to get a subscription?"

"As I told you, they don't deliver the *Times* way out here." I'm sure they do. I'm just too lazy to find out and too poor to get a subscription. I usually look at the newspaper at school.

I hear a rustling of pages. "What are you looking for?"

"An obituary."

"Who died?"

"Juan Carlos's mama."

Silence, then . . . "He called you?"

"Yeah. I just got off the phone with him."

"That's so sad. Last name?"

"Gomez."

Silence. "I don't see a Gomez anywhere. When did she die?"

Oh yeah. It wouldn't be in the paper yet. "Today. Juan Carlos invited me to the wake."

"And you're going, right?"

"He's still my friend."

And he is. He needs me. He needs a shoulder to cry on. I have to go.

The next evening, I arrive at Valley Funeral Service on Peters Creek Road, parking in a nearly empty lot, which means, I guess, that not many people knew his mama. I find Juan Carlos sitting in the front row all alone, wearing a nice suit and tie. He cleans up nicely. I don't look up at the open casket yet, instead making a beeline for Juan Carlos. I wanted to meet his mama, but I didn't want to meet her this way. I also really have trouble at wakes because Death (with a capital D) and I don't get along, ever since my first dog died when I was thirteen.

Juan Carlos stands and hugs me, his body shaking. "She is gone, she is gone," he whispers.

"What happened?" We sit, and I hold his hand, looking up into his unshaven face.

"Cancer," he whispers. "There was nothing they could do."

Cancer? People don't die suddenly from cancer, which means . . .

"She tried to fight, but she was not strong enough."

Oh no! This explains *so* much. "How long was she sick?"

He nods, wiping a tear from his nose. "Three years."

No wonder he worked so much. He had to work overtime to pay for her medicine or her chemotherapy. And somehow . . . My eyes well with tears. Somehow he made time for *me*. I was his reprieve from being around his dying mama. I was the life in his life.

I feel like such a bunta.

"I did not want you to see her, because she wanted no one to see her most days." His voice chokes up. "She lost her hair, Lana. She lost her beautiful hair."

I hold him fiercely, and after a while, I can't tell who is shaking more. Why didn't he tell me that his mama had cancer? I would have understood. At least I think I would have understood.

"Why didn't you tell me?"

"It was her wish." He looks toward the casket. "She was a strong woman. She did not want anyone to know she was not strong. I wanted to tell you." He looks at his hands. "I was on my way to tell you that night. She was feeling better and wanted to meet you that night."

That night. So much went wrong that night. I wish I could have that night back to do all over again.

The funeral director comes down the aisle to us trailed by a beautiful dark tan, dark-haired woman. His cousin? Juan Carlos drops my hand, jumps up, and runs to her. They embrace, and then—

She's kissing him.

On the lips.

Either she's a kissing cousin, or . . .

No, they're using quite a bit of tongue, and at a wake?

They turn to me. "This is Monique," Juan Carlos says.

Monique seems to be a mixture of black and Hispanic, with lighter skin than I have. She also has some seriously bushy black eyebrows.

"Hello," I say.

"We are to be married," Juan Carlos says.

My heart skips a beat. Whoa. They hooked up quickly. They do make a nice couple, but this was my man—or he was one of my men. I have no right to be jealous, but I am. "It's nice to meet you, Monique."

She whispers something in Spanish to Juan Carlos, and his face tightens. "Lana," he says to her without the "ahh" I loved to hear.

And then, Monique kills me with her eyes. Her pupils almost completely disappear, and she literally bares her teeth at me.

"You . . . you are trash," she says in a thick accent. "Get out!"

I don't move. I look at Juan Carlos.

"Perhaps you should go," he says.

I want to tell Monique what a good, fine, decent man Juan Carlos is. I want to tell her how lucky she is to have such a dedicated, hard-working man in her life. And I want to tell him that I'm sorry for all that happened between us.

"Go!" Monique shouts.

I stand, my legs a little shaky. "I came here to pay my respects." I look at the casket. "I will pay my respects, and then I will leave."

"You are not needed here!" Monique hisses.

Again, I look at Juan Carlos, but he is powerless, his shoulders slumping.

I want to tell Monique that I was invited, that I miss Juan Carlos terribly, and that I admire her excellent taste in men. I want to tell him that I shouldn't have taken him for granted, that I still think about him, and that I still smile whenever I hear a Led Zeppelin song on the radio.

Instead of leaving, I go to the casket and see Juan Carlos's mama for the first time. Though she is thin and the wig she wears isn't a precise fit, she is beautiful, the spitting image of Juan Carlos. "I'm glad to finally meet you," I whisper. "You have a fine son." I turn to look one last time at Juan Carlos.

"Thank you for coming," he says.

"Thank you for asking me to come," I say, mainly to Monique.

And I cry my eyes out all the way home.

Chapter 31

Idon't blame Monique for her anger. She thinks I ruined Juan Carlos, but I could never ruin such a truly golden man who has a heart of gold and hands with the golden touch. My stupidity was her gain. I didn't deserve him. I didn't deserve such a golden man.

And then I relive the moments I shared with Juan Carlos. My moving out here *was* a great hardship on him. I was tearing him in two. He wanted to see me, but he didn't want to be so far away from his mama. The times he did see me must have been "good" days for her, days when she could take care of herself, and I took him away from those "good" days. I can't stop thinking about all those times I asked to meet her and the pain that must have caused him. I always thought he was taking care of me, when . . . maybe . . . I was taking care of him, giving him a rest from seeing his mama die before his eyes.

The phone rings a few hours later, the caller ID saying ROANOKE MEMORIAL. Who's calling from the hospital at this hour?

"Hello?"

"This is Pat Swisher, Bobby's mother."

Oh no. A lump forms in my throat. "Yes?"

"We had to take Bobby to the hospital this morning."

"Is he all right?" Please say he has a bad cold or something.

"No."

No. The end is near? I'm not ready for this! "I'm so sorry. I've been meaning to come see him."

"And that kept him going. He had me read that article about you in the paper ten times. I even cut out your picture for him."

Of me in the purple jacket.

"Can you, will you come to play chess with him one last time?"

Oh, God help me. One . . . last . . . time. "Sure. I'd like to do that for him."

"And, um, can you come tonight?"

Oh God! The end is *here.* "I'll be right there."

I stand in front of my dresser staring blindly through my tears at all the bling, all the gifts from the men who used to be in my life. "Nothing gold can stay," I whisper, remembering an old poem. Juan Carlos and Bobby—two golden people in my life—and neither of them can stay.

What can I give Bobby, God? I could take him some of my flowers, but you don't take flowers to a dying child. Balloons? No. He's a young man now. I need something—

My class ring.

Yes. I never wear it. I don't even know why I had Mama spend so much on it. I fussed at her for gold when Duralite would have been enough.

Bobby needs this ring.

And a gold chain. I find the first gold chain I ever bought. It's not as shiny as it used to be, but it holds a few good memories of simpler times in high school, times Bobby won't ever get to have.

Yes. I am going to give Bobby my class ring on a chain.

I am going to be Bobby's girl.

I break every known traffic law on the way from Bedford County to Roanoke Memorial, parking in the no-parking zone.

They can tow it. I don't care.

I carry my magnetic chessboard to the elevator and get in, trying not to think of coming down this or any elevator ever again without Bobby. I go to the nurse's station on Bobby's floor, and a nurse leads me to his room. I take a deep breath, and . . .

"Hey, Bobby Fischer, ready to lose?"

His head shakes slightly as his eyes light up. I will never forget his eyes. So much light! So much life!

I set up the board on his serving tray, willing my hands not to shake. "I have been practicing, boy." I smile at him, and his eyes get bigger. "Yeah, that's right. I've been practicing, and tonight you are going to lose."

His lips twist slightly.

"You don't believe me?"

He shakes his head slightly.

"Just you wait. Do I still get to go first?"

He nods. Can't they take off that oxygen mask for just a little while? I want to hear his voice.

"You are going to be amazed, boy." I move out a knight. "Your move, Bobby, and you better watch out. I'm on to all of your tricks now."

And then . . . we play. He whispers which pieces to move to which square, and I move them while his mama sits in an armchair in the shadows.

"When are you getting out of here, man? I miss our conversations in the elevator." And I will probably never get on that elevator at Patrick Henry again. "Are you still talking to Sunny?"

"No," he whispers, and I can barely hear him.

"No? Why not?"

"No computer," he whispers.

I look at his mama. "We'll have to get him a computer in here, okay?"

She nods.

"So, Bobby, is Sunny your girlfriend?"

"No," he whispers louder, and his face reddens slightly. Oh God, he's so pale!

"Good." My lump returns. "Because I want to be your girlfriend, Bobby Fischer."

I take the gold chain from my purse and string the ring on it. It takes me a while to loop it around his head and clasp it behind his neck because of all the tubes. A tear escapes and falls before I can catch it.

"This means I'm your girl, Bobby, and you can never take it off."

And then my lump goes away. It's as if I swallowed it. I should be crying, but I can't cry because I see joy in that boy's eyes. And the lump doesn't return even when I hear Bobby's mama sniffling in the darkness.

I squeeze his hand. He whispers another move, and we continue playing. Several moves later, I see his "strategy," and it breaks my heart.

He's trying to lose.

He doesn't want to win our last match.

"You're going to let me win? What kind of move was that?"

Bobby's eyes dance.

Wait a minute. He's not guarding his king, but . . . Hey, is he trying to take my queen? No. She's safe . . . If he moves that bishop there, he's got me in check. . . . No . . . Hey, this is a stalemate. He wasn't trying to lose.

He wants us to end in a tie.

"Stalemate," he says, clear as a bell.

My heart leaps, and the lump returns. "You little . . . We tied?"

He nods.

"That is so unfair!" I smile, and swallow my lump again. "I almost had you." I squeeze both of his hands. *His hands are so cold, God. Can't you warm him up just a little bit?* "Well, I will be back tomorrow, and tomorrow I *will* beat you."

"No, you won't."

He's sounding stronger. *Thank you, God. Help him hold on to another day.*

I kiss his cheek. "You take care of yourself now, man. Get some rest, and don't think our match tomorrow will end in a stalemate. I am going to whip your tail."

"We'll see," he says. "Bye, Miss Cole."

I shake my head. "You can call me Lana from now on, okay? I'm your girlfriend now."

"Okay." He blushes. "Lana."

I take the stairs all the way down to my car, which is still there with a nice expensive ticket on it.

And then I cry all the way home.

Again.

Chapter 32

B obby died while I was walking with Hakeem to the lunchroom the next morning. Rachel pulled me aside to tell me. I couldn't cry around Hakeem. He wouldn't understand.

Not that I understand either.

Another man has left me.

And now I'm sitting with Mrs. Swisher at Bobby's funeral inside a little church stuffed to the rafters with people who knew Bobby. That little boy touched so many people's lives! That little boy never complained about his condition, about all the things he couldn't do, about the bad breaks he had suffered. He just . . . lived . . . smiling . . . and blushing at me.

He was a smiling little boy, God, and I hope you're letting him run around for all eternity on two strong legs. And whatever you do, God, don't let him play you in chess. He's good. In fact, don't let him play chess at all. Let him run . . . let him fly.

I sit holding Mrs. Swisher's hand. There doesn't seem to be a Mr. Swisher in the picture, or any other family members around, for that matter, just the people in this church. They are her family now. I've felt sorry for her before for the hardship of raising a dying child, but my heart sinks lower when I realize there's no one here for her on such a tragic day.

No one except me.

But no one in this church is crying. They file in front of us to view a group of Bobby's drawings and paintings set up on easels, then continue on to Bobby's body, and they all walk away smiling, each giving Mrs. Swisher a nod or a hug before they return to their seats. A few even smile and nod at me.

It's our turn. I help Mrs. Swisher to her feet, and we walk up to see Bobby's art. He had quite an artist's eye hiding in those shining eyes of his, using lots of color to draw or paint what he saw from his window: trees, flowers, the house across the street, clouds.

"These are so good," I whisper. And they are. If I didn't know better, I'd say a professional artist did these.

"And he was only ten when he did most of these," Mrs. Swisher whispers.

We then move on to the casket, where a gleam of gold jumps off Bobby's chest.

My ring on the gold chain.

"He's so handsome," I whisper to Mrs. Swisher.

She rests her hand on Bobby's arm. "Yes. Yes, he is. And he's still smiling."

"Yes. Yes, he is."

She leans over and kisses Bobby's cheek. "Take care of my boy, Jesus," she says. "I'll see you when I get there, Bobby."

And then I hesitate. I know that that's not my Bobby Fischer resting there, and that his soul is somewhere else. But I can't bring myself to say goodbye. I straighten the ring on the chain, centering it on his tie. "I'll miss you," I whisper.

"He loved you," Mrs. Swisher says.

And after she says that, I am the only one in the church crying.

Mrs. Swisher has to help *me* back to my seat, and I feel so lost. Bobby probably did love me, and it was the purest kind of love because it was impossible. He let his heart reach out to me, a woman nearly twice his age, and he did it without thinking. He loved me without a second thought. That kind of love is pure. He gave me his smiles, his kind words, his heart. And all I can give him now are my tears.

A distinguished-looking older man steps in front of the casket, his dark black hair plastered to his head, and he smiles. How can he be smiling? The sweetest child I've ever known has died!

"We are all here to send Bobby Swisher home," he says. "Bobby is not here. He is in heaven."

Mrs. Swisher squeezes my hand tightly.

"This is a joyous time, not a time for mourning," he continues. "Bobby is resting in the bosom of Jesus. All his pain and all his suffering are over. And if I know Bobby, he's smiling down on all of us right now. . . ."

I ride with Mrs. Swisher, my thoughts going a million miles a second in a million different directions. Why does Bobby's leaving affect me so much? Is it because he was young? Is it because his life was cut short through no fault of his own?

Or is it because . . . Bobby Swisher truly loved me.

"He was so happy after you left the other night," Mrs. Swisher says. "He wanted to tell me all he was feeling, but he was having trouble breathing. But I knew, Miss Cole. I knew what he wanted to say." She puts her two tiny hands on my tear-soaked face. "He wanted to say thank you, Miss Cole, for treating him like a person, not a person with muscular dystrophy. You loved him, didn't you?"

I can only nod.

"I could tell. Bobby had lots of folks helping him throughout his life, all nice people, mind you, but out of all of them, he talked about you the most. Miss Cole is different, he said. She doesn't see my wheelchair. She sees me." She wipes some of my tears away. "Thank you, Lana. You sent my boy to heaven happy."

The limousine stops. The door opens.

We're at Fairview Cemetery. I didn't know we were going here. Roger's here.

I don't look for him, though. I'm not here for Roger. I'm here for Bobby. I'm here for Mrs. Swisher.

The grass has been freshly cut around the gravesite, a mound of dirt just outside the little tent over the . . . the hole in the ground. I can't look at that hole, so I focus on the tree that will give Bobby shade for eternity right there on Roanoke Avenue. I'll bet I will be able to see his resting space every time I pass by on Salem Turnpike. So many floral arrangements all over the place, roses and lily arrangements, so colorful, so—

There's Roger.

I catch my breath as I catch his eyes, and he doesn't look away. I drop my eyes to Mrs. Swisher's hand, holding my hand tightly. A gray-haired man leads us in a long prayer. We sing several hymns. A few people tell stories about Bobby, but I can't hear them because Bobby is in my head humming while I'm about to make a wrong move in a chess game, and he's whispering his moves, and if I tune him out to listen to these people, I'll lose his voice forever and—

Oh God, there's a red rose in my hand! I don't want to put it on the casket, I don't want to move from this place, I want to stay here holding this flower, I want to save this flower and put it in a vase to put on my kitchen table to remind me of a boy with shining eyes who loved me. . . .

It's as if I'm in a dream. I see the casket get bigger, and bigger and see my hand laying the rose on the dark wood, and then I'm standing and watching the casket being lowered into the ground, into the cold, dark, unforgiving ground, and there's someone singing, and it's beautiful, something about never walking alone, and the song ends, and I'm walking away in the sunshine while Roger—

Roger.

I want to talk to Roger.

I want to cry all night on his shoulder.

He's standing over by that hole in the ground telling two men what to do, and—

"Will you come to the house?" Mrs. Swisher asks.

I look down. I'm still holding her hand. "I . . . I don't think I can."

"I understand."

But I don't! I don't understand! I want to understand this. I have been through the deaths of three relationships, the death of Juan Carlos's mama, and the death of a child who loved me, and I still don't get it! Why is all this shit happening?

Sorry, God, but death is shitty.

I look back at the tent. Roger has his suit jacket off, and he's kneeling down, yanking on something in the hole. The scaffolding, or whatever it is, is stuck, and he and the other two men are working to free it . . . so they can fill in the hole.

"Will you ride back to the church with me?"

I nod.

Roger looks my way. I try to smile at him, but I can't. He nods. Maybe he understands. Maybe he can explain all this to me. Maybe he's the only one who understands and can explain it to me.

On the ride back to the church, I try to count my blessings. I'm healthy. My ankle has healed. It clicks some on rainy days, but it still works. I've become slim and trim. I'm eating better because I'm cooking better. I'm more organized. I have a new direction in my life. I'm coaching a sport I love. I will become a teacher someday. I have a specific future in mind with attainable goals. I have a nice house. I live where the country is so beautiful that I have no excuse to be sad or depressed. I am . . .

I am depressed.

But I shouldn't be! I have no right to be depressed!

But you are, Lana.

God, help me.

Please.

Chapter 33

I call Mama as soon as I get home. When she answers, I ask, "What do you know about depression?"

Silence. "Hello, Erlana. How are you? Fine, Mama. How are you?"

This is no time for manners. "Mama, I'm depressed."

Silence. "Really?"

"Yes."

"What do *you* have to be depressed about?" she asks.

What? "What *don't* I have to be depressed about?"

Silence. "Do you want me to come over?"

I sigh. "No. It's late. I just need some advice. I'm having trouble dealing with all this death lately."

"And that depresses you?"

"Yes."

"Hmm. Does death depress you, or is it because you're having trouble dealing with it?"

Good question. "A little of both, I guess."

"I heard about Bobby. I'm surprised you didn't call me as soon as it happened."

So am I. I called her about Juan Carlos's mama but not about Bobby. Why didn't I call her about Bobby? "I guess I should have."

"It's okay. Tell me about Juan Carlos first."

"Mama, this isn't about Juan Carlos." Is it?

"Well, tell me about his mama's wake, then."

I tell her as much as I can about the wake and Monique. "I was keeping him away from his dying mama. I was keeping him away from taking care of her. All those double shifts he worked so he could afford to pay for her medicine and take me out."

"He is a grown man, Erlana. He made his own decisions."

"I just wish I had been there for him." Monique was there for him, not me. But why would he call me to come to the wake, then? He needed me there for some reason. What?

"Now tell me about Bobby."

I describe my last visit with Bobby at the hospital, the funeral, and the burial. "I wanted to talk to Roger so badly afterwards, but I couldn't make my legs move. He was maybe thirty feet away from me, but I just couldn't go to him."

"Uh-huh. You just couldn't go to him."

"Mama, I was frozen in place. I was numb."

"Uh-huh."

A long silence. "What?"

"Do you want to know what I think?"

"It's why I called you."

She sighs. "It might not be what you want to hear."

"Everything I hear these days I *don't* want to hear," I say. "What do you think, Mama?"

"Erlana, you're feeling depressed because you feel guilty."

I feel what? "No, I don't."

"Yes, you do. Death isn't depressing you one bit."

She's tripping. "But it is!"

"Oh, I'm sure you're sad, and I'm sure your heart hurts for Juan Carlos and that little boy, but sadness and hurt don't add up to depression. Otherwise, we'd *all* be depressed *all* the time. We couldn't function at all if we were depressed all the time. This world wouldn't function, either. You have moments of happiness, don't you?"

"Yes, but they don't last."

"And neither does the sadness and hurt, right?"

I feel like a child. "Yes, but—"

"Most depression is caused by unresolved issues in your life, things from your past that you can't let go."

"That's not it, Mama. That's not—"

"I know what I'm talking about, Erlana," she interrupts, her voice louder. "I've been in the place you're at now, and I know how awful it is. I know how it is to feel guilty for years, *many*, many years. I took you away from your daddy. I still feel guilty about that. I will always feel guilty about that. But what I feel guilty about most is leaving your daddy in the first place because I was afraid he would leave *me* first. There are days, even now, when I say to myself, 'I never should have left that man.'"

I don't know what to say. Mama has been depressed . . . since I was eight. Why didn't I pick up on that?

"I didn't know you were depressed, Mama. You always seem . . . okay."

"On the outside, I am okay. But inside . . ." I hear her sniffle. "Inside, I relive that moment I left Norfolk. I go over and over and over all the regrets I have. All of the regrets. And what has it gotten me? Nothing. Not a damn thing. And the only person on this earth I have to blame for it all is me."

"Mama, you can't blame yourself for—"

"The hell I can't!" she interrupts. "*I* made a decision to leave your daddy, *I* found a job far away from those damn ships, *I* moved us out without him knowing where we were going, *I* cut him off completely from our lives. If I can't blame myself, who *can* I blame?" She clears her throat. "Now listen, and listen good. Your past is depressing you, Erlana. You still haven't put those three men behind you."

"But I have!" Haven't I?

"They may have put *you* behind them, but you're still holding on to them."

"But I'm not! Until Juan Carlos called, I hadn't thought about them at all."

"You're still holding on to them, Erlana. Juan Carlos's mama died, a woman you have never even met, and all you can talk about is how it's affecting Juan Carlos and how much you wish you had been there for *him*. You didn't say boo about his mama at all."

She's right.

"And then Bobby died, a little boy you took care of for a long time, and all you can talk about now is *not* talking to Roger."

She's right again.

"You need to go to them."

"That's not going to happen."

"It has to happen. Otherwise, you're going to be depressed like me for a long time."

I hate this feeling, but . . . "What do I say? What do I say to three men whom I have hurt so badly?"

"Say what I wanted and *still* want to say to your daddy. I made a terrible mistake, a terrible, terrible mistake. I'm sorry, and I want you back in my life to stay."

Whoa. I can't say all that! "But Juan Carlos has a fiancée, and I'm sure that Karl and Roger—"

"Erlana Joy Cole, will you just shut up and use your head for a moment?"

Damn. "Sorry."

"If they're seeing any women, it's on the rebound, right? If they loved you as much as you think they did, these women are only temporary fixes, right?"

Mama didn't see Monique kiss Juan Carlos. That looked like a permanent fix to me. "Right."

"So go to them."

Damn, my hands are sweaty just thinking about it. "I'm scared, Mama."

"I don't believe that for a second. You've never been scared of anything."

"But I am," I say in a small voice.

"Okay, Erlana, what is the worst they can say to you?"

In Spanish? Plenty. "That . . . that they never want to see me again."

"Right."

"But I don't want them to say—"

"They *might*," she interrupts, "and you can't blame them if they do. You hurt three men you claimed to love. One, two, or all three may tell you to take a hike. Could you handle that?"

"I don't know, I just . . ." I just don't want to think about it. Losing them once was hard enough. Losing them forever? Can I risk that? "How is all this supposed to help me become unde-pressed?"

"You'll be able to get your life back from the past, Erlana. You'll be able to live again in the present, and you *will* have a life in the fu-ture."

I want to live again, but I'm still so scared.

"Now I'm . . . I'm sorry I yelled at you," she says.

"It's okay. I'm used to it, and don't take that the wrong way. I've been yelling at myself quite a bit these past four months."

"Well, don't listen to yourself too much, okay? You say things to yourself long enough, you'll start to believe them. Don't be like me. And, if you ever need to talk about anything, anything at all, just . . . call me, okay?"

"I will."

"And not just when you're depressed, you hear? I want to hear good things, too."

"Okay." I close my eyes. "I love you, Mama."

I hear a sob.

"Mama, I just told you a good thing. You're not supposed to cry." And now I'm crying. Geez. I need to buy Kleenex in bulk.

"You'll just have to say it more often so I don't cry so much."

"Okay. I love you, Mama."

"I love you, too, child. Now . . . go get 'em."

I read once that a good friend is someone who hears the song in your heart and sings it to you when you forget the melody.

Mama is and has always been my friend, humming the song in her heart.

Chapter 34

I have to go to the men who used to come to me.
And then I won't be depressed anymore.

It seems like a simple plan, but I bet it's not that simple.

I have no idea what to tell them.

God, I pray, *please give me the words.*

Oh yeah. *And God, help me shut up and think sometimes, and if I do yell at myself, help me not to listen.*

I start with Karl. He was my boo first. He should be the first man I see.

I first try paging him on my lunch break at PH, but the number is no longer in service. I try directory assistance and come up empty for a Karl Henderson. "What about K. Henderson?" I ask.

"There are seven of those."

Whoa. "Um, I don't have a phone book handy." The ones at PH are at least four years out-of-date. "Are all seven in the most recent phone book?"

"All but one."

Maybe that's him? "Is that the most recent listing?"

"Yes."

"Please give me that one."

"Hold for the number."

So, now I have a number for the most recent "K. Henderson" in Roanoke. I know it doesn't mean it's Karl, but what if it is? I punch in the number, hoping he'll answer.

"Hello?"

I am so floored by Karl's voice that I can't speak.

"Wait a minute. Lana, is that you? It sure is."

How did he—

He has caller ID. Karl has a phone with caller ID. Karl, who only used his pager long after it was considered cool to do so, has a *real* phone. Has Karl, my "Wind," blown into town for good? Maybe that deal he was hoping for came through. Maybe he already has his own store. "Uh, yeah, it's me, Lana. How you doin'?"

"All right."

"Good. Um, that's good, Karl. Listen, I really want to talk to you sometime soon about what happened."

"So come over." He gives me an address at Buck Run, an apartment complex in southwest Roanoke County near the Blue Ridge Parkway.

I blink. "You live there?"

"Yeah."

No way. "Um, my friend Izzie lives somewhere over there. You remember Izzie, don't you?"

"Sure, I remember 'Grandma.'"

I laugh.

"So," he says, "you coming over, or what?"

"I'm working right now, and I have practice after school, so—"

"I saw you on the sidelines during the PH-Fleming game."

Which we lost badly, and since Karl graduated from Fleming, he's bound to gloat. "You did?"

"You were so pissed!"

Ha, ha, very funny. "They were crackback and cut blocking on us all night, and the refs wouldn't call shit."

"Even if the refs made those calls, y'all still would have lost."

True. We still don't have much of an offense, and our defense gets tired from being on the field for most of the game. We're exhausted in the fourth quarter. "I can come by around six."

"That'll work."

I really shouldn't say this, but . . . "Should I bring dinner?"

"Nah. I've got that covered. Later." *Click.*

That went *much* better than I expected! And I'm in such a good mood later at practice that I have my defensive ends only run ten sets of hills after practice. I usually make them run twenty after a loss.

Buck Run is nestled in the woods, which is the last place I'd expect to find citified Karl. I pull into an empty spot and get out, expecting to see Karl's Blazer somewhere. I don't. Hmm. Maybe they have garages somewhere around here, too.

Or he's not here. Hmm. Maybe this is a way for him to get some revenge on me. I hope not, but he might still be trying to be hard to find.

I walk up to the door with the number he gave me and knock. A moment later, Karl is standing at the door looking all good with his six-packed, tattooed—

"You know we have nothing to talk about, right?" he says.

"I just wanted a chance to explain. Can I come in?"

He steps out, closing the door behind him. "What's to explain? You played us all, you got what you wanted, and it's over."

But he was so nice on the phone! "It's not that simple, Karl."

"Look, I'm with someone else right now."

Figures. My heart sinking, I look past him to the door. "Is she in there right now?"

"No, but if you're in there when she gets back, I'm going to catch some hell."

I didn't come for a fight with Karl or his new woman. "Okay. Can we talk out here?"

He shrugs.

I turn away and look at the trees. "Do I know her?" I look back at him.

He folds his big arms across that big ol' smooth chest of his. "You said you were going to explain."

He doesn't want to answer my question, which means that either I might know her or it's none of my business. Which it isn't.

But I'm curious. And jealous. "Right, um, for what it's worth, I just wanted you to know . . ." No. That's not the way to start this.

"What?"

I sigh. Time to level with him. "I came over here to see if you still wanted me, Karl. I came over to see if maybe we could try again. I came over to find out if you still had feelings for me." There, I said it. It's his turn.

"What goes around comes around, huh? Why would I want you after what happened? Huh? And why would I want you when I don't even know who you are? Do *you* know who you are?"

I don't answer because I don't *have* a good answer.

"Because after talking to Juan and Roger, I found out that you were a completely different person with each of us. Were you *ever* yourself? And did you love *any* of us?"

"I loved you all."

"Right." He looks over my head. "Look, she'll be back any minute, so say your piece and get to stepping."

His words are making me shiver. "Is there anything you miss about me?"

"Miss about you? Hell no. You were always paging me, digging into my business, trying to control me. You were holding me back."

"From what?"

"From my future, girl. You didn't believe in me, in what I was trying to accomplish. You didn't respect me, and you didn't respect my career. You remember that deal I was working on?"

"Yeah."

"Well, it's happening. I'm about to open my first store."

"Yeah? What will it be called?"

"My Bag."

That's an easy name to remember. "I like the name. Where will it be?"

"In a new strip mall at Shenandoah and Peters Creek, you know, where that Food Lion is. High traffic, lots of parking, no competition whatsoever. There's a Subway to my left and a check-cashing place to my right, a Chinese takeout two doors down. I'll be having my grand opening two weeks before Christmas so I can cash in on the holiday rush, and I already have plenty of orders. My Web site gets a couple thousand hits a day, and I have a couple dozen orders to fill and ship this week alone."

I can't believe what I'm hearing. "You have a Web site?"

"Yeah. MyBag-dot-com. I designed it myself. You should check it out."

If I had only . . . No. Don't listen to yourself, Lana. You're supposed to be living in the present now. "Things are certainly working out for you." I sigh. "I'm sorry we didn't work out."

"I'm not."

Ouch. "So, would you have broken it off eventually?"

He laughs. "Hell, I didn't even know we were together. We kicked it for a while is all."

Damn, that's cold. "You weren't serious about me at all?"

"No. You were just a good time, Peanut. That's all." Karl then throws back his head and sighs. "Shit."

I turn and see a fancy black conversion van with chrome wheels and lots of dark-tinted windows come into the parking lot. "That's her?" And she drives a conversion van?

"Yeah. That's her."

"Where's your Blazer?"

"I traded it in on that. I got a nice deal on it at Berglund thanks to Juan."

But of course. "If you want me to go, I'll go."

"Nah. It's too late. She's already seen you."

The van parks. . . .

And Izzie gets out.

No . . . way.

I look again at the door. This *is* Izzie's apartment. I had visited her only once or twice, when she first moved in. Was the door that color then? It's been painted or something. They've . . . moved in together, just like that, and she's at least two years older than I am. Does Karl even live here? Or maybe they both have their own phones at this address? That makes sense. He'll need a phone for his business, right?

I'm so confused.

Izzie doesn't look confused. She walks right up to Karl and gives him a deep soul kiss right there in front of me. She then turns, grinds her little booty against him, and smiles at me. "Wow, look at you, Lana, all skinny and shit."

No . . . way.

Karl has rubbed off on Izzie in the worst way! She has both ears pierced every which way, and one of her eyebrows is pierced. Is that a tattoo on her neck? I wonder what else is pierced or tattooed. I shudder. No. I don't want to know.

She takes Karl's hands and wraps his arms around her. "Boo, you didn't tell me Lana was coming over."

"She just dropped by out of the blue," Karl says. "And she was just leaving."

"Boo, why haven't you asked Lana inside our apartment?"

Did she say "our" a little louder? Of course she did. "I was just leaving, Izzie." I say. "It was good to see you."

"Oh, do stay," Izzie says.

I see Karl shaking his head slightly. I *know* it's not a good idea, Karl. You don't have to shake your head at me. "That's okay, Izzie. I have a long drive home."

She steps closer to me. "Notice anything different about me, Lana?"

That suddenly you look like a pavement princess? I point to her eyebrow. "That's new."

Izzie turns to Karl. "Go on in, boo. I'll cook for you in a few."

Karl escapes, closing the door quietly behind him. Yeah, Karl has dinner taken care of, and no wonder he has his own store. I'll bet Izzie is paying most of his start-up costs.

Izzie leans in like a conspirator. "I got my nipples done, too. Wanna see 'em?"

"No, thank you."

I have *got* to stop blinking. Is my head shaking? It is. I'm almost having a seizure.

"I've been meaning to invite you over, but Karl was against it for obvious reasons. I hope you aren't offended."

"No. I'm not offended." Shocked, yes. Offended? No. "So, how long have you two been, uh, been . . ."

"Together?"

I nod.

"Let's see . . . three months now."

That was quick. He left me and went to her almost immediately. Damn. She got a phone call that night. . . . Shit! I guess I *was* just a good time to Karl! He hooked up with Izzie later that night? Did I ever really have Karl all to myself?

"And guess what?"

I don't want to guess.

"I'm pregnant."

My legs turn to jelly.

"Now, I know what you're thinking, and you can stop thinking it. I didn't trap him. You know I have a thing about . . . fluids. Karl wanted this child, and I was only too happy to oblige him."

Damn. He really meant what he said to me that night. He really wanted to settle down and start a family.

The door opens, Karl popping his head outside. "You gonna be long, Isabel? I'm starving."

"Oh, boo, I was just telling Lana the good news about our child."

Karl's eyes zero in on mine. "You mean the *great* news, right?"

"Of course," Izzie says. "The doctor says I'll be showing in another month, and I can't wait. I'll have to get my belly button ring taken out, of course. I wouldn't want to have my belly button pop out with the ring in there. The ring might kill someone!" She laughs.

Yeah. How interesting that would be. Ha ha. How funny.

"There's another one a little lower, you know," she whispers. "I'll have to take that one out before the birth."

Oh wow. That is just . . . so gross. Now what? "Well, I'm glad that things have worked out for you two."

"Did Karl tell you about the store?"

I nod.

"Girl, I can't wait till that place takes off, so I can quit working. Did he tell you about his Web site?"

I nod.

"It is the bomb, girl. Every kind of bag you can imagine. And once a customer places an order, we get a printout of what to send and where, and the money is deposited electronically into our checking account."

And *they* have a checking account.

"We're using our second bedroom to store all the bags now." She smiles and looks at Karl. "That's going to be the baby's room. Girl, Karl is blowing up!"

Yeah. Izzie is blowing up, Karl is blowing up, and the Web site is the bomb. I have so much . . . artillery going off in my head right now.

"Well, I have to go," I say. "I'm glad things are working out."

"And you brought us together," Izzie says. "We *should* be thanking you."

Yeah, right. This is all going so fast! I haven't said what I've come to say yet. I look at Karl. "Karl, I want you to know how sorry I am. You were—are—a good man, and I was stupid. I wish you both lots of happiness."

And I do. I want Karl to be happy. He wanted a child, and I didn't.

"You be sure to come visit often, okay, especially after the baby is born," Izzie says. "And call me sometimes. Maybe we can have a girls' night out or something."

"Yeah. Sure." Not likely.

And as I'm walking away, I can't help but think, *Will the baby come out pierced and tattooed, too?*

Chapter 35

I have to get out of the house. If I sit in there any longer beating myself up over Karl, I'll go crazy. He had been homing in on me—on *us*—with his plans, and we were *this close* to making it. And now Izzie is getting the good loving I used to get, and Karl is getting . . . Izzie. And Izzie's money, too.

Karl said I was too controlling, so I took an online survey to see if that was true.

It was.

Whenever Karl and I went out, which was rare, I always got my way. Whenever we watched movies at his place, I held the remote. Whenever we ate out, I chose the restaurant. And all that calling I did to him, all those pages—I was a control freak with Karl, hardly spontaneous at all. The survey told me that I would miss out on great chances for love.

And I have.

I did the same survey with Juan Carlos and Roger in mind, and I wasn't nearly as compulsive or controlling. In fact, I let Juan Carlos control me almost completely, but with Roger, we shared. Roger and I had a balance. I don't usually take much stock in surveys, online or otherwise, but this one . . . This one was absolutely right.

On a warm, sunny, Indian summer October day, I decide to get out of the house and visit Bobby's grave to spruce it up. We've been having lots of rain and wind, and I'm worried that leaves have covered his grave. That wouldn't be right. I mean, you lay down for your eternal rest, and a bunch of crunchy orange, red, and brown. leaves block your view of the mountains and the sky.

Okay, okay. Yes, I want to check on Bobby's grave, but mainly . . . mainly, I want to see Roger.

When I stand over Bobby's plaque in the ground, "Beloved son and friend to many" shines brightly. There isn't a single fragment of a leaf, a stray blade of grass, or even any dust on the plaque. Roger obviously takes good care of these. The grass around the plaque seems cut with scissors, not a blade out of place. A little sconce above the plaque contains a fresh arrangement of orange and yellow mums.

"Hey, Bobby Fischer," I whisper. "How ya doin'?"

I hear the rumbling of a tractor in the distance.

Roger.

"I'm . . . I'm okay."

The rumbling grows louder.

"You know, Bobby, this is a good day to play some football, huh? Not too hot, not too cold, just enough of a breeze to make passes interesting." It might be a little too cold to play naked tackle football, though, but I don't tell Bobby that.

I sit, tracing Bobby's name, the rumbling growing even louder.

"Who am I going to play chess with now? It's no fun playing by myself. I always win, you know? I need some competition."

I see Roger's head in all its blazing orange first, then the tractor, then the little trailer behind him.

"I wonder if Roger plays chess. You think he does, Bobby?"

Roger sees me, and the tractor stops about fifty yards away. Has he shaved off his "man-gina"? He has. I like it.

"Should I wave at him, Bobby? Hmm. I don't want to seem needy."

Who am I kidding? I *am* needy.

I wave.

Roger waves back.

I feel several goose bumps creeping up my legs. "Should I go to him, Bobby? Should I go talk to him?"

Roger and the tractor leap forward, and he moves down another row away from me.

That was pretty obvious.

"The chess game begins," I say, laughing. "And white moved first." I laugh again. "That's Roger, Bobby. I like him. A lot. He's a really good man, and he used to play games with me, football mostly."

And maybe we're playing games again.

I watch Roger work on another gravesite, this one marked by a huge marble headstone. He parks the tractor and leaps off snatching a weed eater and cranking it up. In a few sweeps, the grass around the base of the headstone is gone. He turns off the weed eater, laying it in the trailer and withdrawing a rake. He rakes up the clippings and puts them in a black plastic bag. Then he shines up the front of the headstone with a cloth. He pulls a clump of wilted flowers from the sconce, gets a fresh bunch of mums from the trailer. . . . He's very efficient.

"Well, Bobby, it's my move. I'll visit you soon."

I stand and walk as slowly as humanly possible back to my car, cutting across where Roger has already been. Roger and his tractor cruise off in the opposite direction.

He's making defensive moves, taking his time. I can't blame him. He's playing careful, biding his time. I suppose I can do that, too, though it's not in my nature. I really want to run past all these dead people, tackle his ass, and kiss his freckles off.

In a cemetery? That wasn't on our list. Hmm. We'll have to add it.

When I get to my car, one of my windshield wipers holds a single white rose. I pick up the rose and smell it. Fresh. I look around, hoping to see Roger watching me. I'm sure he is. This is so sweet. But it's white, not red. Red is for love. What's white for?

Oh yeah. White is for friendship.

He wants to be friends. What's that old saying? Oh yeah. "Make new friends and keep the old. One is silver, one is gold."

I'm all up for a golden friendship.

I am definitely coming back here soon.

I mean, it's not every day a living girl gets a fresh flower in a cemetery.

Chapter 36

The football season mercifully over—though I did get Curtis, the Bony One, on the all-district team—and the weather getting colder, I have to get the woodstove going. And once it gets going (and the smoke dissipates some), it puts out a nice, even heat and gives me hot water all the time. I'm so glad that I chopped so much wood this summer. The wood smell is nice, Jenny's dollhouse is cozy, and all that's missing is someone who smells nice to cozy up to.

I need to see Juan Carlos.

I drive up Williamson Road to Berglund after school. I figure that Juan Carlos is married by now, so maybe he'll take some time to talk to me.

After being molested by several salesmen trying to sell me a Chevy Trailblazer "with a rear DVD-player for your kids," I get to the service department. "I'm here to see Juan Carlos," I say. I don't say, "Is Juan Carlos available?"

I'm on a mission, and I won't take no for an answer.

Juan Carlos comes up to me, wiping his greasy hands on a blue towel, and we walk out of the waiting area to the parking lot outside. He leans on an old Chevy van. I don't see a wedding band, but I doubt he'd wear one while working on cars.

"How have you been?" I ask.

"I have work to do," he says.

I have work to do, too. "Fifteen minutes. That's all I'm asking."

"So . . . talk."

This is going well. "I just wanted a chance to explain."

"And to apologize?"

"Yes. I'm sorry for what happened."

He nods.

"You never would have married me, anyway."

He puffs out his chest. "I might have. I was faithful to you."

"Would you really have married me? And be honest."

He looks away, squinting that cute squint of his. "No."

"I thought so." My heart thuds. "Why not?"

"You are not Catholic. You do not speak Spanish. You do not like to do what I like to do."

He didn't like making love to me? "Such as?"

"I like to salsa, to mambo. I love to dance, but where we went that time, that was not dancing. I am a good dancer, and you would have been impressed."

I nod.

"I also like to play soccer and watch soccer on the television. I do not like American football at all."

Or, evidently, American football players.

"I like to work on cars. I like to drink Corona, and I do not need the lime. I love to eat. We have nothing in common. We are so different."

"I like to eat."

He doesn't respond.

"Would you have married me if I was pregnant?"

"Yes, but only if you had been pregnant. That would have been the only reason. I must go back to work."

"You didn't love me at all?"

He steps closer, his voice hoarse. "Yes, I did, Lana, like my heart was on fire all the time. You do not know how hard it is to have a dying mother and a need for a living woman. She was getting sicker all the time we were together, and I did not notice as much because of you. I could have saved her if I had been paying attention."

Whoa. It's time to go. "I am so sorry, Juan Carlos. I want you to know that you are a good man, and any woman would be lucky to have you. I mean that."

"Lahhh-na," he says, and my heart hurts. "I hurt for so long after you hurt me."

"I'm sorry. That's all I can say. Is Monique good to you?"

He smiles. "She will learn. I will teach her."

"Are you, um, married yet?"

"Not yet. Soon. I must go."

I grab his arm. "Why did you ask me to your mama's wake?"

He sighs and looks away. "I wanted to see you."

"Why?"

"To see if my heart was still on fire for you." He looks back at me. "I felt no fire."

"Oh." I shouldn't have asked.

"Goodbye." He walks away.

"Bye."

I had wondered earlier what was wrong with this man, and I think I've finally figured it out.

Juan Carlos was too good for me.

That's what was wrong with him.

He was just too good.

Chapter 37

Two down.

I'm still not sure about the third man, but at least I have a white rose in a vase on my kitchen table because of him.

Most of the leaves outside have fallen or been blown away by the November winds, so checking Bobby's grave on Election Day for debris seems a stretch. Mama will know what to do.

"You want a reason to visit a grave?" she asks.

"Well, yeah."

"You're paying your respects, right?"

"Yeah." And I'm hoping a redheaded tractor driver pays more attention to me this time than last time. "But I can only pay my respects for so long, you know? I need something that will keep me there a while, until Roger notices me."

"Plant bulbs, then."

"Huh?"

"Plant bulbs around the grave so they'll come up in the spring. If you plant the right mix, flowers will bloom there throughout most of the year."

"It's a great idea. How do you do it?"

She explains, and yes, I take notes. I don't want to screw this up.

I carry a spade, some white powdery bulb food, and a garbage bag full of every bulb I could find at Home Depot to Bobby's grave on an overcast, chilly day. Bobby's plaque and the area around it still look pristine. I check a few other plaques and graves to see if maybe Roger is giving Bobby's resting place special care, but they are all just as spiffy.

Then I start digging, following Mama's instructions not to "plant them too shallow or the squirrels will eat them." I don't have a plan, really, mainly because I mixed up all the bulbs. I could be planting a daffodil or a crocus or a tulip—it will just have to be a surprise. I even put several bulbs in the same hole, not because I'm tired, but because I'm curious what will happen this coming spring.

I'm almost halfway done when I hear a tractor. I don't look up, and keep digging. Eventually I smell the exhaust. I still don't look up. I drop three bulbs into my latest hole, sprinkling them with the bulb food. Then I see boots, Roger's boots.

Instead of saying, "What are you doing?" or "You can't do that," Roger takes the spade from me and digs another hole. I look up at him, and he's intent on digging his hole, no expression on his face. I drop in three more bulbs, sprinkle them with bulb food, and he pushes the dirt into the hole, tamping it down with the spade.

"This is a good idea," he says.

I'll have to thank Mama. Her idea brought him within a few inches of me.

"If everyone did this," Roger says, "we'd save a fortune on fresh flowers."

He digs, I drop and powder the bulbs, and he fills in the dirt, his face a study in concentration. We do this until I'm left with one little bulb. I look around the disturbed ground for the perfect place, pointing at a spot centered above Bobby's name. He digs, I drop the bulb and the powder, and he fills in the dirt. We're pretty damn efficient.

"Done," he says.

I hope not. "Thank you." And now for my next move. "How've you been?"

"I am fine. How are you?"

So formal. "I wanted to talk to you after Bobby's funeral."

"So why didn't you?"

"It wouldn't have been appropriate."

"Not appropriate to talk to an old friend?"

He said "old" friend. Hmm. Does "old" mean I'm no longer his friend? "I guess I should have spoken to you." But what would I have said? "I, um, I never had a chance to answer your question, the one you asked that night before . . ." The end.

"It's okay, and in a way, I'm glad you didn't get the chance. You see, um, I'm engaged now."

I have no words. I am numb. How is this possible? What, was I the training bitch for these three men? I am oh for three: swing and a miss, strike three; wide left; incomplete pass on fourth down. . . .

"Lana?"

"Um, yeah. Well." I can't think! "Um, who's the lucky girl?"

"Someone I *know*."

Oh, he said that with attitude, but I deserved that. I really should walk away, but I have to ask, "When's the wedding?"

"Soon."

Oh, I don't know, why not have a *triple* wedding, where I give all three of you away? You'll save a fortune on flowers, and you'll even get a nice group discount on the tuxedos. "Well, um, that's . . . that's nice." They have all gotten on with their lives, so why can't I? I stand, and slap some dirt from my hands. "I guess I'm done." In *many* more ways than one.

"Have you had that dream again?" he asks.

What? "What dream?"

"The one with the milk chocolate baby."

What a time to bring this up! The man has just destroyed any hope I had of getting one of my men back, and he's asking about that dream? I can't tell him that I *have* had the dream, and that the last time, *she* had hair as bright as orange oak leaves.

"No. I don't have that dream anymore."

"Oh."

I don't think I have any dreams anymore.

"I miss talking to you like this," Roger says.

I miss this, too. "Yeah." We did have some good conversations. "It's been pretty quiet for me, too." I gather the garbage bag, what's left of the bulb food, and my spade. "I'll see you later." Though I'm pretty sure that I'll never see him again.

I feel a tug at my elbow.

"Why wasn't I enough for you, Lana?"

I don't have a simple answer for that one, but at least one of my men touched me. That's something.

"Why did you have to have two others on the side?"

I can't even turn to look at him.

"Why was I the last part of your love square or whatever it was?"

I turn because I finally have an answer. I focus on his boots. "You were the final piece to the puzzle, Roger. You were what was missing from the other two."

"So the other two guys weren't enough for you?"

"No."

"I completed the puzzle, huh?"

I look up and see him smile. "Yes. Roger, if it's any consolation—"

"It won't be," he interrupts, his smile vanishing.

No, I'm sure it won't. "I just wanted to say that I thought—think—about you the most. I even wear your boxers every now and then. I've, um, kept them clean. They kind of hang on me now. . . ."

He steps closer. "It wasn't my . . . *turn* that day, was it? I came over when I wasn't supposed to, huh?"

He had already had his "turn" the night before. "No, it . . . it was all kind of random, you know?"

"I don't know, and I'll never understand."

Nor will I. Nor will I. "Well, it wasn't easy."

"It ended easily enough."

Yeah, I'm standing in a cemetery just full of ends today. But I don't want this conversation to end. "Is she nice?" I ask.

"Who?"

"Your fiancée."

"Yes."

"And does she . . ." I have no right to ask this, but I have to know. "Does she satisfy you?"

"Sexually?"

Me and my big mouth. "Not necessarily. I meant—"

"She knows what to do."

"Sorry I asked."

"Glad I answered."

Ouch. How much lower can I get? "I . . . I better be going." I turn away from him, walking in the general direction of my car.

"Lana."

I don't turn, but I stop. "Yes?"

"Am I your last stop today?"

I turn. "What?"

He walks closer, his hands in his pockets. "I mean, have you already spoken to Juan and Karl?"

"Yes."

"And they wouldn't have you back?"

I shake my head. "Karl's with my ex-best friend Izzie, who is pregnant with Karl's baby, and Juan Carlos is going to marry a girl named Monique soon."

"So I'm your last resort? Again?"

Why did I stop? I must have a need for abuse. "You're not my last resort, Roger. It's not like that."

"You could have fooled me. You fooled me in so many ways, Lana, or should I say, Peanut or Lahhh-na." He smiles.

Can I trust that smile? I have no choice. "Y'all must have had quite a conversation after you left me that night."

"We did." He laughs. "That was one of the weirdest nights of my life. Believe it or not, we stopped and tried to fix Juan's car. It was kind of good therapy. We gave up on it, though, mainly so Juan and Karl would stop arguing about the damn alternator. Juan rode with me, and we followed behind Karl—until his Blazer ran out of gas just a few miles down four sixty. Then . . . we all got in my truck and went to IHOP."

No way! "You went out for breakfast?" He has to be lying.

"I told you it was a weird night. We went to IHOP, and we were there from just before sunrise until almost lunchtime. We went back to Juan's car later with a new alternator. I'm surprised you did-n't hear us arguing later that day."

I must have been crying too loudly or something.

"We even decided to meet at IHOP every Sunday morning from then on."

I stare a hole in his head. "You what?"

He shrugs. "We . . . get together at IHOP, the three of us, every Sunday morning. It turns out that aside from you, we have a lot in common."

"You're kidding."

"It's not a Lana Haters Club anymore."

Ouch. "Anymore?"

"Oh, we still mention you now and then, but . . . mostly we just shoot the shit."

And to think that I brought them together for this weekly ritual.

"Karl . . . Karl's a good guy. A little rough, but he's funny as hell. And Isabel likes the Coach bags."

I roll my eyes. "They're knockoffs."

"Oh, she knows they are. The DVDs though. They pretty much suck."

"Yeah."

"Juan's a good guy, too. He tunes up my truck and Karl's van whenever they need it, even getting us discounts on parts."

My friends with benefits . . . are friends? Wait. They're friends who benefit each other. What kind of a three-headed monster have I created?

"We were all out just the other night watching some soccer match at Hooters. Juan knew every player on both teams, and the waitress he could have picked up that night was a knockout. He said, 'No, I must be faithful to Monique.'"

Roger has Juan Carlos's voice down pat. They have been spend-ing a *lot* of time together.

"You heard about his mama, right?" I ask.

"Yeah. That was sad. She was a nice lady."

"You met her?"

"Sure. We had a few cookouts over at Juan's house. Best chili I ever ate."

This is too much! I date and sleep with the guy, and I don't get to meet his mama. Roger eats breakfast with him, and he gets to meet his mama.

"Karl and I went to the wake."

Huh? "I didn't see you there."

"We saw you go in. We were getting gas across the street."

"Why didn't you come in while I was there?"

He shrugs. "Mainly because we didn't want to be part of the fire-works. Monique can be pretty evil sometimes."

Don't I know it.

"And, we couldn't understand why Juan wanted you there at all, so we gave you two some privacy."

Today is getting to be one of the weirdest days of my life. I need to change the subject. "So, how did you meet your fiancée?"

"Lisa?" He smiles.

That jolts me, and not just because he said her name. It was the smile that followed his saying her name.

"Lisa is our favorite waitress at IHOP."

Roger, the future interment director of Fairview Cemetery, and Lisa, the IHOP waitress. How quaint. One serves you food that will one day kill you, and the other plants you. "So you've only known her for, what, a couple of months?"

He shrugs. "I only knew *you* for a couple of months before I asked *you* to marry me."

Oh yeah.

"Yeah. Lisa's something. And she knows *everything* there is to know about you."

Great.

"Now at first, I didn't want to ask Lisa for her phone number, but Karl and Juan insisted. I thought they were trying to weed me out of the equation so they'd have a better chance to get back with you, but that wasn't the case. Karl has Izzie, Juan has Monique. Anyway, that's when we all agreed never to be with you again, no matter what."

They actually made a damn agreement!

"Karl called me the night you visited Isabel and him, and Juan called me when you visited him, you know, to warn me that you might be coming to see me."

I've been under surveillance. I don't know whether to be scared or pissed. "Did you tell them about the day you saw me here?"

"I didn't mention that to them. I mean, we didn't exactly speak to each other."

"We did share a wave, and you did put that rose under my wiper."

He smiles. "I did?"

"Yes."

"Oh yeah. I did. I must have had an extra to spare that day."

I feel like stomping my feet, I'm so mad! But I don't want to wake any of the dead around me. "Y'all actually have an agreement against seeing me?"

"We wrote it all out on a napkin and everything."

And it's written down! Of course it is! And on a damn IHOP napkin. "Well, that's, um, that's great. Just great." I start to walk directly to my car.

"Hey, sorry," says Roger, trotting alongside. "But at least you'll know where Karl is every Sunday morning from now on."

How comforting. I juggle them, let them fall, and they collect themselves every Sunday morning at IHOP for a cholesterol breakfast.

"How's your ankle?"

I'm almost to my car. "It's fine."

"Will you play again next year?"

I shoot a look at him to see if he's being sarcastic. He seems genuinely interested. "I haven't decided."

"Well, you should. You're a good player, Lana."

Was that supposed to be a smart remark? Why can't I tell anymore?

I get to my car, throwing the bag, the bulb food, and the spade into the backseat.

"Wait," he says.

"What?" I say.

Then . . . Roger looks me up and down slowly, and suddenly I feel self-conscious. "And you *look* good, too, Lana."

"Thanks, um, Roger. Bye." I get in the car.

He pantomimes rolling down the window. What else? I roll down my window.

"You really ought to come out here after the first snow."

Why would I want to do that?

He waves his arm over the entire cemetery. "You'll see white fields as far as your eyes can see."

"I'm, um, I'm sure it's beautiful. Bye."

I start up my car and drive off, talking to the dead people I pass.

"Y'all have it easy," I say.

Chapter 38

I t was *only* five months!
Five freaking months!

Twenty weeks and Roger is engaged, Juan's marrying Monique, and Karl and Izzie are expecting a child. I thought they were better men than that! They leave me and fall all to pieces going after a permanent piece. I was the best thing in their lives. . . .

And they were the best things in mine.

I want them all back!

I know I can get Karl to dump Izzie. I know everything about her, and most of it is scary. She plucks her eyelashes and uses false ones. When she takes them off, she looks like a black gecko. She has a false tooth held in her mouth by a bridge. If that bridge should ever fail, she'll be missing one of her top front teeth. And, she has the hairiest toes I've ever seen! I swear she could braid them. Karl wouldn't want her after I told him all that.

Except for the baby.

Which Karl wants.

No.

They seem happy. They have what I want.

Okay, what about Juan Carlos? Roger said that Juan Carlos *could* have picked up a waitress at Hooters. I'm sure I can make Monique jealous enough about that to break it off with him. I'll just go to Monique . . .

Nah.

She might be Haitian and cut me with a machete or something.

And as for Lisa, I almost want to drop in on them at IHOP one Sunday morning just to tell them how childish they're all being. I'd tear up that little napkin, and I'd get to see Lisa in the flesh.

Today is Tuesday. Five days until Sunday. Hmm.

I *could* go to IHOP and talk about my *boyfriend* Roger McDowell in front of Lisa, and then Lisa would be suspicious or break it off with Roger, and . . .

No. That happens only in the movies or on stupid sitcoms. Or in middle school.

I'll just . . . drop in. Yeah. As in right now. So what if it's lunchtime.

I drive from the cemetery to IHOP, slam the Rabbit's door closed, throw open one of the restaurant's double doors, and—

Damn. There are a lot of people here for lunch at a breakfast place.

Only in Roanoke.

While I'm waiting to be seated, I stare at every waitress's name tag and don't see a single "Lisa."

"One?" the hostess finally says.

Oh, rub it in, why don't you? "Yes. Is Lisa working today?"

"She only works early mornings."

Shit.

I follow the hostess to a booth and sit, not looking at the menu. A waitress named . . . Allie comes over with a pot of coffee. "Coffee?"

"Sure."

She pours the cup. Allie looks no older than nineteen, so she might know Lisa.

"Um, Allie, are you a friend of Lisa's?"

"We've worked together some. You know her?"

Shit. I need information. I don't need to be answering any questions from gum-cracking waitresses like Allie from the Valley. "Um, yeah. I know her from high school."

Allie blinks. "You don't look that old."

Lisa is older than me, or at least she seems so to Allie. White folks sometimes have trouble telling black folks' ages, so I don't know how to react. "Thank you," I say.

"You really went to high school with old Lisa Lou?"

Old Lisa *Lou?* Whoa. She must be really old. Roger, I hardly know you anymore! "Oh, I work at Patrick Henry. That's what I meant when I said high school." That was weak.

Allie squints. "I think Lisa's kids graduated from Northside."

Old Lisa Lou is an older woman with children who *graduated* from high school already? What does that make Lisa? In her late forties at least? Whoa. I look up at Allie. "Perhaps we're talking about different Lisas."

"We must be."

"Yeah."

"You ready to order?"

I'm not even hungry. "Bring me . . . a stack of pancakes. To go."

What am I doing? Who orders pancakes to go after waiting in line at lunchtime at an IHOP?

I'm losing it. I swear I'm losing it.

I call Mama when I get back to Jenny's dollhouse while I eat the coldest, soggiest pancakes I have ever eaten. "Mama, Roger is engaged to a woman *your* age."

"And?"

"Mama, that's at least a twenty-year age difference." Unless Lisa squirted them out when she was fourteen. And with a name like Lisa Lou, she may have squirted them out earlier than that. "Twenty *years*, Mama." And now *I'm* saying things twice.

Sigh.

I'm becoming my mama.

"So?" Mama says.

"So?" Mama's not being very helpful tonight. "Don't you think that's weird?"

"No."

Three one-word answers in a row. "Is anything wrong?"

"No."

Make that *four* one-word answers in a row. What's up with her today? "Well, I think it's weird, and I'm going to IHOP Sunday morning to . . ." To do what, exactly?

"You're going to the IHOP on Sunday morning?"

"Yes."

"To cause trouble, huh?"

"Yes."

"Well, at least get your hair done. I gotta go." *Click.*

This *is* the weirdest day of my life. My mama *never* hangs up on me. What could she be doing that's more important than hearing me rant and rave? I put up with all her rantings and ravings all those years! She should at least find a few minutes to hear mine!

She did say I should do my hair. . . . Oh, and my nails.

A makeover.

Yeah.

That's right.

I need a makeover so I can be smoking-hot good-looking on Sunday morning. I will put Lisa to shame, I will put Izzie to shame, and I will put Monique to shame. My three ex–friends with benefits will be salivating more from me than from their eggs, bacon, and toast. They will all regret not coming back to me.

I giggle.

I've never really ever been girly like this before.

It's kind of a new feeling, and I don't even know how to go about being girly. Do I need to go to a spa? I look at my fingernails. I at least need a manicure. I've never had one of those. Do I dare get a pedicure, too? I know that *I* wouldn't do *my* toes. Yuck.

I flip through the Yellow Pages and find several listings for local spas offering half- and full-day treatments. Only one, St. Pierre Salon Spa and Academy, lists its prices.

Damn.

Twenty bucks for a manicure sounds reasonable, but forty bucks for a pedicure? They're the same number of digits! And the nails are smaller on my toes, and one toenail is even missing! Will I get a ten percent discount for the missing nail?

And what the hell is a Lavender Body Scrub with a Seaweed Wrap, and why does it cost fifty bucks? Microdermabrasion for a hundred ten? A glycolic peel for sixty? What the hell is a glycolic peel? It sounds painful, and you want me to pay you sixty bucks for some pain?

I'm not calling them.

Instead, I call Zee's Salon and Day Spa on the outside chance that they have more reasonable prices than St. Pierre. Zee's was, after all, sponsor of the Miss Virginia Pageant in 2003 and was voted "Best Hair Styling Salon" by *The Roanoker* magazine.

Which doesn't say much. *The Roanoker* magazine says that Texas Tavern, a grimy little diner downtown that serves aged chili and cheesy westerns (mystery meat covered with eggs), is one of the best places to eat in town.

"Zee's Salon."

"Yes, I'm thinking of getting a complete makeover. Do y'all have any package deals?"

"We sure do."

A hundred or less, and I'm in there.

"We have something we call the 'Great Escape.' With it you get a full-body massage, a classic facial, a classic or French manicure, a classic pedicure, a mineral-salt wrap, and a shampoo and style, all for only three hundred dollars."

The price is high, and so is she. "Um, I don't think I'm going to need all that." What the hell is a mineral-salt wrap?

"We also have something we call 'Zee's Special.' This includes a mini-massage, paraffin manicure and pedicure, a facial, scalp massage, shampoo, and style, for two hundred."

She's still high. I am a working woman! "Um, well, I'm not sure—"

"How about what we call 'The Athlete in You'?"

At least the name suits me. "What do I get with that?"

"You'd get a facial, manicure, pedicure, scalp massage, haircut, and style, for one-fifty."

D-damn. "Look, I'm on a tight budget, so . . ."

She sighs. "We have something called the 'Time Out,' a mani-cure and pedicure for sixty."

The same total price as the other place. Geez! "I'll, uh, I'll have to call you back."

When I decide I don't want to eat for a month.

Damn.

How can I look fly on the cheap? I mean, I can shave my legs pretty closely for free and put in my own perm for about ten bucks. And if I need a facial, I can use the mud in my yard. And the average emery board does fine for my fingers and toes.

Maybe Mama will know what to do. I call her. "Mama, I need a makeover."

"Yeah?"

"Yeah." And quit giving me one-word answers.

"You know I've been dreaming that this day would come for a long time."

"Huh?"

"All you have to do is come over Saturday, and I'll do you proud."

Ah, no. "Um, Mama, I was kind of hoping you'd float me a loan so I could go to a day spa."

"A what?"

"A day spa. I'll only need"—gulp—"three hundred dollars." I hold my breath.

Mama laughs for a long, *long* time.

"Mama, come on. I'll even let you go with me."

She still laughs.

"Okay, two hundred."

She laughs louder.

"A hundred?"

She stops laughing. "You're doing all this to go to an IHOP on a Sunday morning so you can cause some trouble with three men who don't want to be with you anymore?"

Yeah. It does sound ridiculous. "I want to be da bomb, Mama."

"I can do all that for you."

Can she? "You can give a manicure and a pedicure?"

"A manicure, yes. I am a whiz with an emery board. You're on your own with your toes."

Figures. "What about a facial?"

"Child, you have flawless skin. All you need is some cleaning and a little makeup."

I shudder. Mama used to, um, "paint" me when I was in middle school. "I don't know, Mama."

"Then . . . come over Friday night and we'll practice. If you don't like what you see, I'll pay . . ."

Please say three hundred.

"I'll pay *half* of what it would cost at that spa of yours."

Which would leave me with The Athlete in You. I can deal with that. "Okay. I'll be over Friday night."

"Good. See you then. Goodbye."

It couldn't hurt, could it?

Chapter 39

"Mama, that hurts!"

"Hush up, girl, I'm only trimming your ends."

"You're pulling my hair too hard!"

"You want them uneven?"

"No. Just be gentle, okay?"

She chuckles. "You've always been tender-headed."

And this is the *easy* part.

"When's the last time you had these raggedy ends cut?"

"I can't remember, but whenever it was, it didn't hurt like this—damn, Mama!"

She smiles. "All done."

I look at the hair on the kitchen floor and on the towel around my shoulders. "How much did you take off?"

"Enough."

I finger-comb what hair I have left. "You aren't going to put in a weave, are you?"

"You want a weave?"

"No." I brush out some of the stray hairs. "I want to look natural."

"Does that mean you don't want a perm?"

I hate perms with a passion. "I just want to shampoo and condition it. That's all." I still like looking a little wild.

She leans down to me, taking off the towel. "You *need* a perm."

"Well, I don't want one." I stand and pick hair from my shirt.

"It'll be easier to style later."

I don't answer.

"Less painful, too," she adds.

"No."

"Okay. It's your hair's funeral."

Mama first pulls out a bottle of Kiehl's Protein Concentrate Shampoo for normal to dry hair. "Jill Scott, the singer, she uses this stuff," Mama says.

"Do you?"

"No."

"So you bought it because . . ."

She opens the top and sniffs. "Smells nice."

"Why'd you buy it?"

She pushes me back to the sink. "I knew your hair would need all the help it could get."

After a relaxing shampoo and conditioning with something called Fudge Dynamite—"Oprah uses it," Mama tells me—I follow Mama to her bedroom and the vanity where I've parked all my Golden Hots.

"You don't expect me to use these, do you?" she asks.

"*I'm* doing this part," I say. No way I'm going to let her scar my tender head.

She sits on her bed. "And what exactly are you going to do?"

I look in the mirror. I still look basically the same as I've ever looked. "Something different."

"Uh-huh."

I pick up the blow-dryer. "I might flip it up on top and . . ." I look past my head in the mirror and see Mama looking pitiful. "Okay, Mama. What would *you* do to it?"

She picks up a bag sitting on her nightstand and empties all sorts of stuff, including a bunch of pink Velcro rollers, onto the bed.

"What's all this?" I ask, picking up a bottle of John Frieda Frizz-Ease Corrective Styling Mousse curl reviver and a container of Kérastase Nutritive Masquintense for fine hair.

"It's my first makeover of you. I had to research and read up a bit. Times sure have changed." She picks up some Matrix Sleek Look Styling Cream. "This is supposed to control your frizzies and your flyaways. You have plenty of those."

"All this stuff has to be expensive," I say.

"It's okay. I'm sure I'll find a use for this stuff after we're done. You ready?"

"I am." But is my hair?

Mama says to let my hair air-dry, so I sit there for an hour while she treats my ends with the Matrix cream. "Jada Pinkett Smith gets this done all the time," she tells me.

Mama has been reading *Essence.*

She applies the Frizz-Ease *and* the Kérastase. "Won't my hair explode?" I ask.

"I don't know. I hope not."

She then wrestles with all of my Golden Hots, using different sizes and curling my hair in different directions to make my fine hair look fuller in the back, diminishing my peanut head. She trims a few strays here and there. "Not bad."

"Are you going to use the rollers?"

"Not this time," she says.

"This time?"

"I know you'll be back, Erlana. And I also know you can't be paying three hundred dollars when you can get all this done here for free."

I look at the finished product and see my once-limp hair wrapped around my neck and touching my shoulders. I look . . . nice. I don't mean "fly" or "hot"—just . . . nice. Older. Wiser. Smarter. Sassy. Even . . . cute for real.

"Well?" Mama asks.

"It looks . . . nice."

"It'll look nicer once we fix your face."

"What's wrong with my face?"

"What isn't?" she says. "Come on. Your face needs fixing."

And fix we do. We first go to the bathroom, where Mama uses

Bioré Pore Perfect Blemish Fighting Ice Cleanser to clean my face. Why are the names of these products so damn long? They barely fit on the label. She then moisturizes my face with Nivea Visage Moisturizing Toner (finally a short name!).

She stares at the container, then scans my face. "Your skin should be glowing by now."

The face in the mirror *is* glowing more than normal. "My face looks fine to me."

She opens the medicine cabinet and pulls out Lancôme Aqua Fusion. "Let's try this stuff."

"Mama, how much did you spend on all this?"

"Too much if it doesn't do the trick."

Aqua Fusion makes my face shiny, all right. "Don't worry," Mama says. "I can tone that down some." After that, Mama does some magic with some of her old-timey makeup that gives me lips (I have lips!) and some damn sexy eyes.

"How'd you do that?" I ask.

"Magic," she says.

I look like someone else. Damn, I almost look like a girl.

She pushes me out of the bathroom and back to her bedroom. "Now, what are you planning to wear?"

"Whatever it is, it will be tight and show lots of skin."

Mama sighs. "Can't you for once just be classy?"

"I am classy."

She coughs. "You are classy now from the neck up, but we need to make the rest of you look just as classy."

"I want to be a queen."

"Uh-huh."

"Okay, a princess, then."

"I have a few possibilities in my closet." She goes to her closet and opens the double doors.

"I don't want to wear your old-fashioned clothes."

"They're not old-fashioned." She pulls out several outfits or dresses (I can't tell) that are still covered in plastic, laying them on the bed. "They're classy. Classy clothes never go out of style."

I stand and watch as she removes the plastic. Hey now, that's nice. Jade green with gold buttons—oh, burgundy. I love burgundy. Whoa, black satin! "What's all this?"

"I bought these for you once upon a time, you know, for dances, prom, graduation."

And she saved them all these years, just waiting for this moment. I didn't go to the prom, though I did have a date. I was in my "Black Power, White People Suck" mode during my senior year. I went to a "black prom" party—really an overgrown house party—instead. And during graduation, I wore rolled-up sweatpants and a Nike T-shirt under my gown.

"You saved these?" For when I would finally become a girl.

"Try"—she picks up the jade dress with the gold buttons—"*this* on for size."

"It can't possibly still fit."

"You stopped growing taller when you were sixteen, and you've lost enough weight since your injury. Try it on."

I slide into the dress, and it slides onto me. It's a little snug in the hips, mainly because I didn't have hips in high school.

"I can't tell," Mama says, "whether that dress lightens or darkens your eyes."

I pose in the long mirror on the back of Mama's door. "It lightens them. It's all the gold accents."

She returns to the closet. "I always knew there was a girl in there somewhere crying to get out." She pulls out a shoe box. "Your feet haven't grown, either. Try these on."

"Matching shoes?"

She nods.

I slip them on and . . . Oh, these are ouchy shoes. My pinkie toes are folded over the toes next to them. They look perfect with the dress, but . . .

"Just make sure you sit at a booth so you can kick them off, and whatever you do, get there early so they won't watch you trip all over yourself."

I smile. "Sounds like a plan."

She goes back to that closet. What's next? "It's going to be cold, so you'll need a coat." She pulls out a long, black, wool overcoat. "Classy women wear these."

And when I put that overcoat on and look in the mirror, I realize something: I never knew that a goddess lived inside me. I bet no one would suspect that this goddess would rather be sacking a lesbian quarterback or breaking number 39's kneecaps.

"This is all just too much!" I stand straighter. "How do I look?"

"Like a lady."

I feel tears forming behind my eyes, so I turn away from her. "I'm . . . I'm going to have to sleep standing up or something so I don't mess up my hair."

"You could stay the night here. It's closer to IHOP, right? When are you getting up on Sunday?"

"Four thirty."

"Why so early?"

"I didn't ask what time they met." I turn to her. "I want to get there before the sun rises."

"All right. As soon as you get up, I'll do a little more magic." She looks at her hands. "You could even stay tonight and tomorrow night. There's a college game on ESPN tonight, and Virginia Tech plays UVA tomorrow. Tech will probably win, but you never know when those two teams play."

I blink. "How . . ." I'm sure she checked the *TV Guide* for who's playing whom, but how does she know about Virginia's major football rivalry? Mama has been researching more than just hair and skin products.

"And I have Velveeta and salsa and those chips. . . ."

I smile. "Sure, I'll stay." I take off the overcoat. "What are you going to do?"

She takes the coat and hangs it up. "Something I've never done before." She laughs. "I'm going to watch a couple football games. You're going to explain what's going on, right?"

"I'd love to."

She checks her watch. "One game starts in fifteen minutes, Louisville versus somebody. We better get ready. . . ."

By the time we watch our *fifth* college football game twenty-four hours later on Saturday night, I have my mama screaming at the refs to "throw a damn flag!" and at the coach to "pass the ball, fool!" I doubt she understands everything about the game, and I'm sure she has better things to do, but for a little while at least, she tries to understand why I love football so much.

Sleeping in my old room in my old bed with its old posters of Venus and Serena Williams, Althea Gibson, and Jackie Joyner-Kersee isn't as hard as I thought it would be. I actually sleep pretty soundly, despite the fact that the room is half the size of my room at Jenny's dollhouse and that the sounds of traffic are so damn loud. But, I realize that Mama's house is almost as nice as my own.

Almost. I miss the sound of the wind.

At four thirty, at least six hours before I usually get up on a Sunday, I wake and sit at Mama's vanity while she rushes around me, turning me back into the classy lady in the jade dress. She pulls out a camera when she's through.

"No, Mama."

"I've never seen you look so beautiful, Erlana. I want to capture this memory."

I let her take my picture, standing right there in Mama's bedroom next to her dresser.

"Thank you, Mama."

"Thank you, Erlana Joy. Now, go get him."

I laugh. "Which one?"

"The way you look, you might bring back all three of them. But this time, choose one man, just one."

I fake a pout. "What if I come back alone?"

"You won't."

"But what if?"

"You won't. Trust me."

"But . . . what if?"

She pushes a strand of hair from my cheek. "I'll be here. You know I'll be here."

That's right. Mama will always be here waiting for me to come home. "Um, Mama, if I get lucky, I may not be coming back here at all today."

She shakes her head. "Just you make sure to hang up the dress before you all . . ."

"I will." I kiss her cheek. "Is this anything like the prom?"

"Well, it kind of is, except that no boy is picking you up. You're going to pick up a man."

"At IHOP."

She laughs. "At IHOP." She steps back and looks at me one more time. "Damn, you're fine."

I am.

And she's the reason.

She has *always* been the reason.

Chapter 40

It's five AM, and it's still dark outside.

I am sitting in a corner booth with a view of the front door.

I am a queen, an African lady, looking sharp, feeling sharp.

I have clear polish on my smooth and long nails, and I enjoy hearing them tapping on the table, a sound I don't think I've ever heard before.

I am ready.

And my ouchy shoes are down under the table somewhere, where they belong.

An old waitress shuffles up to my booth, flipping through an order pad. She smiles. "What can I get you?"

Her name tag reads "Lisa." *This* is Lisa? She has to be sixty! And is that an engagement ring on her finger? Roger's hooked up with a lady he can hook up with a burial plot? She's older, with kids as old or older than Roger is!

"Good morning," she says. "Are you awake, honey?"

"Oh. Sorry."

"What can I get you?"

"Are you the only Lisa who works here?"

Lisa looks up at the ceiling. "Yeah. Why?"

"This is going to sound very strange, but . . ." Do I bust out and ask if she's engaged to Roger? Classy ladies don't "bust out" on anyone. "Do three men come in here every Sunday morning?"

She looks up at the ceiling again. What's up there? "I'm sure they do. We have lots of regular guys."

"No, you'd remember these particular gentlemen. One is African-American, one is Hispanic, and one is white."

She nods. "Oh, them. Yeah. Great tippers." She waves the ring right in my face! "Got this in a tip, can you believe it? I tried to return it, but they said they couldn't think of anyone more beautiful to give it to. They said it was really for some girl who did them all wrong. You should hear the stories they tell about her."

Ouch. Classy ladies are not supposed to feel pain.

"Most of their stories are so far-fetched," Lisa says. "They can't all be true."

Believe it.

"They are some sweet boys, though. Do you know them?"

I nod.

Lisa blinks. Lisa looks at the ceiling. Lisa looks at me, blinking. "Are you Lahhh-na Peanut?"

Oh shit! Classy ladies are not supposed to even think profane thoughts. "Yes. I'm Lana."

Lisa smiles, and then she *sits* across from me. The nerve! "I have heard so much about you."

"I'll bet you have."

She looks side to side. "Did you really, uh . . . you know."

"Yes," I say. "I really, uh . . . you know."

She slaps the table and holds out her hand. "I want to shake your hand."

I hesitate, then shake her hand once.

"You must be really something to get all three of them at one time. I mean, I'm a born flirt"—she fluffs her hair—"so I can get some nice tips, right? But you . . ." She leans closer. "You are a hero to most of the single girls who work here, and even to some of the married ladies."

Oh my.

She checks her watch. "They're usually here by six, six thirty, sometimes seven."

"And where will they sit?"

She raps the table with her knuckles. "Right here where you're sitting. This is their booth."

I start to get up. "Why did the hostess sit me here, then?"

She shrugs. "She must have thought you'd be gone by the time they got here. Do you want to move?"

If I stay here, they'll come straight to me. "What do you think?"

She touches my hand. "I think you're a brave woman." She winks. "But if you stay right here, you'll be the bravest woman who ever lived."

I sit. "I will stay."

"Good. What can I bring you while you wait?"

I close the menu. "Three eggs over easy, a stack of pancakes with real butter and blueberry syrup, and a large glass of OJ."

Lisa stands. "Oh, I remember you. You're that football player who used to order that very thing."

I feel so welcome! "Yes."

"Putting your game face on, huh?"

"Yes, ma'am."

She winks again. "Be right out with your order." She takes a step, and then she steps back to me. "If you, um, see folks staring at you, it's, well, it's because I just can't contain myself!"

"It's okay," I say. "I'll try not to let you all down."

"You won't."

And then, I wait for my men to come to *me* at least one more time.

Chapter 41

W ell.
   Lisa is obviously not Roger's fiancée. She can't be. Roger could-
n't go from me to her even if he were the most desperate man on
earth. He just gave away my ring in a fit of spite. Lisa got the ring as
a tip. Roger isn't engaged, and maybe Monique isn't really marrying
Juan Carlos. She wasn't wearing an engagement ring at the wake,
was she? I would have noticed. Maybe it was just an act . . . though
the way she kissed him at the wake does make me feel a little
queasy. And since Izzie didn't look like she was showing, maybe . . .
   Six thirty. Ah, there's the sun.
   Well.
   It's possible they're all scamming me, getting their revenge the
only way they think will hurt me. Karl wouldn't let me into the apartment at Buck Run. Maybe he isn't living there at all, and the number I called was his cell phone or somewhere else.
   Seven.
   Well.
   Who'll be first through that door? Let's see. Karl is the night owl
of the bunch, so he probably hasn't even been home yet. He'll be
late. Juan Carlos? He was pretty punctual. I'll bet Roger rolls in first.
He is a morning person.

Seven fifteen.

The doors open and . . . Karl . . . with Izzie?

Hold up, here.

This is supposed to be a guys-only thing. What's Izzie doing here?

They bypass the hostess and walk directly up to my booth.

Izzie slides into my side of the booth, and I have to scoot down to the window. "Hey, girl," she says.

Karl says nothing and slides in next to Izzie. We must look strange, the three of us sitting on one side of a booth.

"Hey," I say. Do classy ladies say "Hey"? They do today. "Um, what are you doing here, Izzie? I thought this was only for the guys."

"Izzie and me had a late night," Karl says, and the two of them smooch! I feel the over-easy eggs getting uneasy in my stomach. "Hey, Lisa!" he yells. "Two coffees!"

"So," Izzie says, "how have you been?"

I check out her bling, and she's blinging more than I ever did, gold bracelets jingling and jangling on both wrists. "Fine."

She waves a gaudy diamond ring under my nose. "Guess what I have."

A gaudy diamond ring? "You got your nails done."

She sighs. "No, girl. I'm engaged."

"To whom?" I ask.

"Funny." She pulls up her shirt, right there in the IHOP. "I'm showing now. See?"

I see a little mound puckering out from her stomach. "Wonderful."

She pushes her shirt down and takes Karl's hand. "We're getting married next month. You'll come to the wedding, won't you?"

I look at Karl, but he's looking only at Izzie. Damn. He might actually be in love with her. "Sure. I wouldn't miss it." Mainly so I can see it really happen. Karl is getting married? Amazing!

"Here comes Juan," Karl says.

I see Juan Carlos and Monique come through the door. Or should I say, I see my ex–fire brother and a dark brown head bobbing above two enormous girls. Damn, where did Monique sprout those? She wasn't that buxom at the wake, was she? Maybe it was too dark for me to see them, but . . . d-damn! So, Juan Carlos likes them big. My girls are pouting in my bra. Both Juan Carlos and Monique are dressed nicely, he in a suit and tie, she in a loud red churchy dress . . . and she *is* wearing a diamond engagement ring.

"Karl," I whisper, "is Monique Haitian?"

"Hell," Karl whispers, "I don't know. She's from Nicaragua or something."

"Can barely speak English, girl," Izzie says, a little too loudly. "Always has a bad attitude."

Juan Carlos shakes hands with Karl and nods at Izzie, and he and Monique slide across the opposite bench seat until she's directly across from me. Monique's eyes narrow to little dots when she sees me staring at her. I'm not staring at her—I'm looking at those tig ol' bitties she has propped up on the table. Where will Lisa put Monique's plate?

"Where is Roger?" Juan Carlos asks.

"He ain't coming cuz it's his turn to pay," Karl says.

I feel like I'm the fifth wheel, and I can't escape because I'm pinned in by Izzie's fat thigh to my left, the window to my right, and the table and Monique's girls in front of me. "I better be going," I say, but then the door opens . . .

And Roger enters with a big grin. I see him kiss Lisa on the cheek, and she laughs. Roger looks good in a black fishnet sweater and faded blue jeans.

"You leavin' already?" Karl asks.

"Uh, no," I say. "I'll stay."

Roger gets some dap from Karl and from Juan Carlos (I never would have believed it!), and slides in at the other end of the table, next to Juan Carlos. "Sorry I'm late," he says. He waves to me. "Hi, Lana."

"Hi," I say. Wow, I have a small voice when I'm cornered.

"Y'all already order?" Roger asks.

"We're just having coffee," Karl says. "We're beat."

Izzie grabs my arm. "Oh, girl, we were down in Greensboro at this little club Juan told us about last night, and it was thick, girl. Oh, I did me some dancing last night. Whoo!" She lets go of my arm and pats her stomach. "I hope you can dance like your daddy, little one."

Creepy.

Lisa comes over with two coffees, setting them in front of Karl and Izzie. "What can I get for you, Juan?"

Monique spews a whole bunch of Spanish just then, and Juan Carlos's eyes pop.

"Um," Juan Carlos says, "just two coffees. To go."

Damn, Monique has a tight leash on Juan Carlos.

"We go to eight o'clock mass," Monique says, still eyeing me.

Lisa puts her hand on Roger's shoulder. "What will you have, honey?"

Roger winks at me. "I'm hungry, Lisa. I'll have a western omelet and a large coffee."

Lisa writes it down. "Be back in a jiff."

Well, the gang's all here, but not for long. If I'm reading this right, only Roger and I will be left at this booth in about . . . ten minutes.

No one speaks for a full minute. Lisa returns with two Styrofoam cups, setting them in front of Juan Carlos.

"Uh, see you next week," Juan Carlos says.

Roger stands, and Juan Carlos, Monique, and Monique's chest start to slide out.

"Wait just a second," I say.

Juan stops, and Monique's girls bounce off his back. That had to hurt, for him probably more than for her. What are they made of? Petrified Jell-O?

"What's going on here?" I demand. Classy ladies are allowed to be demanding.

No one speaks.

"Why is everyone leaving?" I ask.

More silence.

"I can see no one wants me here," I say, standing and reaching for my coat. "Juan Carlos, Monique, don't leave on my account."

Karl laughs. "Girl, sit down. We're all here on account of you."

"You did," Roger says, "bring us all together."

I sit, but I don't take off my coat. "And five months ago, you wouldn't even be here, right?"

The three men nod. Izzie drums her nails on the table. Monique scowls, and her girls wobble. Is the table moving? D-damn. They must weigh ten pounds each.

"So why can't I be a part of what I started?" I ask.

"Well," Karl says, cradling his mug of coffee, "there's this agreement we signed."

"Where is it?" I ask. "I want to see it." So I can tear it up. Classily, of course.

"What agreement?" Juan Carlos asks.

"The agreement y'all put on that napkin," I say.

Karl and Juan Carlos look at Roger. "You told her," Karl says.

"Yeah," Roger says. "Sorry."

"You got it?" Karl asks Roger.

Roger shakes his head. "You have it, Juan?"

Juan Carlos shakes his head. "I thought Karl had it."

I'll bet there isn't even an agreement at all. This is all part of the scam. "Look," I say, "I came here to . . ."

"To do what, Peanut?" Karl asks. "Why did you come here? It wasn't for the coffee. The fancy stuff you made was much better than this stuff."

Izzie sighs. "Like I told you, boo. She adds some hot chocolate mix. There's nothing fancy about it."

I feel five sets of eyes on me. "Look, I came here just to see you guys, okay? I just wanted to see you."

Roger smiles. "Here we are."

"No, I mean, I came here to—"

Monique puts a finger in my face, ripping into me with staccato bursts of Spanish.

"What's she saying?" I ask Juan Carlos.

Juan Carlos blinks rapidly. "You do not want to know."

Other diners around us are looking our way, first to listen, and then to watch Monique's girls bobbing up and down.

"I didn't come here to cause a scene, Monique, and you can quit cussing me in Spanish," I say. I wait until she takes a breath to swat her finger from my face. Then I stand and lean over the table. "I do not want your man. Juan Carlos only wants you." And your boobies. "Grow up."

Monique looks ready to cut me. "That is right. He wants me. He has tried the rest, and now he has the best." She pushes Juan Carlos past Roger, out of the booth, and through the other tables and booths to the front door.

Bye, Juan Carlos. I hope you and the "twins" have a nice life.

The other diners go back to their food, and silence reigns at the table again.

Izzie makes a big production number out of finishing her coffee, slurping the last little bit. "Let's go home, boo."

"Yeah," Karl says. He stands. "Good to see you again, Peanut. Later, Roger."

And they leave.

Roger hasn't moved from the other end of the table. The chess game continues. It's my move.

"I met your fiancée."

"She's something, huh?" he replies.

Hmm. "Aren't you going to move down here?"

Roger shrugs. "I just warmed up this seat."

A stalemate. Great. I slide to his end. "Now, do you have—"

Lisa arrives with Roger's breakfast, and he immediately digs in. Great, just great. He looks up every now and then, the tiniest smile on his lips.

"Are you enjoying yourself?" I ask.

He nods. "I knew you'd come."

"You couldn't have known I'd be here this morning."

"Sure I did. You're too much of a competitor not to be here."

Huh? "And who or what am I competing against? Lisa?"

He wipes his lips with a napkin. "Ah, she's a great gal. She serves me food, smiles at me, likes my jokes. She even flirts with me."

"I do all that."

"Did."

I hate the past tense. "Okay, I *did* all that."

"Times three," he says.

Ouch.

"The first time we came here, you know what happened?" he asks. "We talked of nothing but you, Lana. Just you."

Should I be flattered? "Why? I just hurt you all."

"Oh, we cussed you up and down, too. Juan knows some really cool curses. Want to hear some?"

"I've heard them all."

He nods. "Oh. Yeah. He told us about that. Did you really say he had PMS?"

Geez, what *didn't* they talk about? "Yes."

"Remind me never to go dancing with you."

"As if you'd ever let me dance with you."

He squints. "I might. As long as there isn't a crowd. I don't like crowds."

So many hidden meanings today. "Is there anything y'all *don't* know about me?"

He looks at the ceiling. "I . . . No, I don't think so. We discussed every inch of your body in detail. It made me right horny. Looking at you now . . ." He grunts. "Your body is talking to me again."

I know I am blushing under all this makeup. "But did y'all have anything nice to say about me?"

He squints. "Other than about your body? Hmm. Let's see . . . After all the cursing died down, we said lots of nice things about you, but we agreed right here at this table not to—"

"I know, I know," I interrupt. "Not to be with me again."

He sits back and squirms a bit. "Oh. I do have it." He brings a folded napkin to the table.

I try to snatch it, but Roger pulls it back. "Let me see it, Roger."

"Why?"

"I need closure or something."

"Why? What's being closed?"

"Look, y'all have gotten on with your lives, and . . . I need to start mine over. So, show me the damn napkin." The classy lady has officially left IHOP.

He unfolds the napkin and spins it around to me.

Above the signatures, I read: "We the undersigned agree on this day not to be with Lana Peanut Cole ever again unless one of us doesn't have a lady in his life."

My hands get a little sweaty. Does this mean what I think it means? "This isn't what I expected."

"Life rarely is," Roger says. "Let's see . . . Karl has Izzie, or is it the other way around? Hmm. They have each other. And Monique definitely has Juan. I already pity him. So that leaves . . . me. Again. I'm once again the last possible choice, the bronze medalist."

Who isn't bronze! Well, his freckles are kind of bronze, but . . . "What about Lisa?"

"Oh, I'm afraid I'm much too old for her. She likes 'em young."

I re-read the agreement. "So you don't have a lady in your life."

"Nope. I'm single. The name's Roger." He sticks out his hand.

But my hand is too sweaty! I shake his hand quickly. "Erlana Joy."

"Erlana Joy?"

I can't look at him. "My daddy's name was Earl, and Mama's name is Lana. Earl-Lana. Erlana Joy."

"Nice to meet you, Erlana Joy."

"Nice to meet you, too."

Silence. It's as if we're starting completely over. I don't want to take this slow. I want to jump back in where we were before. I mean, we have a history, right? We have plenty to talk about, and here we are listening to the sound of forks and spoons hitting plates around us. I'm sure if we listen really hard, we'll hear old people pooting.

"You know what?" he asks suddenly.

"What?"

"I'd like to ask you out on a date, Erlana Joy."

Oh, my heart! "A date?"

"Yeah. That's how folks usually start relationships, you know."

Hope? Is that what I'm feeling? "Yeah. I guess they do."

"Not that we'll have a relationship. We'll just have to, you know, take it slow, see what happens."

"Right."

"I mean, how would it look if we just suddenly, oh, I don't know, made love on the floor of my apartment on our first date while people are walking by outside?" He smiles. "You know, I don't think we ever really had an official first date."

"No," I say, "we didn't." I look up into those hazel eyes. "Roger, do you still want to be with me after all that's happened?"

"Well . . . Yes and no."

I hold my breath.

"You see, I once knew this woman named Lana. She did me wrong. She hurt me bad. She broke my heart. She ruined my life. She made my life a living hell. She made me—"

"I get the picture," I interrupt.

"No," he says, "I'm not sure you do. I was down on my knees in front of this woman with an engagement ring, and I was so sure she was going to say yes. Instead, her other two boyfriends showed up." He stares hard at me, and I look away. "You can imagine how . . . lost and how hurt I felt. I never want to feel that way again."

"I'm so sorry, Roger."

"Why should you be sorry? I was talking about a girl named Lana. Your name is Erlana Joy, right?"

I nod. "Right."

"And while I don't agree with your methods, I am willing to give you another chance." His voice catches. "Yeah. I'm willing to . . . to try again, but only if we take things slow, okay? I'm not going to be in a rush to get on my knees again."

I nod, though my heart hurts.

"But, if I ever had to get on my knees again for anyone, it would be for you."

My eyes well with tears. I think I've finally found the man of my dreams.

"Now, I know all this is a big step for you, Erlana Joy," he says.

"What is?"

"Settling for just one guy." He wags a finger at me. "I've heard an awful lot about you. I know all your secrets."

There's a scary thought. He probably knows more about me than I do.

"But, I want you to know that I've been practicing my Spanish."

Huh? "What?"

"I've been practicing my Spanish. I bought some tapes and everything, and I listen to them every night. Juan helps when he can, too, and now I'm pretty sure I can ask just about anyone in Mexico where the bathroom is. *Donde esta el baño?*"

I laugh, and a tear spills down my nose onto the table.

"I even listen to Led Zeppelin. I play a mean air guitar, let me tell you."

"Roger, you don't have to—"

"And Karl's going to help me be a better plot salesman," he interrupts. "He's going to help me talk people into buying 'eternal real estate'—that's what he calls it. And if I cut your grass enough without my shirt on all *next* summer . . ." He pauses and looks into my eyes. "If I do that all next summer, all my freckles will congeal into one dark orangish-brownish color, which you seem to like so much."

I stand and slide in next to him, taking his hand. "I love you just the way you are, Roger."

Damn. I just said the word "love" to a man. I need to wring out my hands!

"And I love you *any* way you are, Erlana Joy," he says, and then, well, we make out right there in the booth at IHOP.

With lots of tongue and some, um, wandering hands.

When I let him catch his breath, I ask, "Can you please get my ring back from Lisa?"

"You want *her* ring?"

"It was meant for me, not to be worn by Old Lisa Lou, a woman serving pancakes at an IHOP."

"But why would you want her ring"—he pulls out a black velvet box from his back pocket, popping it open—"when *this* is the ring I wanted to give you?"

I look into the box, and I'm looking at the only bling I'm going to need for the rest of my life. "Then what ring is Lisa wearing?"

"Some ring Karl had in his pocket that night."

I squeeze the life out of his hand.

"It wasn't a ring Karl planned to give to you, Lana. It was cubic zirconia or something, and I tipped Lisa with it."

"Oh."

The ring is still in the box. It shouldn't be in the box. It should be on my finger.

"Aren't you going to put it on me?"

Roger sighs and sits back. "I don't know. I mean, I've just said I want to take it slow, and if I suddenly just . . . gave it to you, then I'd be contradicting myself. I don't like to contradict myself." He shrugs. "Maybe someday, but . . . not right now." He closes the box.

Oh no!

"But I have been looking at it for so long, imagining how it would look on your finger."

"So stop imagining!" I shout. I stare the other diners back to their omelets.

Roger sits back. "You'll forgive me if I hesitate, I mean, I have to know about a thousand things about you first."

A thousand? "I thought you knew everything about me."

"I know a lot, but I don't know everything."

"What do you want to know?"

"I wrote down everything I need to know about you at the apartment, right on the back of that list we made. Do you remember that list?"

I nod. "I have a few more places to add to that list."

"You do?"

I nod. "This booth, for one. Have you heard about something called the 'Mile High Club'?"

He nods.

"I haven't decided whether I want to do it in an airplane or a hot air balloon."

"Why not both?"

"Yeah, why not?"

He exhales a long, slow breath. "Well. Hmm. Well, I'll have to remember the new list I made from memory." He looks at the ceiling. "Oh, the first one was: Do you have any more men in your life? For all we knew that night, we might have been only three of maybe six or seven in your life, like maybe you had one for every night of the week."

I cradle his face with my hands. "I am looking at the only man for my every night of the week and for every one of my dreams. Any more questions?"

He looks up at the ceiling again. "Uh, that response answered the other nine hundred ninety-nine." He squeezes my leg. "You'll need to stand up for a second."

I stand, and he slides by me.

Then he kneels—here it comes!—and he . . .

He picks up a napkin.

"Scoot down," he says. I do, and he digs back into his breakfast.

What the? It was the *perfect* time! I *would* have said yes! And he picks up a damn napkin? The nerve!

"I talked to your mama about all this the other night, and she told me how difficult you might make this."

No . . . he . . . didn't! And no *she* didn't!

"Remember the night you called your mama about getting a makeover?"

I nod. Mama knew the whole . . . damn . . . time! She was making me over just for this moment! She was making me over for Roger!

"I was there when you called, and your mama and I, um, well, we came to an agreement of sorts."

"You did?"

"Yeah, and it wasn't easy. She's a tough lady."

I nod. She is. And I'm as tough as she is. Now.

"She says that as long as I let her visit us out in the country, and that I make and *keep* you happy, I can marry you one day. I hope I can do all that. If I ever did ask you again, would you marry me, Erlana Joy?"

There's only one possible answer to this. "Yes, Roger."

He's fidgeting in his seat. Oh, he's trying to dig out the ring, I just know it!

He pulls out his wallet.

"Have you paid for your breakfast yet?"

Damn, my heart is jumping up and down. "Uh, no, not yet."

He pulls out a twenty. "My treat."

I'd rather have the ring!

He kisses me tenderly on my newfound lips, and then . . . he begins eating his breakfast again!

"Roger, what the hell are you doing?"

He shovels in another mouthful of omelet. "Finishing my breakfast. This is some good stuff."

If I blink any harder, I'll blink off my eyelashes. "But you just . . . You almost just asked me to marry you."

"Yeah." He drinks more of his coffee. "And?"

"And?" My jaw is scraping the table. "And you're finishing your breakfast because it's 'some good stuff'."

He nods. "Yeah. And?"

"Well, Mr. McDowell, I got some good stuff, no, some *better* stuff back at my house." And if I give it to him properly—and I will, oh yes, I will—I will get that ring *today*.

He stops chewing. "Got any eggs? You could make an omelet or something with lots of mushrooms, cheese, and green peppers. Or you could make me some pancakes. Or, you could make me—"

"A baby," I interrupt.

He swallows. "Oh. You have *those* kinds of eggs. How many eggs do you want to spare?"

"How many do you need?"

"Well, for the omelet I'm planning, at least . . . eleven. I want us to field a football team."

Oh yeah.

I have found the right man for the job.

Now, in the movies or on those dopey sitcoms, I would be wearing that ring. Juan Carlos, Karl, Izzie, and even Monique would be just outside the window clapping or something. Lisa would be leading cheers with the other waitresses inside, and I bet all the diners would give us a standing ovation. My mama and maybe even my daddy would come out of hiding, the music would swell, and Roger would carry me to a convertible with me holding on to my ouchy shoes. Then we'd drive off into the sunset as the credits roll.

I used to hate those kinds of movies.

I might actually like them now.

So, instead of all that drama, I walk out of an IHOP—barefoot, somewhat crusty toes and all, and ringless—with the man of my dreams, my earth brother, my Mr. Meat 'n' Potatoes, my soul, tears drying on my face, ouchy shoes left under the table where they belong, wondering about our future, our future that will one day—maybe this time next year—involve another threesome.

Just me, my man, and our child.

Ah, who am I kidding? I'm not wondering about any of that at all, really—except for the ring. I mean, I haven't had any good loving in five months, six days, and two hours (I've been counting), and I can't wait to get back to Jenny's dollhouse so we can make us a milk chocolate baby girl.

I hope it rains all weekend.

Maybe we can work in a little football, too.

It would be so cool to say that we made our first baby during a football game.